THE TRACKER'S DAWN

INGRID SEYMOUR

PenDreams • BIRMINGHAM

Published by PenDreams
Cover design by "Covers by Juan"

Manufactured in the United States of America

ISBN-13: 978-1-7360612-4-4 HARDBACK

CHAPTER 1

Grief was a creature of many teeth, eating me alive.

Every night as I went to bed and every morning as I woke up, my first thought was of Rosalina. At once, my heart tightened, and it remained completely clenched for the rest of the day, making me feel as if I was asphyxiating.

It had been like that for two weeks. Today was no different.

I sat up with a jolt in one of the guest bedrooms in Eric's house. Burying my face in my hands, I exhaled, certain I hadn't slept a drop even though I'd gone to bed early, hoping to get some much-needed rest before today's tracking trance.

I kicked off the bed sheets, went into the bathroom, and then took a scalding shower to loosen my stiff muscles.

Jake would be here later to help me. He'd wanted to stay last night but was way too busy with his new pack leader responsibilities. Since his grandfather's murder, there had been all kinds of things to take care of: legal matters to sort out, businesses to tour and familiarize himself with, pack squabbles to settle, people to meet—a bunch of things he wanted nothing to do with at the moment. Not with everything else going on in our lives.

I had given him a crash course on sign language, and the things Rosalina did to help ease the side effects of my trances. He insisted on learning as much as he could and assured me he would make me as comfortable as possible.

"You'll never have to do this alone again," he said to me yesterday before he left to meet his grandfather's lawyer or, more accurately, *his* lawyer.

I knew he was trying to help, but his words only managed to upset me because Rosalina wasn't here, because I hadn't found her… The thought of never seeing her again was something I fought off every second of the day. I could not accept that possibility.

She would be back soon.

Today, even.

This morning's tracking would reveal her location for once and for all. We'd thought of a way we might find Rosalina, even if everything else had failed. And I wouldn't let her down. I would rescue her from wherever that godforsaken Midnight Witch was keeping her.

I hopped out of the shower and quickly got ready. I had a stash of clothes and toiletries that seemed to grow every day. How I'd ended up practically living here came as a surprise every time I thought about it. If a month ago anyone had told me that I would be this close to Eric Cross, I would have laughed in their face. But here I was, living under the same roof as one of the most feared werewolves in St. Louis.

I'd only been back to my place to pick up my stuff. Jake, Eric, and even Damien had insisted I shouldn't be alone—not with Mekare Graves still at large. It had been twelve days since we'd last seen her. Though now, it was more than only us trying to stop her. Law enforcement was also keeping an eye out for her. The witch had attracted everyone's attention with her antics, which, on top of harassing us, murdering Stephen Erickson, and kidnapping my partner, included distributing rhabo all over St. Louis.

Just two days ago I visited Tom Freeman in his office and finally told him everything. Well, almost everything. I couldn't tell him anything relating to the Pack Rule, but I told him about the rhabo cure, our battle at the coven temple, Mekare Graves, my kidnapping by her, Rosalina's disappearance, and everything else I was free to share.

He was mad, of course.

"I can't believe you waited this long to tell me, Toni," he chided me, looking very disappointed.

"I've been busy, looking for Rosalina."

"Did it ever occur to you that I could help? I do have a host of resources at my disposal."

"A big help they've been," I said, bitterness thick in my voice.

He only raised an eyebrow and regarded me sadly, his fatherly expression making me feel guilty.

"Sorry," I said. "These past few days have been rough."

"I can only imagine. A lot of what you've done is… against the law," he said, measuring his words.

"Are you gonna arrest me?" If he did, I would deny everything. I would not be put in jail—at least not until Rosalina was safe.

He didn't answer my question. Instead, he said, "You didn't do any of this alone, especially that massacre at the coven temple. That is clear. Who helped you? I'm sure I can guess, but…" He raised his eyebrows, inviting me to name names.

I kept my lips sealed tight. I would not betray my friends. I loved Tom, but screw the law. We hadn't done anything morally wrong.

He sighed and rubbed the back of his neck.

"The vampires who died that day were bad people, Tom, and the entire city is better off without them. They killed an entire pack, only two people survived. All in all, it was self-defense."

"I'm sure it was, including using magic to erase all the evidence from the crime scene. Damien Ward did that?"

I shrugged. "I don't know anything about any evidence."

"And what about Walter Knight's death, do you know anything about that? He was your boyfriend's grandfather."

"I know it's been rough on Jake. It was an untimely death."

"Why was he killed?"

"I don't know. Stephen Erickson killed him."

"But now Stephen is dead and you said…" he looked down at his notes, which he'd started scribbling furiously as soon as I started spilling the beans, "Mekare Graves killed him."

"She did. I guess you'll have to ask her why they decided to kill an old man."

I couldn't tell Tom about the Unholy Vessel. I had been sworn to secrecy at Wolfskeep. Still, he needed to know about the possibility that hybrids might become a problem, that packs of innocent werewolves might be turned into monsters we had no other choice but to kill. He knew about their existence. One of them had killed Liliana Ward, Damien's daughter. Em, Liliana's neighbor, and I had prompted him to look into her murder, though he'd discovered nothing, except another crime scene scrubbed of all evidence—Mekare's doing for sure. Mages and witches were handy like that.

"You sure you don't know anything about Walter Knight's death?" Tom pressed.

"I'm sure." I kept my face impassive as I answered his question. It surprised me how easy lying to him was becoming.

"I don't know why you don't trust me, kiddo. Perhaps, you're not at liberty to speak." He cocked his head to one side, encouraging me to acknowledge his comment.

I thought of lying again, but there was no point, he understood. So I gave him a small nod. He knew Skews had their ways. He knew that the goings-on in our city had taken me into the heart of the werewolf community.

Tom shook his head, his expression full of regret. "I appreciate you confiding in me," he said, to my surprise. "I know it must not be easy. I won't speak of your involvement in any of this with anyone. By my job and duties, it's wrong of me. But it's right by you, and that's what matters most to me. Be careful, though. There are others who wouldn't think twice about bringing you in."

Tears pooled in my eyes, and it took a monumental effort to hold them back. "Thank you, Tom." I walked to the door, but before I left I offered him a warning. "I think… I think things are about to get very bad. That Midnight Witch is dangerous and can control those monsters, the hybrids. I think soon she'll make a move, and she may have an army of her own to use against us."

Tom had looked grim at my words, which let me know they had sunk in. "I'll keep my eyes open," he'd said as I left his office.

Now, I shook away the memories, put on my arrow bracelet, and pocketed the heavy metal key Prince Kalyll had given me. It belonged to Gonira, his cousin, and the person I would be tracking today. I had put off trying to find her, just as I had put off tracking Mr. Taylor's mate. The man was the only customer the agency had, and probably also the last. In fact, I was going to call him today and tell him we wouldn't be able to work with him due to unforeseen circumstances.

Since my run-in with Mekare and my recovery after she tried to turn me into a charred piece of grilled meat, I'd spent all my energy searching for Rosalina. I'd tried to track her several times, all with the same result. Nothing, not even a small spark of light, a minor scraping sound, or the faintest scent. Every time it had been as if I was tracking a dead person, but I refused to believe she was gone. I knew magic was involved. Mekare was concealing my friend's location from me. The witch knew I would be looking for Rosalina. She knew I would never give up. But more importantly, she knew that my friend's absence was killing me. The witch hated me, and I had no doubt she was enjoying torturing me.

Gonira's key was heavy in my pocket. As I left the bedroom, I berated myself yet again, wishing I'd thought of tracking the Fae female earlier. I had been so focused on Rosalina, that it hadn't occurred to me that finding Gonira might lead me to the Midnight Witch. Gonira had been working with Bernadetta and Stephen from the beginning, so there was a chance she was still with Mekare—a small one, perhaps, but still a chance. For all I knew, the Fae had been loyal to Mekare and not the others.

Jake had thought of questioning the Dark Donna about Gonira, the only problem… the vamp was keeping to herself, and said that she'd see us when we had the cure with us and we'd better hurry if we didn't want to face her wrath. Or more likely her coven's wrath since rhabo was slowly turning her into a withered husk.

She'd actually used the word "wrath." But I wasn't intimidated by it. Lately, there was only one thing I feared, and it was *not* finding Rosalina.

It wasn't as if the Donna could kill me. If she did, she would be signing her own death sentence. No one except Jake and I knew where the leftover cure was, and even if she found out, Prince Kalyll wouldn't turn it over to anyone else but me. So it was a catch-22 for the vamp.

I left the room and meandered through the large house on my way to the kitchen. As usual, Eric was already there, drinking coffee and scrambling eggs. From the smell of it, this morning, he also made bacon. He wore a sleeveless gray shirt that was stained with triangular patterns of sweat at the neck and back. His dark brown hair was wet around her ears. It didn't seem like he skipped a day of training no matter what was going on in his life. He hadn't asked me to join him again, though. He'd been uncharacteristically gentle, but I had a feeling he was losing his patience. Maybe, once I recovered from today's trance, I would join him again. It would do me good.

"Good morning," I said as I filled a cup of coffee with his strong brew.

"Hey." He nodded as he plated a mountain of eggs and several strips of bacon. "Here." He offered me the food, his blue eyes assessing me.

I blinked at the platter. It was huge. Normally, my appetite was big but not this much.

"Umm, thanks." I took the hefty breakfast and walked to the table with it.

"I didn't know how much energy you would need for your trance." He served his own plate, which contained half the amount mine did.

"This is great. Thank you." I doubted I would be able to eat everything, but I decided to give it my best try. Red was a pig most of the time. Besides, I didn't want to discourage any civilized gestures from him. He was making strides, acting more personable than the ogre I'd met in the beginning.

"Gah!" someone said as they entered the kitchen, startling me. "I swear a layer of grease jumped on my face as soon as I walked in here."

I blinked up at Damien, who had just stormed into the kitchen, apparently materialized out of thin air. "Where did you come from?"

Tiredly, Eric glanced up from his cup of coffee, looking annoyed at the mage. "He does this sometimes. He knows a way around the house's protection spells since he's the one who installed most of them in the first place. I warned him one day he might get mauled, but he won't listen."

Damien Ward was wearing his top hat and satin-lined cloak, and dabbing at his face with two fingers, his mouth twisted in disgust. His hair was perfectly white and recently trimmed. "Besides ungodly amounts of grease," he said, "bacon contains nitrates, did you know that? They are terrible for your health. You should think about that before you…" He gestured toward our plates.

Right after his short stint as a cat, Damien had seemed a bit subdued, but he was quickly getting back to his original self. I was starting to miss Blaze.

"What are you doing here?" I asked.

He exchanged a look with Eric as he removed his hat, neatly folded the cloak, and deposited his ridiculous attire on the center island. "Eric said something about tracking Rosalina, so I figured I might be of some assistance."

Damien felt guilty for Rosalina's disappearance. He had been in his cat shape when Mekare came for us at Eric's cabin. At the exact time, he had been out in the woods chasing squirrels, possessed by his feline instincts, which had come and gone at random times, driving him completely wild and leaving him unable to hold onto any of his human qualities. When he came back to the cabin, we'd been gone and only the sour scent of magic had lingered behind. He knew immediately who was responsible for our abduction. I just wished he also knew why we hadn't found Rosalina yet.

"I'm not tracking Rosalina, but Prince Kalyll's cousin," I said.

Damien walked to the coffee machine, picked up the carafe, lifted it against the light, and swirled it around, judging its contents. "I know that." He sniffed the brew, then turned to Eric. "What brand is this?"

Eric crossed his arms. "The same one werewolves use to give mages enemas."

The mage set the carafe back in place. "I know better. I should've stopped somewhere for a proper cup."

"Jake will be here to help me," I said, wondering if Damien's presence would only cause a distraction. He and Eric were like an old married couple, always going on about one thing or another.

Damien sat across from me, his nose wrinkling as he examined the mountain of food on my plate. "Yes, well, then at least I can get the news as soon as you come out of your trance."

"Also," Eric put in, "if you come up with a location, Damien and I can go straight away."

It seemed they'd been making plans behind my back. I shook my head. "No, you're not going anywhere without me."

Eric set down his fork. "But you might be incapacitated for hours."

"I'm going."

"I think you should stay here with Jake." Damien smoothed one of his white eyebrows and rubbed his thumb and forefinger together as if he were really removing bacon grease from his face.

"I said I'm going," I insisted.

"Time could be of the essence," Damien argued.

That was true. Still, I wanted to be there. If we found her—no, *when* we found her—Rosalina would want to see a friendly face, not Eric's or Damien's.

I stared pointedly at the mage. "She thinks you're dead. If she sees you, she'll freak out."

Eric nodded. "She has a point."

"That won't be a problem. I can change my appearance."

"But—"

Suddenly, my cell phone started ringing in the back pocket of my jeans. My heart and my lungs froze at the customized ringtone, one I hadn't heard in twelve days. Hands trembling, I stared at the screen in his belief. My thumb fumbled erratically as I tried to pick up.

"What is it?" Eric and Damien asked in unison.

The caller ID showed a name that seemed to flash, leaving me like a deer in the headlights.

I met their curious stares and said, "It's Rosalina."

CHAPTER 2

"Hello," I answered my cell in a shaky voice, my heart swelling with hope.

"Hello, dear."

I lifted my free hand to my chest, willing my paralyzed heart to start beating again. I recognized the voice, and it wasn't Rosalina's. The person on the other side of the line was Makare Grave.

"Where is she?!" I demanded.

"No greeting? After what we've been through?"

I clenched my teeth to repress a sob. Silence roared in my ear, seeming louder than a scream.

Mekare sighed. "Okay, straight to business then. I know you're looking for her."

"Of course I'm looking for her! And you're going to tell me where she is right now or I swear I'll make you wish you'd never met me."

"The Prince's offer must've been quite something."

Huh? The Prince's offer? What was she talking about?

"I don't see why anyone cares about this wretched Fae. There's nothing particularly special about her, and she is a *royal* pain in the ass."

I blinked at Eric and Damien who wore twin questioning expressions.

"Who are you talking about?" I said, feeling as dumb as a thumbtack. She must be referring to Gonira, but I didn't want to believe that. It was Rosalina I needed to know about. I was aware it was a selfish feeling, but I didn't give a shit about anyone else right now.

"Gonira Loraerris, of course. Who else? Like I said, I know you're looking for her. Better yet, I know of your little deal with the Prince. I will save you the trouble of using your pathetic powers and ending up like a clueless mole. I have her, and I'm willing to make an exchange."

What? How did she know I was looking for Kalyll's cousin? I shook my head. It didn't matter.

"Where is Rosalina?" I asked between clenched teeth, my words as jagged as a serrated knife.

"Who?" she asked innocently, a hint of mockery in her tone.

"Quit the bullshit! You have her phone."

Mekare let out another tired sigh. "I found this in that dreadful cabin. Anyway, if you're going to waste my time talking about this Rosalina, I guess I'll have to hang up."

"No, wait!" Whatever game she was playing, I needed to go along with it. I quickly hit the speaker button, set the phone in the middle of the table, and mouthed the Midnight Witch's name.

"That's better," she said in a simpering voice as Eric and Damien glared at the phone. "I still want that elixir. I guess someone promised it to Bernadetta Fiore to get her on your side, but I can't have her recover from that very *fortunate* illness." At once, her voice did a one-eighty, turning into a near growl as she said, "I want her dead. Truly dead. If you give me the elixir, I'll give you Gonira. I'll even throw in the other two in the bargain."

What? Other two? My heart pounded against my chest, its

erratic beating filling my ears.

"What other two?" I asked.

"Wouldn't you like to know?" She laughed a cackling laugh very appropriate for a witch. "I'll meet you at your little agency tonight at midnight. Don't be late. Come alone. And of course, bring the elixir. And don't, for a second, dream you will be able to fool me. I'll know if you try to replace the cure with a fake one. Bitterthorn is something I'm adept at spotting."

"Please tell me—"

The call disconnected, leaving me at a loss, a feeling of utter disorientation making my head spin. Last night, I'd gone to bed with a plan, and in a matter of minutes, Mekare had smashed it to pieces.

That fucking bitch!

Scrambling for the phone, I picked it up and dialed Mom's number.

"Good Morning, Antonietta!" She greeted me.

"Mom, where are you?"

"At home, where else would I be at this time of the morning?"

"Where's Lucia?"

"Getting ready for school."

"You've seen her."

"Yes, I've seen her. What is this all about?"

"And Dani?"

"I don't know. You're starting to worry me. What's happening? Do we need to hide again?"

"I don't know. But maybe it's best if you stay home today."

"This is—"

"Sorry, I gotta call Dani." I disconnected, cutting Mom off mid-sentence.

When my older sister picked up the phone, she sounded groggy and angry. I had woken her up after a late shift at the hospital.

"Sorry, I just needed to know you were okay," I said.

"I'm okay, Toni. But what about you?"

"I'm fine. I'll talk to you later."

"Witchlights, this has got to stop! Your life is a constant turmoil, and you're putting everyone in danger."

"I don't mean to."

"I know you don't, but…" She exhaled and gave me a tired warning. "Please be careful, whatever is going on."

"I will be."

Eric and Damien bore my panic with stoic expressions. When I started to dial Jake's number, Eric shook his head.

"He's here already. I've let him in." His eyes flicked toward the phone in his hand, which allowed him to control the security system that wired the entire house.

The tight knot that had formed in the middle of my chest loosened a little. "Who *other two* was that fucking witch talking about?"

"Maybe she's just pulling your chain," Eric said.

I looked at Damien for his opinion.

He was stroking his chin. "Something tells me she isn't," he said after a moment.

"Then one of them is Rosalina," I said. "It has to be. But who could the other person be?"

Eric thought for a moment. "Tom Freeman? Your brother?" He lifted his hands and shrugged as if to say *that's all I've got.*

I pressed a hand to my forehead as if to squeeze an answer out of my brain. I could call Tom, but I had no idea how to contact my brother.

With my enhanced wolf hearing, I caught the sound of Jake's steps out in the hall. Without thinking, I jumped to my feet, rushed out of the kitchen, and ran straight into his arms. His eyebrows raised in surprise as he wrapped me in a tight embrace.

"What is it?" he asked, sounding a bit panicked. "Is everything all right?"

I shook my head and inhaled his fresh scent, trying to find some comfort in it. He stroked my hair without asking any more questions and held me until my panic subsided. When I pulled away, his silver eyes scanned my face.

In a quiet tone, I explained everything as we stood there in the hall. His hands rested gently on my waist as his eyebrows pinched together in concern. When I was done, I dragged him into the kitchen, where Eric and Damien sat making conjectures.

"How do you think that damn witch knew about Toni's plan to track Gonira?" Eric asked.

"Maybe just a logical deduction," Damien answered.

"I think she does have Rosalina," I said as we approached.

Damien cocked his head to one side. "How are you so sure?"

"She used her phone, besides it's the only way she could've learned about my deal with Kalyll. Mekare got the truth out of her. It's the only explanation. The Prince wouldn't tell anyone, and none of us would've either."

Eric nodded as he thought about it. "Quick thinking, Toni. It makes sense."

"And the third person?" Damien asked. "Who could that be?"

I grabbed my phone again. "I have to rule out Tom. I'll call him. I don't have a way to reach my brother, though. No one knows how to get in touch with him. God, I hate him sometimes," I added as I pulled aside and dialed Tom Freeman's personal number.

To my relief, I quickly verified that Tom was all right. He was also at home, getting ready to go to work.

"What's happening? Everything all right?" he asked with considerable suspicion after we exchanged greetings.

"I just wanted to make sure you're all right. I read about that raid in the news this morning. I didn't know if you were involved." While I was brushing my teeth, I'd perused the news on my phone for a few minutes. The local police, with the help of the feds, had busted a rhabo operation overnight. Shots had been exchanged, and a few people had died. It was the perfect excuse for my call.

Tom seemed to buy my story. "Thank you for your concern, kiddo, but I wasn't involved. There are other things keeping me occupied these days."

"Good. I'm glad, Tom. I have to go now. Please, be careful."

"You too."

I whirled and faced the table again, a horrible feeling crowded my chest like the worst heartburn in the history of heartburns.

"So not Tom," Jake said. "And probably not your brother since he's not around."

Eric rose from the table, taking his still-full plate with him. "A safe assumption, I would say." He scraped the food into the garbage can and rinsed his utensils before putting them in the dishwasher.

"It *has* to be Rosalina," I said.

Damien threw his hands up in the air. "No use in racking our brains trying to figure this out. Our time would be better spent preparing for tonight. We need to plan what we'll do when we get there."

"No, she said I had to come alone," I protested. "If I don't, she might hurt Rosalina."

"Yes and Gonira and whoever else," Damien said, giving me a narrow-eyed look as if to point out my disregard for the other captives. "But you don't really think we're going to let you go alone."

"I have to. I can't risk Rosalina getting h—"

"Don't waste your breath arguing," Eric interrupted.

"Yeah," Jake said. "No way in hell we're letting you go by yourself. We're coming with."

CHAPTER 3

Sometimes, being surrounded by alpha males—werewolves or otherwise—sucked. All three ganged up on me, insisting that whether or not I took them with me, they would be there. They knew the rendezvous location and time, after all.

"It will be fine if we come with you," Jake reasoned. "Mekare won't hurt anyone until she has the elixir. If that was her intention, she would have done it already."

"For all we know, she did."

"Shh," Jake pressed a finger to my lips. "Up until now you haven't allowed any of us to be negative, so I'm not letting you do that. Rosalina is fine, and she'll be there tonight."

I nodded. He was right. I shouldn't lose hope now.

"Also, I doubt the witch will be there alone because she knows there's no way we would *not* go with you," Jake added.

"Besides, it's our chance to get her," Damien put in, hatred flashing in his copper eyes.

"No! Nah-ah. You have to promise not to do anything stupid. Getting Rosalina out alive… and the others, too, of course," I added quickly, "is our priority."

Rather than giving me one of his flippant answers, the mage bowed respectfully. "Most certainly." His demeanor appeared sincere, but still, I needed to make triple sure.

"Promise. All three of you."

"We promise," they said in unison.

"The elixir doesn't matter," I added, giving Damien a pointed look. I was willing to make the exchange regardless of Damien's promise to Bernadetta to give it to her.

He sighed. "The Donna will come after me, but I guess that's a riddle for another day."

Eric shrugged. "You could hold your own with her even when she was healthy, shouldn't be a problem now."

"I doubt she'll come alone, but like I said, I'll worry about it later," Damien said.

"*We*," I corrected. "We'll worry about it later."

He smiled crookedly, a grateful expression shaping his features. Then his copper eyes twinkled. "Though perhaps…" he paced in front of the kitchen sink, rubbing his pointed chin.

"Perhaps what?" Eric pressed him.

"Just a thought. I need to let it… congeal for a little bit. Now, I think you'd better go to Prince Kalyll to retrieve that cure."

I had been so focused on the idea of meeting Mekare and rescuing Rosalina that I hadn't even realized I had to go to Elfhame.

"What if I can't find him?!" I asked, a surge of panic sending my heart into a frenzy.

"We'll find them," Jake assured me, squeezing my shoulder for comfort. "But Damien is right, we should leave right away."

My gaze darted to Damien again. He pulled the wooden token out of the breast pocket of his jacket. I had given it back and thanked him for letting me borrow it.

"I always carry it with me," he said. "It's one of my most prized possessions." He handed it over. "I trust you will take care of it, just as before."

I wrapped my fingers tightly around it. "I will."

"Then go, *shoo,*" the mage made sweeping motions with both hands.

A million thoughts crowded my mouth, but I didn't have time to vent them. It could take hours to find the Prince. Though, hopefully, he would find us first as soon as we materialized in his realm. He'd done it last time we'd used the token.

Feeling restless with anticipation, I turned to Jake and grabbed the hand he extended toward me. We interlaced our fingers and, as I thought of the Fae realm, the world around us began to wash away, all the color melting to nothing then building back up into the vibrant forest on the outskirts of Elyndell.

It was daytime, a crisp morning filled with birdsong. The Seelie capital was fit for a fairytale and could take your breath away upon sight, but Jake and I wasted no time gawking at it as we normally would have, and, instead, started walking away from the forest and headed directly for the idyllic city, veering in the direction of the Vine Tower, the place where the royal family lived. I kept waiting for the Prince to appear in our path like last time, but no such luck.

We were practically running as we crossed the large prairie that separated the woods from the city limits. Finally, we intersected one of the many moss-covered paths which meander through the picturesque Fae dwellings. Self-consciously, we slowed to a brisk walk, and continued hand-in-hand in search of the Prince.

Despite the early hour, it seemed that everyone was up and around. People watched us from the path, the round windows of their treehouses, and the hanging bridges that stretched from branch to branch overhead. We stood out like two fat sore thumbs, and I worried someone might say something, but they simply observed us quietly, their keen eyes holding a warning not to do anything stupid.

Jake walked, staring straight ahead, his chest rising and falling—

not from exertion, I realized, but from an effort to ignore his hyper-alert wolf instincts warning him of potential hostiles that could attack us at any moment. Red felt the same way, but my fear for Rosalina's well-being was the predominant emotion, the one thing that would make me walk in front of a fire-breathing dragon if it meant seeing her again.

As we neared the center of the city where the Vine Tower stood, the tree canopy above us thinned gradually, allowing us a view of the beautiful structure. It stretched toward the sky, tapering as it rose. Its white walls were dressed in twining vines that crept in through doors and windows, undisturbed. As we moved closer, I was able to perceive a sweet scent that seemed to come from tiny flowers gracing the vines.

"We're almost there," Jake said. "This way, I think."

Pulling on my hand he led me around a stone structure with a roof of what looked like terracotta Spanish tiles, except these were made of tree bark. As soon as we rounded the corner, we came to an abrupt stop as a line of people appeared before us. It stretched for about thirty yards from the Vine Tower's outer gate.

"Shit," I cursed, remembering something.

"What?"

The people standing at the back of the line turned to watch us over their shoulders, their expressions turning distrustful right away. I smiled and waved, wiggling my fingers. Slowly, I pulled Jake off to the side.

"I think those people are petitioners," I said. "I remember something from the first time I was here. Foreigners are supposed to stay in the back of the line and wait their turn."

Jake followed the length of the line, measuring it, and frowned. "That could take forever. We don't have time."

"I know."

"What do we do?"

I thought for a moment. Anything else besides waiting in line like the rest would be rude as hell.

"Maybe the line will move fast," I said.

Jake raised an eyebrow, indicating he didn't think luck would be on our side. Still, he walked to the back of the line and joined it. I stood behind him, craning my neck to look ahead and judge the speed at which things were moving.

"Hey," I said, getting the attention of the person that stood ahead of us, an older woman with a long white braid down her back and ears as pointed as a fennec fox's. "Um, at what time did you get here?"

She frowned as if she didn't understand what I was saying. A little boy I hadn't noticed pulled away from behind the flowing leaves of her garment.

"My Meior-la doesn't speak your language," the little boy said, causing my ovaries to coo at the sight of his cute, cherub face. He spoke in a lilting accent, and his magenta eyes were so big he looked like a Disney character.

"Oh, jeez!" I exclaimed. "Tell her I'm sorry. I shouldn't have assumed."

They both stared at us impassively.

"Um, do you know how long you've been waiting?" I asked the little boy.

He shrugged. "Since after breakfast."

So not *helpful.*

"Hey, buddy," Jake interjected, "could you tell us when you expect to make it to the front of the line?"

"Whenever we do," the little Fae said.

Jake and I exchanged an annoyed glance.

"Maybe by lunchtime?" I said helpfully.

"Lunchtime?"

"Um, the next time you have to eat. Noon. When the sun is straight up ahead."

He turned his huge eyes toward the sky, thought for a second, then opened his mouth to answer. "I think—"

"*Falie! Sareh Nanan,*" his grandmother cut him off.

Looking chastised, he pressed his lips together, straightened his back, and turned away from us, facing the front of the line.

"What just happened?" Jake asked.

I shrugged hopelessly.

Just then a creaking sound accompanied by the thumping of heavy steps drew my attention. I glanced back and did a double-take at the sight of someone familiar.

"Yalgrun?!" I said under my breath. He was the Fae that owned the store where Rosalina and I got our ingredients to make our customers' potions.

The seven-foot-tall creature lumbered to the back of the line and came to a stop, his all-black eyes focused on the Vine Tower ahead. His body was made entirely of tree branches, and two of them protruded from his head to form horns.

Jake stared up, his jaw unhinged. It seemed obvious he had never seen a Bladuhian.

I was about to greet him but bit my tongue when I noticed he had five fingers on each hand. No, he wasn't Yalgrun. my Bladuhian only had four fingers on each hand. It was something I always noticed whenever he delicately packed my purchases.

At last, this Bladuhian looked down and noticed us. His twig eyebrows drew together.

"Foreigners," he said as if it were a curse word. He blew air through his nose and a puff of dust or pollen, I wasn't sure which, blew out. None too gently, he stuck his heavy trunk-like arms in front of himself and parted them, pushing Jake and me aside as if we were nothing more than two saplings. With us out of the way, he stepped forward and took our spot.

Jake's clear eyes flashed in anger. Double-quick, I ran around the Bladuhian and dragged Jake back. "C'mon, it's just how it's supposed to work. We can't do anything about it."

It took a hard shove to move him, but I managed to get him past the end of the line and then some more.

"I should teach him some manners," Jake said between clenched teeth.

"I think he'll turn you into pulp before you teach him anything. He's seven-foot tall, Jake. Besides, picking a fight is not going to help us."

He kept glowering at the creature over my shoulder.

I grabbed his face and directed his gaze to mine. "Focus. Don't forget why we're here."

Reluctantly, he relaxed, unclenching his jaw and shaking his arms at his sides.

I leaned closer and whispered in his ear. "Maybe we can find another way in. We could jump the wall."

His sharp eyes glanced about as he nodded. "Let's do that."

We abandoned our spot in the line, walked back the way we'd come, and found a route that took us closer to the outer wall. The structure appeared to be made of vines and to surround the entire perimeter of the Seelie Court's home. We strolled along a row of buildings along its perimeter, examining it closely.

Witchlights! Why didn't we ask Kalyll to give us some sort of password that would let us through the front gate?

"There are guards every few yards," Jake said, leaning close to whisper in my ear.

"And they're watching us," I said, waving at one of them. He stood impassive, showing no reaction to my greeting. "Maybe if I tell one of them I need to see the Prince, they'll call him."

"I doubt you would be the first one to try that, so I don't think it'll work, but give it a go."

Rolling my shoulders, I walked closer to the wall and cleared my throat. "Hi, there," I called out to the closest Fae who stood guard on the parapet. He ignored me.

"My name is Toni Sunder, and I need to see Prince Kalyll. Do you think you could call him for me? I assure you he'll want to see me."

The guard barely blinked. For all I knew, he didn't speak English, and I was wasting my time.

"Please," I said in my best groveling voice.

Still nothing.

Giving up, I turned back to Jake and shrugged. He scratched the back of his neck, considering. After a moment, he gave me a wicked grin.

"What?" I asked.

In answer, he shifted, his clothes falling to the ground in tatters, and ran straight at the vine-covered wall.

CHAPTER 4

"Oi!" The Fae guard yelled, swiftly nocking an arrow and shooting it down at the wolf.

Jake's leap took him as high as the middle of the wall. He hit it with his front paws, then bounced back just in time to avoid the arrow.

I cried out a warning, my heart jumping into my throat. "What are you doing?!" I demanded. "You're going to get yourself killed, you idiot."

Another arrow flew in his direction as he flipped in midair and hit the ground. It whizzed by his tail, shaving a few hairs off.

"Don't shoot him, please," I begged. "He means no harm."

This time one of the arrows came at me, missing my head by a mere inch as I ducked out of the way.

"Dammit, Jake!" I ran to the left and hid behind a sparse bush that offered little protection.

The hubbub quickly attracted more guards, who came running along the parapet with their arrows nocked and ready to shoot. Jake, for his part, was running in crazy eight shapes, weaving in and out of the way of the many projectiles that started raining down.

The guards shouted at each other in their language. I had no idea what they were saying, but I was sure more than one had cursed Jake's mother and all his descendants.

"Jake, stop!" I cried out, unable to see the point of all this nonsense.

Just as I said this, he leaped out of the way of one arrow but fell limp to the ground as another one struck him.

"No!" I ran from behind the bush, waving my arms. "Peace, peace!" I demanded. The arrows stopped, I knelt at his side. "Jake!"

An arrow was stuck to his side. My hands hovered over it as I tried to decide what to do. I searched for a wound, for blood, but there was nothing.

"I'm fine, Toni," his voice broke into my thoughts.

He opened one silver eye and winked at me.

What the hell?

On closer inspection, I could see that the arrow was tucked in between Jake's side and the top of his front leg, where he was squeezing it in place.

"Make a scene," Jake spoke inside my head again.

I didn't see how making a scene could help, but at this point, I guessed we had to see where this craziness would lead. Most likely to the dungeon somewhere, but he had gotten this ball rolling, and I had no choice but to play along.

Squeezing my eyes together and scrunching up my face, I did my best to muster tears and began fake-wailing.

"Oh, what have you done? You killed him. You awful, awful people." I leaned forward and pressed my forehead to his fur. "Oh, Jake. What am I going to do without you?"

Exaggerated sobs racked my body. A few reluctant tears made it out of my mostly dry eyes. I blubbered for several seconds until I heard the rustling of plants behind me. Pulling away from Jake, I blinked at the top of the wall and found several of the guards lithely climbing down the vines. They all wore tunics with the royal seal on their chests. Bows and arrows still in hand, they stared at us with distrust.

"Look what you've done," I wailed at the top of my lungs. "You killed my mate. He was only playing. He wasn't going to hurt anyone." I beat my chest, working up a few more tears.

"Wow, I didn't know you had acting in your veins," Jake spoke inside my head.

I almost busted out laughing and disguised the impulse with another huge sob.

Rushed steps sounded to the side. I glanced over as a group of about ten guards approached from an adjacent street. I blinked up at them, searching each face, hoping to see Prince Kalyll among them, but to my dismay, he wasn't there.

There was another face I recognized, however.

Swatting the tears off my face, I jumped to my feet. "I know you!" I pointed at a female with blond hair and green, feline-looking eyes. "And you," I pointed at another one that looked like her doppelgänger. I had met them the first time I'd been here with Damien. They were the guards who ambushed us as we rode Glimlock's ponies in search of Prince Kalyll. They shrank as all the other guards turned to look at them.

"Um," I knocked my head with a closed fist, trying to remember their names. I snapped my fingers as they perched on the tip of my tongue. "Oh, yes, Misra and Ladresel, right?"

"Do you know them?" An imposing male asked in perfect English. He appeared to be their leader, judging by the slight differences in his uniform. For one, it was expensive-looking, had a high collar, and a slightly different emblem embroidered in his tunic. He stood with regal confidence, had long brown hair pulled into a ponytail, leaving his pointed ears in full display.

"Yes, Captain Loraerris," Misra said, stepping forward and inclining her head, causing her straight blonde hair to fall forward like a silken sheet. "She is an… acquaintance of Prince Kalyll."

Loraerris? Why did that sound familiar?

"So she does know him?" One of the guards who had climbed down the wall asked. She had red hair, pulled back into a tight braid that draped over her shoulder.

Misra nodded and so did Ladresel.

"She was yelling at us to get the Prince for her, that it was an emergency," the redhead added.

Captain Loraerris stepped sideways for a better look at the wolf lying at my feet. His keen eyes scanned Jake's body, stopping at the protruding arrow. One of his pencil-thin eyebrows went up, and I could tell by his expression that he was reading clearly through the charade.

I let out a nervous laugh, snatched the arrow from under Jake's armpit, and threw it to the ground. "This is Jake. He's fine. Aren't you, Jake?" I nudged him with the tip of my shoe.

He opened his eyes slowly and grinned a wolfish grin. The guards who had been up on the wall shuffled uncomfortably as Jake got to his feet and playfully sidled next to me. I patted his head and smiled like an idiot.

A long silence stretched as Captain Loraerris scrutinized us, his expression growing more shrewd by the second. This charade had gone too far. It was time to explain and quickly.

"My apologies for… this." I gestured toward the arrow. "I admit it was a ploy to attract attention.

"I deduced that much," the Captain said, "and I must say, it is in poor taste—not to mention disruptive of our cherished peace."

Heat rose to my cheeks, and I lowered my head feeling like a chastised brat. "I apologize, but it really is an emergency. We need to see Prince Kalyll, and I assure you he will want to hear what I have to say."

Captain Loraerris turned to Misra and Ladresel as if to consult what they thought of my claim. They could have easily dismissed my claim, but instead, both appeared unsure, which was enough to make the Captain curious.

He turned back to us. "What is it you need to tell him?"

"I'm sorry. I'm not at liberty to divulge that." I had no idea if Gonira's situation was something the Prince's family discussed publicly. Either way, no one needed to know about the elixir and the fact that Kalyll was keeping it safe for me.

The Captain thought for a moment, then gestured toward the side, inviting me to a little privacy. My nerves prickling with restlessness, I walked with him a safe distance away from his guards. Jake stayed at my side, his sharp gaze never leaving the Fae male.

"You may talk freely now," he said.

"I'm afraid I can't."

He sighed with irritation. "I am Kalyll's uncle. I assure you it is quite safe to talk to me."

I frowned, feeling unsure. For all I knew, he was Kalyll's shoe shiner. I had no way of telling if they were really related. "Sorry. I need to talk to him personally."

"Well, he's not here. He's away on business."

So that was why he hadn't come looking for us when we first crossed into Elyndell.

"When will he be back?" I asked, my heart threatening to sink to the pit of my stomach.

The Captain thought for a moment, then asked, "What is your name?"

"Toni Sunder," I responded.

He stiffened, his narrow eyes going wide. "Is this about Gonira?" he asked in a halting voice.

I was taken aback. I hadn't expected that. So maybe the Captain was, indeed, close to the Prince.

When I didn't respond, he said, "Gonira is my daughter."

Holy shit!

I glanced down at Jake. *"Jackpot,"* he said inside my head.

My gaze returned to the Captain. "Yes, it relates to Gonira."

"Is she all right?" he asked with a hint of desperation in his voice.

"She's in danger," I said.

He flinched.

"But I hope I can help her tonight, so she can return to you."

"I'll do anything you ask." He straightened his spine, looking like a soldier ready for battle.

"Prince Kalyll has something of mine," I said, carefully examining the Captain's face.

He made no indication that he knew what I was talking about.

"I need it back. Without it," I shook my head, "I'm not sure I can… help your daughter."

The Captain's nostrils flared. "Whatever you are referring to, I am not aware of its existence, so I have no idea where to look to procure it. My nephew is due back tonight, is that soon enough?"

"I need it before midnight."

His gaze darted to and fro as his thoughts seemed to race. "He could be delayed. Anything can happen on the road." He spoke mostly to himself, venting his concerns out loud. After another moment, his jaw set in determination. "I will ride out to meet him and make sure he comes home in haste. You may wait in the palace if you please. I assure you he will be back in time. Or you may ride with us if you prefer."

His resolute tone left me no doubt he would do everything in his power to make sure of the Prince's timely return. It was no substitute to Kalyll's actual presence here, but it was better than nothing.

"Thank you." I inclined my head. "I count on you to do everything in your power to reach him and bring him back as soon as possible. I wish I could stay and wait for him, but I have to prepare for tonight." My presence here wasn't necessary. I knew nothing of riding horses in haste, and I was likely to become a *liability* instead.

"I understand. I will leave at once."

Quickly, I gave him Eric's address as well as the address to the agency. He assured me he had memorized it and said Kalyll would have no trouble finding me.

When that was settled, he retreated with a bow. "I leave immediately."

I held up a hand to stop him. "You should know, it isn't only your daughter who is in danger. Someone I care about deeply is also involved. Good luck."

He pressed a tight fist to his heart, whirled on his heel, and ordered his men to retrieve the horses immediately. I hated to leave without the elixir, but I had to believe everything would be all right.

CHAPTER 5

When we got back to Eric's, he was waiting for us in his study, pacing in front of the fireplace.

"It took you guys long enough. How did it go?! Did you find him?" He asked as soon as we walked through the door.

I shook my head. "No, but his uncle is going to find him and deliver a message from us."

"He'll be here," Jake said, placing a hand on my shoulder and giving it a reassuring squeeze. We had swung by the training room before we came looking for Eric, where Jake had retrieved a pair of dark jeans, and a gray button-up shirt.

"Where's Damien?" I asked.

Eric's mouth twisted to one side. "He took off as soon as you did. Didn't say where he was going or anything." He didn't sound very pleased about that. Not at all. "He's going to get himself killed again, if he does I'll dance on top of his grave."

"You might squish him if he has become a worm again," I pointed out.

"Precisely."

Jake chuckled. I elbowed him in the stomach.

He rolled his eyes. "What? It was funny."

"No, it wasn't. Just like you acting like a fool in front of those Fae wasn't either."

"Do I want to know?" Eric asked.

I exhaled. "No, you don't." I rubbed my forehead. "What do we do now?"

"We come up with a plan."

We sat around the coffee table across from the fireplace, Jake next to me on the sofa, and Eric across from us in an armchair.

"I think there'd be no point in trying to conceal our presence," Jake said. "A Midnight Witch… she'll know if we try to hide, so I say we just all walk up to the agency."

"I agree," Eric said.

I nodded. I had to trust them. They had more experience than me on this type of thing. "What do we do if Prince Kalyll doesn't come?"

"He will," Jake assured me again.

"But what if he doesn't?"

He exchanged a defeated glance with Eric. They didn't think things would go well if we didn't get our hands on that elixir to perform the exchange.

I wrung my hands together. "I'll beg her for more time. She'll have to understand."

"I don't think she's the understanding type, Sunder," Eric put in.

"Yeah, I don't think so either." I hated to agree.

"In fact," Jake said cautiously, "I feel like she won't care either way. Whether or not we have the elixir, she will…" He stopped as if to spare me from his dark thoughts.

But I knew exactly where he was headed. "She will get to make someone miserable," I finished for him.

"Something like that," he admitted with a nod.

If we gave her the elixir, she would get rid of Bernadetta Fiore, and if we didn't, she would get her revenge against us. We had thwarted her efforts against the Dark Donna, and she hated us for it. She wanted the vamp dead, and Damien had gone and offered Bernadetta the cure in exchange for helping them find me after Mekare took me from the cabin—not that we'd hurried to deliver it.

"So is there anything at all we can do to prepare?" I asked.

"Of course there is," Damien said, appearing at the door.

"Where the hell were you?" Eric asked.

"Preparing, of course." He waltzed in, discarding his top hat and cloak on a side table. "I have a plan, and you need to help me polish it to perfection."

ജ്ജ

Driving with his headlights off, Eric's Mercedes rolled slowly up the road. We were a couple of blocks from the agency and had no trouble finding a parking space. Damien parked behind us, driving separately in a second car. Eric shut the engine off, and we got out and convened on the sidewalk, no one saying a word.

We all knew the plan. We'd discussed it until we could recite it by heart. I had no idea if it would work, but I felt glad we had one, especially since Prince Kalyll hadn't made an appearance at Eric's house.

I checked my watch. We were fifteen minutes early. I had told Captain Loraerris that if Kalyll couldn't make it to Eric's place, he should meet us at the agency. There was still time, and I was doing my best not to lose hope.

Damien reached out a hand and deposited a small vial in my palm. It was filled with a clear glittery liquid that looked exactly like the rhabo cure. The mage had concocted it in Eric's kitchen using water, sugar, clove, and a slight touch of magic. He said the scent might be able to fool Mekare into thinking it contained bitterthorn.

Though, he doubted it. He *seemed* to have a healthy degree of respect for the witch. She had bested him, after all. It scared me to see the uncertainty in his copper eyes. He'd never been anything but confident. But when it came to Mekare Graves, it was a different story.

My heart knocked inside my chest with wild ferocity. I kept thinking of Rosalina somewhere nearby. She must be so scared. I feared the witchy bitch had hurt her. I feared my friend might not be the same after the ordeal, but mainly, I was afraid she would be done with me. Everything that had happened was my fault. If she hadn't met me, she would've never started a hopeless business that did nothing more than getting her into debt and a heap of trouble.

Jake leaned close and gently deposited a kiss on my temple, then whispered in my ear. "Rosalina is fine. I feel it in my bones." He pulled away, his silver gaze locking with mine.

Whereas I saw only caution in Damien's eyes and calculation in Eric's, Jake's gaze showed me self-assurance and resolve. I had no idea where he got his inner strength, but I was grateful for it because it gave me the confidence I needed to stand firm and do what needed to be done. I would crumble if I lost hope.

"She is," I said, willing every cell in my body to believe it and finding that I did. No other alternative was possible.

When there were only five minutes left until midnight, Eric, Jake, and I started walking toward the agency. Damien stayed behind as part of the plan, and he quickly started weaving his hands in the air, crafting a spell.

Eric was on my left and Jake on my right. Our steps synchronized of their own accord. If it had been a movie, there would have been badass music playing as we advanced in slow motion.

Because we *were* badasses.

The effect was probably spoiled by my darting gaze, which kept searching, trying to spot Prince Kalyll. I imagined him running in my direction and bringing the cure back to me in the nick of time, but there was no sign of him.

In truth, I didn't want to have to be a badass tonight.

All I wanted was to make the exchange exactly as Mekare wanted it. I would hand over the cure. She would let her hostages go. And I would run to embrace my friend in the tightest of hugs while blissful relief washed over me.

But without the real elixir in my possession, there was no hope for a peaceful resolution. There would be a fight, no question about it. Hopefully, the fake cure would buy us some time, though.

Turning the corner at Giovanni's Pizzeria, we marched down the middle of the street that crossed in front of the agency. At this hour, it was deserted—all the businesses closed and no cars parked by the sidewalks.

Heart in my throat, my attention immediately homed in on the second to last building on the left. The place looked just as peaceful as all the others, the windows dark, the door closed. I threw a panicked glance at Jake. Had the witch left when she realized I hadn't come alone?

God! Had I messed everything up by refusing to listen to these stubborn men?

A sickening feeling tightened my stomach, and my legs began to tremble. Cold sweat slid down my back, and only Jake's hand in the small of my back allowed me to keep walking.

"Rosalina is fine. I feel it in my bones." His words echoed inside my head, and I held on to them for dear life.

When we reached the front of the agency, we turned to face it, peering into the darkened interior. Nothing stirred inside.

"Where is she?" I whispered.

But before anyone ventured a guess, white-blue light sprang from the sidewalk and rose upward. A few blinding flashes made me squint as they crackled on the building's façade. Through my lashes, I saw shapes forming behind the random blasts of energy, which dissipated as they climbed past the second floor.

When the light show was over, three women stood in front of the agency, facing us.

I nearly fell to my knees in relief when I laid eyes on Rosalina's beautiful face. Her green eyes widened as she saw us. She mouthed my name and made as if to move forward but discovered her feet were rooted to the ground.

Clenching my fist, I stopped myself from running in her direction, and instead, tried to convey through my expression that everything would be all right, that we would take her home to safety, and she would never have to go through anything like this again.

It took a few beats before I glanced at the other two people who had materialized in front of us. One was Gonira. I would never forget those fawn horns and slitted gaze. The other person was someone I would've never imagined finding here.

It was Em, Liliana's neighbor.

How in the hell had she ended up in Mekare's clutches? It made no sense. My mind raced as I tried to figure it out, but nothing came to me. Except… the day that Makare had walked into the agency pretending to be a customer, Em had been there, too. She'd been asking for my help to convince the police that a monster, a hybrid, had put an end to her neighbor *and* suburban bliss. Maybe Mekare had assumed we shared some sort of meaningful connection. But how and when had the witch kidnapped her?

"You're lucky I'm in a good mood," Mekare's voice traveled up and down the street as if through an amplifier, tearing my attention from the three women. "You didn't come alone."

We scanned the street, trying to spot her, but she was nowhere to be found.

"Up here, dear," she said.

We tipped our heads back to look at the top of the two-story building. Dressed all in black, the Midnight Witch stood on the edge of the roof. The gossamer fabric of what appeared to be a cape glittered and billowed in the wind. Blond, green, and black hair blew around her as she produced her own wind to give her an eerie aspect. *Dramatic much?!*

I would've liked to say she didn't impress me, but when she jumped off the ledge and easily floated down to take a spot in front of her three hostages, I couldn't stop my insides from turning to water.

She let her dark eyes examine my companions. "I guess I can forgive you for bringing these two, and that *pathetic* mage," she said, looking unimpressed and waving her hand in the general direction of where we'd left Damien.

Shit! She knew he was here. I tried not to let my disappointment show. He *had* said that she would probably be able to spot him, but could she detect more than that? Could she sense his spell and what it was supposed to hide?

"Well, do you have the cure?" She went to the point.

I patted my breast pocket. "I have it, but first, let them go." I nodded toward the women behind her.

Mekare waggled a finger at me. "Oh, no, no, no, that's not how it works. I set the rules, not you." She paused, letting that sink in, then added with a tone of command, "Bring it here. Now!."

"No! She's not going anywhere near you," Jake spat.

"Do you think I can't harm her from where I stand?" She cocked her head to one side, putting on an innocent expression. "She already disobeyed me once. Don't test our patience."

Our patience? What was she talking about?

Noticing our surprise, she pointed toward the top of the building. At first, there was nothing but the empty roof's ledge against the backdrop of the midnight sky, but a second later, several shapes stepped forward ruining the view with their ugly mugs.

Hybrids! At least ten of them!

So she'd been busy making more. We should've figured she would find werewolves to turn despite the warnings the St. Louis packs had sent out.

I stared in horror at the beasts' malformed faces with their short snouts, patchy fur, and crazed eyes. My skin itched as Red fought to come to the surface, but not yet.

Mekare crooked her finger and made a *come here* motion. Next to me, Jake blew air through his nose, expressing his fury.

"It's okay," I said.

He nodded reluctantly, and I took a step forward, clenching the fake cure in my hand. The liquid inside the vial looked exactly as it was supposed to, but I doubted the witch would be content with simply looking at it. She was probably going to open it and smell it, and then she would know we were trying to trick her.

Where was that damn prince?!

I took another step forward, focusing my attention on Rosalina. She appeared scared, but there was something else in her gaze, a fierce darkness that hadn't been there before. My heart ached, and I feared some essential part of her might be forever altered by whatever had happened since she'd disappeared.

My panic grew with every step. My throat felt tight, and I was itching to shift and rip Mekare to pieces. It was all I could do to keep Red at bay.

She would turn you into a slug before you got within an inch of her throat, I warned her, and there was no doubt she believed it as well as I did.

When I was but a couple of feet away from the Midnight Witch, I stopped and met her gaze. Immediately, she put a hand out, demanding the elixir.

"Let them go first."

"Not until I make sure you've upheld your end of the bargain."

She wiggled her fingers. I lifted a trembling hand and deposited the vial on her open palm. She picked it up with her opposite hand,

and without preamble uncorked it. A sweet scent identical to the elixir Josh had taken reached my nose. Damien had done a good job creating the decoy. With my sharp wolf senses, I could discern no difference in the smell. I hoped to God Mekare wouldn't either.

The witch's nose twitched as she took in the scent. I watched for any change in her expression as she poured a drop of the liquid onto her index finger and rubbed her thumb over it until it was gone. The entire time her face remained unchanged, no hint of suspicion or anger. I dared hope she would be fooled, but when she shattered the small glass container against the sidewalk and shot her hands up in my direction, energy crackling between her fingers, I knew we were screwed.

I was on the verge of letting Red free as we'd planned when a strong voice resounded down the street. "Stop! I have what you want."

My head snapped to the side, and I nearly fainted with relief at the sight of Prince Kalyll Adanorin. He was confidently marching toward us, a cloak billowing behind him.

CHAPTER 6

"I apologize for my tardiness," Prince Kalyll said with a bow as he came to stand in front of me. He was dressed in a midnight blue tunic and leggings that perfectly matched his hair. A broadsword clung to his back, its hilt protruding above his head. "My uncle ran into a few delays before he was able to reach me, but I'm here, and it seems," his cobalt gaze cut toward Mekare for an instant then returned to me, "not a moment too soon."

"The Seelie Prince," the witch said. "How unexpected."

As her focus rested on the Prince, I glanced around quickly and saw that both Eric and Jake were in their wolf forms. They had managed to shift in that spare second in which Mekare discovered our trick. Man, they were fast! My shifting speed had improved since the first time, but I still had some catching up to do.

I dared another glance around, searching for Damien. He'd also been somewhere, prepared to intervene the moment things inevitably went south, but I didn't spot him. He had held back until the very edge of chaos. Or, for all I knew, he was standing next to me, invisible. At least that was what I chose to believe because I didn't like thinking that, if Kalyll hadn't shown up when he did, I would've ended up like hybrid chow.

Wasting no time in ceremony, the Prince pulled a vial out of the folds of his tunic. "I believe this is what you want." He thrust the cure within an inch of Mekare's nose.

She blinked and leaned her head back, looking offended.

Kalyll stared at her, his expression impassive, his extended arm steady. There was no hint of fear in him at all.

Behind the witch, Gonira was gawking at her cousin with a mixture of relief and surprise. I thought the Prince must be a truly honorable man to risk his life for the weaselly likes of her. There was nothing about Gonira that made me think she deserved any sort of sacrifice from him, or anyone else, for that matter.

Mekare's vicious gaze slipped away from the Prince and focused on me. Her upper lip twitched with disdain. "You think yourself so clever, you and your friends. But you have tangled with the wrong witch."

In one swift motion, she snatched the elixir out of the Prince's hand, and in the same movement, flung it to the ground, smashing it and leaving behind nothing but a wet stain.

I stared at the spot in dumbfounded disbelief.

The witch put on a forced smile. "No need to double-check. I'm sure that was the real thing. Now, let me see, how shall I teach you a lesson?"

She lifted both arms. Magic streamed from her fingers and, thrusting both hands backward, shot it toward her hostages.

"No!" I screamed as time seemed to slow to a crawl.

The Prince drew his sword. Jake and Eric leaped forward, and I just stood there frozen with shock.

As the magic hit Rosalina, Gonira, and Em, they flew backward, crashing against the agency's window and smashing through it, glass and magic rained down like spent fireworks.

Jolted by a second shock, I started to skirt around Mekare to go after Rosalina, to save her somehow, when something hit the back of my legs, and I fell flat to the blacktop. A bolt of magic flew from Mekare's fingers and whizzed above me, just where my head had been a split second ago.

"Shift, Toni!" Jake ordered inside my head as he got between the witch and me. He had saved me, knocked me out of the way, and if I didn't keep my focus and did what he said, we would both end up dead.

It was Damien's job to keep the hostages safe. Not mine. That was the plan. I needed to trust him to do his job.

Getting on all fours, I let Red loose. She burst to the surface, ready to clamp her jaws around Mekare's throat and not let go until the damn witch drew her last breath. I was barely done shifting when a blast of magic hurled toward us. Swiftly, Jake and I leaped out of the way, narrowly avoiding the attack.

Just as we landed, the sound of beastly roars filled the night. A glance toward the top of the building revealed Mekare's hybrids falling from the sky, their naked bodies grotesque.

I assessed the situation in a split second. Prince Kalyll was lightly stepping backward, his sword crackling with what must've been a magical attack from the witch. It seemed he had a way to defend himself against spells, so his self-assurance hadn't been in vain.

I spotted Eric next. He was taunting Mekare, snarling, and feigning attacks as he inched closer. He didn't seem worried at all about the Midnight Witch's magic—his trust relying completely on Damien, who even as a cat had been able to make her magical attacks ineffective. He had warned us not to get too complacent though since his attention would be divided among a number of things—the most important of them: concealing the presence of a few last-minute allies.

As if I'd conjured them with my thoughts, two hosts of vamps rushed in, coming from each end of the street. They attacked with more than just their natural given powers but also with weapons, which ranged all the way from knives to automatic rifles.

Getting the vamps help had been Damien's idea, and he had done it behind our backs. It hadn't been smart of him to go to Bernadetta when we still owed her the cure. To say the least, she had been irate and ready to use the mage as a disposable blood bag. But when he promised she would have the cure tonight as well as her retaliation against the traitorous witch, she had agreed. I doubted the Donna would've been so eager to comply if her life wasn't on the line. Lucky us. Hopefully, this wouldn't come back to bite us in the butt.

Instantly, the Donna's vamps engaged the hybrids, their advantage greatly increased by their numbers. There were three times as many vampires as there were hybrids, and though the beasts were hard to kill and fought without any regard to their lives, they were not invincible.

With the hybrids otherwise engaged, we were free to turn our attention back to the witch.

She still stood in front of the agency, against the backdrop of the broken window. Kalyll, Eric, Jake, and I formed a semi-circle around her—somewhere, hopefully not far away, there was also Damien, making sure Rosalina and the others were delivered from Mekare's control.

She looked unimpressed by the threat that surrounded her, and why shouldn't she? She had escaped us before. After giving everyone her undivided attention for a few beats, she concentrated entirely on me.

"I was willing to make a fair exchange. Truly, I was." Her expression was sincere, which meant I had been right to make the exchange our first plan of action.

If only Kalyll had arrived on time…

"But instead, you decided to play with your friends' lives."

I lowered my head and shook it, denying it.

"The last time you bested me, fair and square," she continued. "But today, there was nothing honorable about what you tried to do, so now you owe me, and I think I know how you will repay me."

A buzzing panic filled my head as I tried to figure out what she had in mind.

"Goodbye, dear," she said as she started levitating upward the way she'd come. She cast a dismissive glance toward her hybrids—some of which had already fallen while others still fought, maiming whoever dared stand in their paths. It was obvious she didn't think much of them. They were expendable, like bullets, or, in their case, huge missiles bent on indiscriminate destruction.

As she floated away, I leaped, snarling and biting the air, but she reached the rooftop in no time.

Someone shoot her! Guns or magic would do.

I held my breath waiting for something to happen. The few seconds that ticked by seemed to stretch for an eternity, then at last, she lifted one hand and snapped her fingers.

As the sound echoed in my ears, the agency exploded.

Debris flew out, whirling through the air. Huge flames followed. Instincts taking over, I ducked, though, in my heart, I wanted to run into the fire to meet my end alongside Rosalina.

The debris settled, though the flames continued to burn, its heat lapping mercilessly. I lifted my head. A patch of fur was singed off my shoulder, and bits of glass from the exploding door stuck to the side of my face. I winced in pain as I struggled to my feet and turned to face the pyre that our mate tracking agency had to become.

The street before me was littered with bodies and remains from the explosion. The strong tang of Mekare's magic burned in my nostrils. I blinked trying to get my bearings. When my head stopped spinning, I quickly marked Jake's position. He was also recovering from the blast, shaking himself and sending bits of glass flying in all directions. Eric and Prince Kalyll were also all right. The Prince was shedding his scorched cloak, which had caught the worst of the blast. He stared at the conflagration in dismay, surely contemplating how to deliver the message of Gonira's death to his family.

My gaze drifted to the roaring flames that had now reached the second floor and were making the wood groan.

Rosalina!

I started toward the building, but Jake was there in an instant, blocking my path.

"No, Toni!"

"Get out of my way."

"No, listen—"

"I have to get her out," I shrieked, all logic gone.

I snarled and snapped my teeth an inch from his snout. He would not stop me. I had to get Rosalina. I would not abandon her. Blind with desperation, I slammed my body into Jake's, pivoted to one side, and dashed toward the fire. I'd almost made it to the sidewalk and was about to leap inside the building when I smacked into something hard and invisible.

Seeing stars, I shook my head. It took me a moment to figure out what had happened.

Damn you, you fucking witch! Let me through!

I scratched at the barrier with my sharp claws, desperately trying to tear it.

Eric appeared at my side in his human form. He was fully clothed and looking down at me with a mixture of pity and irritation.

"Quit it, Sunder. We need to get out of here."

"Fuck you! I'm not leaving her."

"Oh, ye of little faith." He rolled his eyes. "Rosalina isn't in there. She's safe with Damien, I assure you. That mage doesn't fail. Let's get out of here before the cops show up."

CHAPTER 7

As soon as we entered Eric's garage, I leaped out of the car and left my three companions behind. Prince Kalyll had come with us since his cousin was also here. It was where we'd agreed to reconvene, preferring Eric's house to Damien's because it had never been compromised—Blake and that annoying Copper Mage, Jensen, had gotten in Damien's place.

I ran all the way to the second floor in my wolf form, taking huge leaps up the stairs. I skidded to a stop on the main floor, my claws sliding on the floor until I gained purchase on one of the rugs. The surrounding glass walls were dimmed and a few of the lamps were on. That was where I found Damien, kneeling in front of a couch in front of Rosalina, obstructing my view of her.

I approached hesitantly, my heart beating loudly in my ears.

Rosalina. God, are you okay?

I wanted to shift to my human form so I could talk to her, but the last thing I wanted was to immediately flash her. That wouldn't be pleasant for either of us, so I stayed as I was. When I reached her, I coyly sniffed her hand which lay limply at her side.

Noticing me, Damien pulled away, and I was finally able to see my friend. As soon as she realized it was me, she raised her hand to the top of my head and petted me.

"Toni," she said in a very weak voice that broke my heart and at the same time made it sore with happiness.

She was fine. Rosalina was fine. The jeans and T-shirt she'd been wearing the last time I saw her were filthy, and she looked like she'd lost a few pounds. There were huge circles under her green eyes, but she was alive.

Damien allowed us a few minutes of basking in each other's presence, then he said, "she needs some rest." Getting closer once more, he pressed the tip of his index and middle fingers to her temples and spoke a quiet incantation.

Rosalina's eyes grew heavy, then they closed, and her face relaxed, the tension dissolving and leaving behind only peacefulness.

Damien deposited a gentle kiss on her forehead, then drew to his full height. "She'll feel much better when she wakes. Now, I must tend to the others."

I glanced around, noticing Gonira and Em for the first time. They were lying on a couple of the additional sofas that were strewn about. There were four seating areas in this front room, all delineated by rugs.

I'd never asked Eric why he needed so many of them, but I figured it was just to fill the large space. He didn't spend any time here anyway, so I was sure it would be all the same to him if the area was filled with S&M implements. Em was curled up in the fetal position, hugging herself and shivering. Her frame was so petite that she looked like a child. Her green hair was stringy and matted to her face. Gonira, for her part, was rubbing her eyes with closed fists and blinking at the ceiling as if making a huge effort to draw her attention to the here and now.

Jake, Eric, and Prince Kalyll finally joined us. Jake was fully dressed and had a set of my clothes draped over his arm. We kept several spare outfits in the training room. He nodded and draped the clothes over the back of an armchair.

"Thank you," I said.

"You're welcome. Are you all right?"

I nodded.

"Rosalina?"

I nodded again and glanced in her direction.

"Good," he said, a smile of relief lighting up his face. "I told you she was fine."

Prince Kalyll's dark blue eyes scanned the room until they found his cousin. His face tattoos stood out sharply against his pale skin. It was strange seeing him here with his tunic, pointed ears, and sword strapped to his back. It made me understand how the Fae looked at us when we appeared in their realm wearing our jeans and T-shirts.

Sternly, the Prince approached Gonira. When she noticed him, she gave her head a good shake and struggled to sit up. She managed to get to her feet by pushing against the arm of the sofa, though it seemed to take all her strength. She kept her head bowed, appearing scared and contrite.

Kalyll scanned her from head to toe as if to make sure she wasn't missing any important bits, when he was satisfied, he asked, "Are you well?"

Gonira nodded once.

"Perhaps this time, you have learned your lesson. Could we be so lucky?"

She said nothing. I remembered her defiance that time at the repair shop when we found Stephen Erickson. She'd seemed fierce and wild, but there seemed little left of that person. Maybe now, her mother and father would finally have some peace.

Damien approached the Prince and inclined his head. "It's good to see you again, Your Majesty."

"I'm glad to see you are alive." Kalyll inclined his head in response.

When the building exploded—something I was blocking at the moment for fear of crumbling in defeat—Kalyll had been certain that his cousin had perished in the blast. He'd had a hard time believing she could possibly be alive, but during the ride home, Eric gave him a quick explanation of the events.

"I must thank you once more for coming to our aid," Kalyll said. "First you delivered us from the reapgrubs, and now you saved my dear aunt's daughter. How could my family ever repay you? Do you perhaps require more bitterthorn to repay your debt to that vampire? Your friend explained your dilemma on our way here." He gestured toward Eric. "It wasn't easy to convince my parents the last time, but it is their niece you delivered from harm, so perhaps, it won't be so hard to persuade them again. That is," he turned to his cousin and stared at her sharply, "if their affections haven't spoiled."

Gonira shrank, her shoulders caving in.

"Thank you for the offer, but…" Damien reached into his breast pocket and retrieved the cure.

I stared dumbfounded. *How?!*

"How?" Kalyll echoed.

"Oh, it wasn't very hard," Damien said. "Mekare was too distracted to notice the small spell I used to save it."

Kalyll chuckled. "I'm glad it all worked out for you." Stiffly, he turned to Gonira. "We will leave now. I'm sure my family is anxiously awaiting news." His cobalt gaze stopped at Damien, Eric, and Jake, with deliberate attention. "Thanks to all." He, then, turned to me and pressed a fist to his chest. "Especially you, Antonietta Sunder."

"She says *thank you* back," Jake repeated the words I'd projected forward.

Kalyll's mouth tipped with a crooked smile. "I have a feeling this won't be the last time our paths will tangle together."

His long midnight blue hair swung about him as he whirled to face Gonira. He extended a hand, and she took it. Immediately, their outlines blurred, their colors dimmed, then they were gone. We were silent for a moment, transfixed by the disappearing act.

With a sigh, Damien turned his attention to Em. Jake and Eric also moved closer to where she lay. Seeing my chance, I took a step backward, shifted, and quickly slipped into the clothes Jake had gotten for me. Everyone respected my privacy and kept their attention on Em. Once dressed, I twined my fingers with Jake's. He blinked in surprise, then gave my hand a reassuring squeeze. His silver gaze was so expressive I could almost hear his voice in my head.

I'm glad you aren't hurt. I'm glad Rosalina is fine. I love you!

I squeezed his hand back, echoing the same feelings.

"How did *she* end up as Mekare's hostage?" Eric asked, gesturing toward Em.

The petite woman shrank into an even smaller ball as Damien knelt in front of her and scanned her for injuries.

"Who is she?" Jake and Damien asked in unison.

"Her name is Em," I said, feeling stupid for not knowing her last name. "She was your daughter's neighbor, Damien."

At the mention of Liliana, Damien's expression darkened. Em watched him carefully, a mix of suspicion and fear in her eyes. There was a certain edge to her demeanor that made me think she would spring on Damien like a cat if he made the wrong move.

"You knew Liliana?" he asked.

Em nodded.

"Maybe you can tell me a bit about her when you feel better. But for now… do you hurt anywhere?"

She shook her head this time.

"I'm glad. Would you like to sleep? I can help you." Damien rubbed his hands together, a bit of magic crackling between them. "You will feel much better when you wake up."

She hesitated for a beat, then answered in a weak voice. "Is it safe?"

"Quite safe, I assure you." Damien smiled with fatherly tenderness.

"Okay."

As he'd done with Rosalina, he placed two fingers at each of her temples and spoke an incantation. Instantly, Em's eyes closed and she began breathing in an even rhythm.

Damien stood and turned to us. "All's well that ends well."

"I doubt the authorities will agree," Eric said. "We left quite a mess back there."

Jake turned to me, looking sad, and I knew right away what he was going to say.

"Rosalina's life is the only thing that matters," I cut him off, a lump suddenly forming in my throat. "Material stuff can be replaced."

The mage ignored my preemptive strike and spoke anyway. "I'm sorry, Toni. I tried to save the agency, but it was more than I could handle."

I put both hands up and waved them. "I don't want to think about that right now. I just want to enjoy the fact that Rosalina is back." I turned to look at her, and my heart swelled at the sight of her peaceful expression.

"We will get it all figured out later," Jake said firmly. "It will take some work getting things back into shape, but don't worry about it, we'll take care of it." His tone brooked no challenges, and my heart swelled a little more, knowing that I had his unconditional support. I was glad the explosion hadn't damaged his office. Mekare's magic had been well-targeted.

"So tell us, Mr. Copper Mage," Eric said, "how did you get them out of there before the explosion?"

"Ah, I'd love to tell you all about it, but only over a stiff drink. Anyone else care to join me? I think Eric keeps some oakfire for this type of occasion."

"I wouldn't mind some of that," Jake put in, and I had to agree.

Eric glowered at Damien, none-too-happy about the disclosure of this secret. Oakfire was expensive, and the only thing able to get a werewolf drunk. After a moment, he shrugged, though. "Follow me, it's in my study."

I shook my head. "You all go. I'll stay with Rosalina. I don't want to leave her alone."

"Never mind, I'll bring the bottle and some glasses here." He left with a wave of his hand.

"Bring me some Scotch," Damien called out.

"Let's sit here." Jake guided me toward the seating area right across from Rosalina.

We sank down with relief, glad everything had turned out okay.

Eric came back a few minutes later, and as we sat there, enjoying the heat of the oakfire in our chests, we listened to Damien's explanation of how he'd saved the hostages from Mekare's evil clutches.

CHAPTER 8

"Odd to think that I owe my life to the Seelie Prince," Rosalina said, looking bewildered.

We were sitting cross-legged on the bed of her room in Eric's house, facing each other. It was the morning after our confrontation with Mekare, and she appeared much recovered thanks to Damien's spells. She was freshly showered, her black hair wrapped up in a towel and piled on top of her head. She had no makeup on and wore an overly large T-shirt and a pair of basketball shorts that belonged to Eric. Dressed like a princess in a potato sack, she still looked absolutely beautiful.

"And Damien, of course," she said. She shook her head in disbelief. "God, he's alive. I thought I was dreaming when I saw him."

"I bet."

I had caught her up on everything that happened since Mekare took us from Eric's cabin. She did the same, relating how while I was in my tracking trance trying to find the witch's supposed soulmate, the door to the cabin slammed open and a blast of magic hit her, rendering her unconscious. The next thing she knew, she woke up in a dark cellar, alone. She didn't see Gonira or Em, not until last night.

Now, there was only one thing left for me to tell her, and I didn't know how I would manage. Our agency was destroyed, all our hard work gone in an instant. I guessed the insurance would pay for the damage, but the lost time would still hurt our business. And with everything gone, the inevitable question arose… was it worth starting over? The way things had been going, I wasn't so sure. In fact, if I was being objective, the answer would be *no*.

My heart squeezed tightly. Our dream's slow death had started that day at Ulfen Erickson's party. Blake's body hanging over the miniature model had been the first sign that everything was doomed. Then, last night, it had all ended with a massive heart attack that would need weeks if not two months of constant CPR to revive it.

"If I could have," Damien had repeated last night as he recounted how he saved Rosalina and the others, "I would have saved your agency. I know how much it matters to you both, but keeping everyone safe took all of my power."

"As it should have," I said. "You don't have to apologize for that."

After he had stayed behind by the car, Damien had begun the job of keeping Bernadetta's vampires' presence hidden from the Midnight Witch. The deed was a combination of magic, distance, and death. The vamps were several blocks away from the agency, shrouded under a concealing spell and waiting for the signal to attack. The fact that they were dead, for all intents and purposes, had also contributed to keeping them undetected.

Once he finished that piece of work, Damien approached the agency, positioning himself at a safe distance, also doing his best to magically conceal his presence from Mekare.

The moment the witch sent Rosalina, Gonira, and Em flying backward through the agency's window, Damien made his move.

Relying on his concealing magic, he carved a hole in the building's back wall and quietly entered. It wasn't easy with his magical abilities taxed to the max—keeping the vampires and himself from notice was hard enough, not to mention fashioning a door by removing one brick at a time—but he managed. Beautifully.

"I wanted to blast the damn thing out of the way," Damien had said last night, "but that would have drawn Mekare and her hybrids' attention."

It took him several agonizing minutes to form a hole big enough to step through, but once he did, he went into the building and found the three women lying on the floor, unconscious.

"Taking that wall part was hard, but not as hard as not going after that bitch," Damien said. "She was right there within reach. I could see her back as she threatened you. I wanted to…" He grunted in frustration. "But keeping the women alive was the priority."

His copper eyes spoke the rest, revealing what he was unwilling to say out loud—that he wasn't sure if he could best the Midnight Witch and that trying and failing might've meant a bigger mess and, possibly, everyone's death.

After healing Gonira who had suffered a cut to her side and was bleeding profusely, Damien levitated the women out of the building one at a time, starting with Rosalina. Not a moment too soon, he got all three out, saving them from the explosion. Then, additional spells were cast to protect them from the fire and debris and to quickly levitate them to his car two blocks away.

As she listened to the replay, Rosalina unwound the towel from her head and set it aside. She ran her fingers through the wet strands, spreading them over her back to help them air dry. She let out a trembling sigh.

"Did she… did she hurt you?" I asked her, afraid of the answer.

"No, not physically," Rosalina said.

"But…"

Another trembling breath, then, "she… she told me you were dead."

I gasped as tears filled my eyes, pooling at the edges. Leaning forward, I wrapped her in an awkward hug. The worry that she might be dead had been torture, and only the hope that we would find her safe and sound had kept me going. Had Rosalina kept the same hope? Or had Mekare managed to crush it with her lies?

"I'm sorry," I whispered. We held each other for a long moment. When we pulled apart, we were both crying, salt streaks staining our cheeks.

"I tried not to believe her," she said. "I told myself that she wouldn't keep me hostage if you were dead. I thought maybe you had escaped her at the cabin, but every day that went by, it got harder to convince myself."

I squeezed her hand, understanding all-too-well how she'd felt.

We were quiet for a long moment as I contemplated how to give her the news about our agency. I heaved a heavy sigh, met her eyes for a moment, then glanced at the floor.

"There's something else, isn't there?" she asked, reading me like an open book.

I nodded, my insides doing weird things. She had been through enough already. This news might devastate her.

"Just rip off the Band-Aid." Rosalina straightened her back, preparing herself for the blow.

"Mekare, she… she blew up the agency."

All the air seemed to go out of her. Her shoulders caved in. Her chin fell to her chest. Her breath grew agitated, and I thought she was crying, but when she looked up, her expression was twisted in anger.

"That bitch! That bitch!" Her hands tightened into fists, and I was sure that if she'd had one of her guns in her grip, she would've started shooting holes in the ceiling.

"I'm sorry." Guilt washed over me. Her life had turned into

such a mess because of me, and now her livelihood had been blown to smithereens. "I'm so sorry."

"Quit apologizing," she said dryly.

I glanced up from the patterned quilt on the bed. Her expression was fierce, nothing but anger reflected in her eyes. I expected despair and tears, but it was quite the opposite.

"I know you think this is your fault," she continued. "That I would be better off if we had never met, if we had never started a business together. You need to stop thinking that way. I make my own decisions, Toni, and I'm not the kind to regret my choices, especially when they are the right ones. My life would suck without you. It would be dull as hell. I would probably be stuck in some cubicle, surrounded by people who hate me and try to stab me in the back while they ask where I bought my cute outfit.

"Besides, bad things can happen to anyone, no matter what. At least, I have *you* to face them with, an unconditional friend, someone who would never abandon me. What else could I ask for?"

When she finished, I was blubbering like a baby. We embraced again, and I let my tears flow without trying to stop them. But I wasn't crying for what we'd lost or because I felt guilty. I was crying because I was the damn luckiest person in the world.

I had the best friend anyone could ask for.

CHAPTER 9

I left Rosalina to rest, closing the bedroom door softly behind me. She was still tired and weak. The witch had fed her only a few times, it seemed, and Rosalina had missed several meals for almost two weeks.

As I made my way to the kitchen, I ran into Jake in the hall.

"Hey, how is Rosalina doing?" He came closer, a line of concern etched in his forehead.

"She's resting. She's still a little weak. I told her about the agency."

Jake winced. "How did she take it?"

"Not the way I thought she would."

"How so?"

"She's pissed. Super pissed."

"That's understandable."

"Don't get me wrong. I'm pissed too, but she's off the charts. I've never seen her like that."

Jake raised an eyebrow. "Maybe that's why it seemed so magnified."

"Yeah," I nodded. "She's always been so easy-going, it's hard to see her like that." I started walking toward the kitchen again. "I need some coffee, might help with this headache."

Jake followed me. He had spent the night here, slumped on the sofa despite the fact that there were enough rooms in the house to host a football team. He and Eric had almost polished off the entire bottle of oakfire, while Damien took care of the Scotch. *Bunch of drunks!*

With good reason, this morning, Jake looked a little worse for wear. He had on the same clothes, his hair was standing on end, and his silver eyes were bloodshot.

"I could use a little coffee, too," he said. "I don't know how Stales get drunk all the time. I feel like shit. Oh, I should tell you, that girl, Em, she left."

"She did?!" I was surprised. She had seemed so out of it, weak like Rosalina, and distressed by the entire ordeal. She had still been asleep on the sofa the last time I looked, appearing as fragile as an orphan child.

"She asked me to call her an Uber."

As we walked into the kitchen, I made a beeline for the coffee maker. A big pot had already been brewed by some kind soul, and I was thankful I didn't have to wait to get my fix. I poured two cups and handed one to Jake.

After a few sips, he said, "I asked her how she ended up with Mekare."

"What did she say?" I asked curiously.

"Well, apparently, she was on her way to see you at the agency to ask if your detective friend had any news about Liliana's murderer when someone hit her over the head. She said the next thing she remembers is waking up in a dark room."

"It sounds exactly like Rosalina. Mekare must've thought we were close or something."

We were quiet for a bit. Jake appeared pensive as if there was something on his mind. A few times, he seemed on the verge of speaking but stopped himself. He was acting exactly the way I had before I told Rosalina about the agency.

"Is something the matter?" I asked.

He set his coffee cup down on the counter and took a deep breath. "It's about the wedding."

My heart stuttered. I knew where this was going, but I braced myself.

"Craig made good on his threat to move the date up."

I put my cup down too for fear I would smash it on the floor in a fit of anger. "When?"

"Saturday."

"Damn it all to hell!" I cried out, stomping a foot on the floor and tearing open my palms as my claws unsheathed themselves into my angry fists.

It was Monday. We only had a few days to figure a way out of Jake's unbreakable pact. It wasn't enough! We'd been trying to come up with a plan to perform the spell we'd found in Eric's book, but finding and rescuing Rosalina had taken precedence.

Jake slammed his fist against the counter. "I tried to buy us more time, tried to convince him there was no hurry, but he's a stubborn bastard."

His face contorted with a mixture of anger and deep frustration. There was a certain quality in his eyes that made me suspect he was losing hope. When it came to Rosalina, he'd never allowed doubt to become a factor. He was certain we would find her and made sure my faith didn't waver. But when it came to his personal situation, he seemed at a complete loss.

I couldn't allow that.

Reigning in my own feelings of frustration along with my claws, I took his hand in mine. "We'll figure it out. There's nothing to stop us now. Rosalina is safe, and I don't have to worry about the agency or tracking anyone. It's time we focused on *us*. Screw everything else that's going on. Let the police, the packs, and the covens deal with Mekare and her hybrids."

"What if we can't find a way to make the spell work, Toni?"

"We will."

"What if we don't?"

I shook my head. "You have to stop thinking like that."

"I couldn't stand losing you. Life wouldn't be worth living without you." He gathered me in his arms so tightly that I had a hard time breathing. His desperation was palpable and crackled all around him, pent-up energy that needed to be spent or else he would implode.

I pulled away from him. "We'll get right to work. Damien has been doing some research already."

"I'm such an idiot. If I hadn't let my grandfather entangle me in his schemes, if I hadn't allowed him to make me feel so guilty, we wouldn't be in this mess."

"Regrets won't solve anything. Look at me!"

His gaze had lowered to the floor but, at my command, it snapped back to mine.

"We *will* figure this out." My voice rang with conviction. I wasn't going to let the man I loved slip through my fingers.

Not without a fight.

CHAPTER 10

I lured everyone to the kitchen with tacos for lunch.

After checking Eric's bachelor pad refrigerator and pantry, I had to call for a pack-sized grocery delivery and started cooking as soon as it arrived.

Now, we were all seated around the table. Even Damien, who proclaimed his favorite was French cuisine, was there on time, though it was possible he'd come to feast his eyes on Rosalina instead of his stomach on tacos. Unlike Jake, Damien hadn't spent the night. He had gone home and returned in a freshly dry-cleaned suit and cloak.

Eric sat at the head of the table, followed to his right by Damien and Jake, and to his left Rosalina and me.

"It looks really good, Toni," Jake said, eyeing the food that sat in the middle of the table.

"Sure does," Eric agreed.

"I learned from the best." I gave Rosalina a sidelong glance. Though her roots were Cuban, she also cooked mean Mexican fare and taught me how to do the same.

I'd made both beef and chicken to accompany either corn or

flour tortillas. I preferred the former but to each their own. To garnish the tacos, I'd cut up onions, tomatoes, cilantro, cabbage, and lettuce. I'd also made green and red salsa, and crumbled Cotija cheese and grated cheddar cheese. Everyone could put together their own traditional tacos, or they could pile whatever they wanted on top. I liked combining different flavors, and always ate more than my fill. Anticipating that Jake and Eric would also eat their weight in food, I prepared enough food for fifty Stales. Still, I was worried it might not be enough.

We all dug in, passing the different condiments around and enjoying a companionable silence.

"I didn't know you could cook, Sunder," Eric said, licking his fingers after his third monster taco.

"I only know how to make a few things, but I think I've perfected them."

Jake took a swig of his cold beer. "You certainly have."

"That's a compliment coming from you," I said. "Jake isn't a bad cook himself."

Eons ago, when we used to share an apartment, he did most of the cooking. His specialty was chili. He made a killer pot, spicy and rich.

Damien watched Eric scarf down a fourth taco while he was still working on his first. "I'll never figure out where you werewolves put all that food." He daintily took a bite of his taco with a fork. He'd been cutting small pieces with a knife, while Rosalina and I exchanged glances and snickered.

The two of them had been stealing glances at each other, and I could practically feel a current of electricity traveling between them. Before Damien *died*, their budding relationship had been getting back on track after we called the police on him. Understandably, he got furious at us for doing that, but he eventually came around, and it had seemed as if they were going to pick things back up where they left off. Then Mekare attacked him, we thought he died, and when he returned, he had four legs and fur all over his body. Maybe now that he was human once more, they would be able to make up for lost time.

When Jake, Eric, and I finally started slowing down on our seventh or eighth taco, I cleaned my hands on a paper napkin and explained why I'd brought them together.

They listened with care and no mockery, even Eric who claimed to hate discussing matters of the heart. At this point, they understood how Jake and I felt about each other and knew we wouldn't stop until we found a solution to our problem. The strong friendship we'd all developed made them care. They didn't want Jake and me to do something stupid and hurt ourselves in the process. They wanted us to succeed and be happy. It was the same way I felt about each of them. I'd grown to care about Eric and Damien very much.

"And are you sure there's nothing you can do about pushing back the wedding to its original date?" Damien asked.

Jake shook his head. "I tried. Craig won't budge. He wants to get the alliance finalized as soon as possible. The situation has him nervous."

"He's always been a stubborn asshole," Eric said. "That's why he got along so well with your grandfather."

Sheesh! Eric had the tact of a rhinoceros sometimes.

I winced at the comment—not because I didn't agree with him but because the old man's death was so recent. Jake's expression betrayed nothing, however. He was the kind to grieve privately, and though it seemed Walter's death had hit him hard in the beginning, he quickly compartmentalized his emotions. I felt awful at the thought of him grieving alone. With Rosalina missing, I'd been no comfort to him. On the contrary, I'd been a burden, and he'd been my rock the entire time. Without him, I wouldn't have been able to hold it together.

Smiling gently at him, I promised myself to change that.

"Have you been able to figure out a way to perform the spell?" I had given him the copy of *Blood Treaties: My life in France* to read over and decide whether or not the demon spell would solve our problem.

Damien rubbed his chin, looking thoughtful.

"I've had a few ideas," he said. "However, nothing that makes me one hundred percent confident yet. It's a difficult spell and extremely risky for Jake. In spare moments, I've tried to find other alternatives, but I'm disappointed to say I haven't run into any other incantation that would break the pact—not even remotely. So the demon spell, which is a cleansing of sorts, still seems our only viable option. Especially now that the deadline has been moved up."

"You know, Jake," Eric interrupted, sounding hesitant, "you can always… divorce Allison after you marry her. You could also step out on her."

This time, Jake flashed a furious glance in Eric's direction. Still, his voice remained even, void of anger. "The first one is not a possibility. There was a stipulation in the pact to prevent that. And the second, I would never do that to Toni. *Never.* I respect her and love her too much to make her a mistress. She's my mate, Eric. My mate. I couldn't share her with anyone, and you know the same goes for her."

Eric waved a hand in the air. "It bore mentioning it."

"I *have* to break the pact, and whatever it is, whatever it takes," Jake said, "I'm willing to do it."

I shook my head. "Not if it's reckless."

His clear eyes connected with mine across the table. His expression was unfamiliar to me, etched with emotions I didn't recognize. It unsettled me because I'd thought I knew him well enough to read him like an open book.

"I'm sorry, Toni," he said, "but it's my decision."

The words felt like a blow. My anger surged. "So I don't have a say?!"

Eric twisted uncomfortably in his chair.

"We can discuss this later," Jake said.

"No! We'll discuss it now!"

He rubbed the back of his neck, looking resigned. "Okay." He stared pointedly at me, inviting me to begin the discussion, with the same even temperament as with Eric.

My mouth opened and closed a few times before I eloquently blurted out, "You can't die."

"And I can't live without you."

"B-but you're saying *I* can. Because if the spell goes wrong that's what I'll be doing… living without you."

"And what if I don't try, Toni? What if I marry Allison without taking the risk? What kind of lives would we live, huh? I would forever hate myself for being a coward, and you would, too. Soon enough. I don't want that." His eyes wavered slightly. "I would rather you love my memory than hate my worthless living ass."

"I wouldn't hate you."

"Are you sure about that?"

"Yes. I'm sure, and you want to know why? Because after you left me, I tried. For almost two years, I told myself that I was over you, that I hated your guts. And see how well that worked out?"

"Maybe you're right," he conceded. "But I wouldn't be able to live with myself. What would be the point? Put yourself in my shoes, Toni."

His gaze filled with sadness, much deeper than I'd ever seen in him, and for a moment, he seemed lost in his own despair as he contemplated what our future apart would be like.

Put yourself in my shoes.

I tried to imagine what it would be like to marry someone I barely knew, renouncing all possibility of ever being happy. It took me a moment to really let the idea sink in, and that was when I finally understood. I couldn't condemn him to such a life. I couldn't ask him to marry someone he didn't love when I wouldn't do it myself.

Lowering my eyes to my lap, I gave in. "Okay."

A taut silence stretched for a long minute, and it might have gone on forever if my phone hadn't vibrated. It was sitting next to my empty plate. Absently, my eyes flicked to the screen. It was my mother. I pressed a button and silenced it, deciding to call her later.

"Toni, I promise you I will put all my efforts into figuring out the safest way to carry out the spell," Damien said, trying to reassure me.

"Thank you." I began gathering the dishes.

Rosalina grabbed my hand and squeezed it supportively. "No way. You cooked. We clean up."

Damien made a face that suggested he wasn't cleaning anything, but a glare from Rosalina had him on his feet collecting utensils and empty cups.

Doggedly staring down, I refused to peer up at Jake. I was angry at him for making me see things his way.

My phone buzzed again. This time it was a text from Mom.

Call me now. It's Lucia.

I snatched the phone in a flash, my heart in my throat.

Something was wrong with my little sister.

CHAPTER 11

Everyone stared at me as I jumped from my seat and started to call Mom's. "It's my sister. Something's wrong."

Mom picked up on the first ring. "Toni!"

"What's the matter, Mom?! Is Lucia okay?"

"I don't know." Her voice sounded choked as if she'd been crying. "It's on the news. Their school is in lockdown. There's some sort of hostile situation going on. I called Daniella. She's on her way here. She told me to stay put. Not to go to the school, but I'm going crazy here."

Lockdown. Hostile situation. My mind raced. What exactly was going on? An active shooter? Something else? A terrible feeling crawled over my skin.

I turned to Eric. "Is there a TV anywhere in the house?" I'd never seen one anywhere, so I had no idea.

He hurried to one corner of the kitchen and pressed a button on the wall. A device lowered itself from the bottom of the corner cabinet. It looked more like a computer than a TV. He reached inside a drawer, pulled out a remote control, and clicked the TV on. He scanned through a few channels and stopped when he got to the local news.

A red banner scrolled across the screen reading *Roosevelt High School in emergency lockdown.*

The image depicted an aerial view of Lucia's high school—the same one my siblings and I had attended—surrounded by armed cops, their cruisers parked all around the building, blue and red lights flashing.

A woman reporter in a smart dress came on the screen next.

"The nature of the emergency is unclear, but a student that was able to get out of the school before it all began says he saw something that chilled him to the very bones."

"Antonietta, are you still there?" Mom asked.

"Just a sec."

The screen flashed again, and this time, a pimply kid appeared. His eyes were wide with fear, and he kept glancing from the camera to the school over his shoulder.

"I've never seen anything like that before," he said. *"I asked for permission to get my homework out of my car, so I came outside. Then I heard a super loud crash behind me, and when I looked, there was this huge… monster smashing down the door. It tore it off the freaking hinges like it was nothing and flung it down."*

The screen switched to the image of a battered door lying on the ground, then back to the kid.

"I already told you I don't know what it was, but there were more. They hauled ass after the first one got rid of the door. I just hid in my car and dialed the cops."

Eric muted the TV. A ringing had started in my ears as soon as the kid explained what he'd seen. My hands were sweaty, and my heart thudded out of control.

"It's the hybrids," Rosalina said in a quick breath.

"That fucking witch!" Jake exclaimed.

"She's not an alpha, so how can she command them?" Eric

wondered out loud, lost in his own thoughts.

I muted the phone. "She's targeting my sister," I said, not a hint of doubt in my mind.

No one tried to deny it. How could they? What was the likelihood of my sister's school being attacked by hybrids?

"She wants revenge, and she'll stop at nothing to get it," I added, still standing frozen in place. With a jolt, I came back to my senses and unmuted the phone. "Mom, I'm going there. You stay put. I'll call you."

She started to protest, but I disconnected the call.

I didn't wait to judge anyone's reaction. I just ran out of the kitchen and headed for the garage. I was about to fleet there when I heard footsteps behind me. I glanced back just as Eric got ahead of me.

"I'll drive," he said. "Your two-door Camaro, it's a bitch."

Everyone else was hot on my heels, even Rosalina.

"You needed rest," I protested.

She shook her head. "No way in hell I'm staying."

Within minutes, the five of us were stuffed in Eric's black sedan. He drove while Damien sat on the passenger seat and Rosalina, Jake, and I occupied the backseat. When we got close, I gave Eric a few directions toward the high school.

A few moments later, he brought the car to a halt behind a line of vehicles blocking the street. From the looks of it, we weren't the only ones who had rushed here after hearing of the awful events on television.

I jumped out of the car and rushed toward the school down a familiar street. It led straight to the front of the high school.

"Excuse me. Excuse me," I pushed past several people, the others following close behind.

When I made it to the front of the crowd, I was met by a line of cop cars and a police barrier. A line of officers stood behind it, facing the crowd, making sure no one snuck past. And even more police officers stood behind them, focusing their attention on the school.

My eyes roved around desperately as I tried to figure out a way to get by unnoticed. I needed to get in there. I needed to save my sister.

"Shit!" Eric grumbled behind me.

I turned to Damien. "Any way you can get us by?"

He shook his head, his copper eyes flickering about. "There are alarm spells in place already," he said. "Mage cops act quickly."

"Dammit!"

"Toni, look," Rosalina pulled on my sleeve and pointed toward the right. "It's Tom."

I followed her finger's trajectory and spotted Tom Freeman standing behind the open door of an unmarked sedan. He stood with his hands at his waist, a deep frown on his forehead as he stared fixedly at the school. He was with his partner, whose name I couldn't remember. Maybe he would let me go in there to get my sister. Fat chance, I knew, but, at the least, he might explain the situation.

Scooting past a group of concerned parents, I sidled my way in Tom's direction and called for him when I got close. His dark eyes searched the crowd. I waved desperately until he spotted me. He said something to his partner and peeled away.

"Toni!" He grabbed my hand as I reached out for him, standing on the other side of the barrier.

"What's happening?" I asked.

He did a quick assessment of me and my companions. He blinked when he caught sight of Damien. "Weren't you… dead?"

"It's a long story," the mage said. "I still owe the authorities a visit to set the record straight. But that's a matter for another day."

Tom shook his head and returned his attention to me. "Lucia is here?" he asked, realizing immediately why I was here.

I nodded.

"I was afraid of that." He let out a frustrated exhale.

"What's happening?" I asked again, my tone insistent.

"We haven't heard much. Some of the kids are texting their parents." He pointed toward a group of cops surrounding a few civilians, which I assumed were the parents in question. "They're huddled up in their classrooms, in their safe spaces. They're reporting growls and shouts and crashing sounds. One of them went silent and hasn't texted again. We're about to send a team in. They're ready. SWAT, a mix of highly trained Stales and Skews. They'll get them out all right."

"How many?" Jake asked behind me. "How many hybrids?"

"Hybrids?" Tom asked. "Like those monsters we found dead in front of your agency last night. What was that all about?!"

Oh, shit! I didn't want to think how many fucking red flags were tacked over my name. But we had no time to discuss that.

"Tom, listen to me," I said, looking deep into his eyes so he didn't miss the importance of what I was about to say. "I don't care how highly trained those people are. They've never dealt with what they're about to encounter. You have to warn them."

A million questions flashed behind Tom's sage eyes. No doubt he was remembering what I'd told him about the strange *creature* that had killed Damien's daughter.

He shook his head. "It's too late to stop it."

Just as he finished saying this, a barrage of shots began within the school.

CHAPTER 12

Panic shot through me. What if the SWAT team made everything worse? What if they didn't reach my sister in time?

"How many hybrids are in there?" I demanded of Tom.

He shook his head. "We don't know. Twenty? Thirty?"

Oh, hell!

The SWAT team didn't stand a chance—not without knowing what they were about to face. Rosalina had emptied full clips of high-caliber bullets into Stephen's hybrids, and they had kept coming and coming. And not only that, even after she took them down, they healed and quickly got back on their feet. What was worse, shooting them only pissed them off and increased their violence. And if the SWAT team didn't stand a chance, the students would fare even worse. Soon, the school would be nothing but a stage for carnage.

Shaking my head, I backed away from Tom.

"I'll talk to the captain," Tom said. "Try to reach them on the radio. How do you kill those… hybrids?"

Damien stepped forward to answer his question while the

others stepped back with me. We mixed with the crowd and came out behind them.

"I gotta go in there," I said, my skin tingling with restless energy. "I have to find Lucia."

Jake shook his head but said nothing. He understood well. That was my little sister in there, and I wasn't about to sit here doing nothing.

"I'll go with you," Eric said.

He and I were the only ones who could fleet. We would be able to move fast enough to avoid detection.

"Please be careful." Jake squeezed my hand.

Rosalina set her jaw. "Kick their ass."

I nodded, then Eric and I were off, circling the main police barrier from the side. Once we made sure no one had noticed us, we let our fleeting power unfurl. The world around me seemed to come to a complete stop. All the sounds became garbled and the spectators froze. Eric and I ran at full pelt. He was a lot faster than me and quickly got ahead. I was able to perceive his legs and arms moving at an unnatural rate, but only because I was also moving at a crazy speed. If I hadn't been, he would have practically appeared invisible.

In an instant, he was at the side entrance with the demolished door. He stepped just past the threshold and stopped to wait for me. I skidded to a halt a few paces in front of him. I still had trouble estimating my momentum and stopping in time.

I bent over panting. Fleeting was a bitch. It drained me too quickly.

"Let's save our energy," Eric said.

I nodded, itching to shift, but urging Red to stand down. My human shape would serve me better here.

At the end of a long hall, a group of men dressed in black and carrying body shields moved in unison. They faced no opposition as they methodically advanced, but it was clear by the sound of shots elsewhere in the building, that there must be another team that had penetrated the school through a different entrance.

"Do you know where to find her?" Eric asked.

I shook my head. "Not yet, but I'm about to find out."

I pulled out my phone and quickly fired off a text to my little sister. I had tried earlier, but she hadn't replied. I figured they'd put a spell around the school to avoid panic.

"Where are you? What classroom?!!!" I could feel my heartbeat in my temples as I waited for a reply.

None came.

It was possible Mom had Lucia's schedule and might be able to tell me where to find her, but she might have a heart attack if she realized I was in here, too.

"C'mon, Lucia," I hissed under my breath as I shook my phone. I glanced up at Eric, feeling my hope deflate.

What now? Did we canvas the school, knocking on every locked classroom door? That would take forever. Just as despair reached out for my throat, my phone buzzed. I lifted it and read Lucia's response.

"PE the gym so scared."

"Do you know where that is?" Eric asked.

"Yes. I used to go here not that long ago." Since my graduation, they could've moved classrooms around, but there was no way they could move the gym.

I quickly typed a response as garbled as hers. "*Stay put dont do anything stupid im coming 4u.*" I slipped my phone into my back pocket and ignored it when it buzzed with another message.

We were standing at an intersection of two halls. The SWAT team had disappeared, but I didn't think it would be wise to go in their direction, so I hooked my finger to the right.

"This way," I said.

We passed several offices, which looked empty. It seemed that maybe some people had been able to escape since they were close to an exit. We rushed to the end of the hall toward a flight of stairs. We climbed them two at a time, slowing down when we reached the top. There, we pulled the door open and peeked out.

"Shit," I spat under my breath.

Around the bend, I could see someone's booted feet. From their position, it was clear the person was lying on their stomach. We slunk in that direction, head nervously swiveling from side to side. When we peeked around the corner, I gasped. Several bodies were strewn on the floor, puddles of blood spreading over the beige linoleum floor. The walls and ceiling were riddled with bullet holes and blood splatters. Entire sections of sheetrock were punched in. It looked as if a bomb had gone off.

There wasn't a single hybrid among the bodies. They were all SWAT team members who had come in with no idea of what they would be facing.

"It was a massacre," Eric said. "They never stood a chance.

Gingerly, we stepped over the bodies. I tried not to look, tried not to think of their families and all of those who would be mourning their tragic deaths. Eric was less squeamish, squatted next to a couple of men, and took their weapons. He offered me one of their handguns. I took it, aware that the best it could do was buy me a couple of seconds. Though sometimes, that was all you needed to make a difference.

There was a tiny beep that caught our attention. It'd come from the dislodged headgear from one of the fallen men. The beep was followed by a set of orders.

"Use wolfsbane bullets and grenades," a voice said. *"Aim for vital organs. When the hostile goes down…"* there was a pause of hesitation, then the rest of the order came in a halting tone, *"cut their heads off or they'll get back up."*

It seemed Damien had gotten the message across loud and clear. I hoped that would be enough to save some lives today.

When we made it to the other side of the hall, we went down

another corridor. Huge paw prints stamped in blood stained the floor. Droplets of blood followed the same trajectory. As we went, the drops got smaller, then disappeared. The beasts healed quickly. Too quickly.

"We're almost there," I said. Only a few more corridors then—

There was a horrible crashing sound followed by hysterical screams. My heart took a tumble. They were coming from the gym. Without thinking, I ran. Walls and doors blurred by, and I was there in an instant. I skidded to a halt in front of the broken gym doors. They were smashed in as if they'd been pummeled by a gigantic ramrod.

Beyond that point, it was chaos.

Two hybrids stood in the middle of the basketball court, roaring and pawing at the polished floors, tearing huge gashes in the wood. The sound of their bloodcurdling growls mixed with the students' screams, creating a discordant echo within the hollow space. The students were hiding under a set of bleachers that had been pulled away from the wall. They were huddled together, caged and helpless. The beasts seemed bewildered as if unsure of how to get to them.

"Help the students. I'll distract the hybrids!" Eric said, startling me. I figured he'd fleeted here since he caught up with me so quickly. "Go!" He urged as I hesitated, then he shifted in a fluid motion, his tawny wolf leaping forward without a care for his own safety.

Shots rang out in the distance.

Witchlights, keep all the children safe.

Doing my best not to let my concern for Eric get in the way, I ran towards the students. When I reached the bleachers from the side, I peered under them. Several pairs of round eyes stared at me in paralyzed horror.

"C'mon," I hissed. "Let's get out of here."

The person closest to me—a girl with black lipstick and several eyebrow piercings— simply stared at me, frozen.

"MOVE!" I screamed.

She jumped, then did as I ordered.

"Run toward the stairs in the far corners, then go out through the side door, the one in front of the back parking lot. The way is clear."

I could only hope this was still true, and the other hybrids were occupied elsewhere. The kids might be forever traumatized by the brutalized bodies on the floor and the sight of all that blood, but it was the best I had—certainly a plan better than death.

As the first girl ran toward the exit, the rest followed. I waved my arms back and forth like a crazy person, urging them on. I threw a quick glance, searching for Eric. The sound of something breaking drew my attention toward the back of the gym. Eric was on the performance stage. One of the hybrids tried to use a table to leap up, but it collapsed under his weight, and sent the creature spread-eagle. The second hybrid made the jump without assistance and went after Eric.

"Toni!" Lucia crashed into me, wrapping her arms around my neck.

I allowed myself a second to feel relief, then pushed her away. "Go! Run! Get out of here!"

"I'm not going anywhere without you."

I knew how stubborn she was and arguing would be a waste of time, so I went back to waving my arms, screaming at everyone to go faster. When the last student and the teacher were out, I grabbed Lucia's wrist and ran.

"Eric, let's get out of here!" I yelled, glancing over my shoulder. "Dammit, where is he?" I desperately searched for him at the same time that I tried to push Lucia forward.

"There!" my sister said, pointing as the wolf ran from behind the stage curtain, caught its corner with his teeth, and ran around the pursuing hybrid, wrapping him like a burrito. The beast roared in frustration and thrashed so hard that it brought the gigantic curtain down from its perch, tangling itself further.

Eric took a huge leap off the stage and hit the ground running. The second hybrid, which had just climbed onto the stage, hopped back down, his enormous clawed hands and feet leaving gouges in the floor as it tried to gain traction.

Suddenly, a stream of basketballs flew up in the air from a wire cart and hit the hybrid straight in his hideous mug. The balls went one after the next like giant bullets, tripping the creature and sending him in a blind rage. My eyes flicked toward my sister in surprise. She was using her telekinetic powers to fire the balls at the beast and buy Eric time to escape.

Using what must have been the last of his fleeting energy, Eric made it to us, shifted in one fluid motion, and ordered us to run as he stretched to his full human height.

He didn't have to tell us twice. We ran without looking back. When we reached the hall littered with all the bodies, Lucia hesitated. I pushed her forward, skipping over fallen officers and doing our best to avoid the slippery blood.

Half tripping, half running, we rushed down the stairs and rallied toward the exit. Lucia's classmates and teachers were already running across the lawn toward the line of policemen and first responders. Officers came to meet them and help them as many collapsed on the ground in near hysterics.

When we made it to the barricade, Tom came to meet us. He stared at me, astonished. There was a strange look in his eyes, a combination of relief and disappointment. He was glad my sister was safe, but he couldn't believe I had taken matters into my own hands.

"I had to, Tom," I said.

He stared at the ground, then back at me. He gave me one curt nod. "Of course, you did."

"The SWAT team… some of them…" I shook my head.

"I know. They're not responding."

"I'm sorry."

"They were doing their jobs. Still are doing it." He gestured toward the far side of the building where a stream of students was running out, guarded by a group of SWAT officers. "They've taken down a few of the… hybrids, and they'll take down the rest. Now, get out of here before I…" His teeth snapped together as he shut his mouth.

His anger toward me seemed to be brewing to an unmanageable level. As I stood there trying to catch my breath, I found myself regretting all the lies I'd told him. I felt terrible. I knew I'd let him down. Big time. I hadn't wanted to, but I'd had no other choice.

Still, it had been wrong. I retreated with a sigh, a hand around my sister. I didn't know how, but I had to make it up to him. Hopefully, he would let me.

ଌଓ

Lucia jumped out of the Uber and ran toward Mom, who stood on the porch of her little two-story cape cod. As they embraced each other, Mom sobbed with relief.

Jake and I got out of the Uber after her. There hadn't been enough space for everyone in Eric's car, so he, Damien, and Rosalina had returned to his house while Jake accompanied my sister and me.

As we walked up the pathway, Daniella came out of the house. I hurried forward, climbed the steps to the porch, and joined in a four-way hug, while Jake watched awkwardly from the sidelines.

Intense emotions washed over us. We were so, so, happy that nothing had happened to our baby girl. Of course, she wasn't anywhere near a baby anymore. She was hardly even a girl. Womanhood was just within her reach now that she was about to graduate. But to us, she would always be the baby.

Once the bulk of our emotions were unloaded, we shuffled into the house. Mom, not fully calm, set about brewing a pot of coffee and arranging biscotti on a plate. Once she poured a hot cup for everyone, she remained on her feet, her hands wringing nervously in front of her as if she'd forgotten something.

"Mom," Daniella called from her spot at the table, "sit and enjoy your coffee." She patted the chair next to her.

Mom shook herself and did as her older daughter suggested, and finally seemed to let the fact that we were all safe sink in.

"Are you all right, honey?" she asked, noticing the way Lucia was staring into the depths of her coffee.

Lucia shook herself. "Yeah, I'm fine."

Daniella and I exchanged a glance. We knew our little sister well. She was too cool to ever let anything get to her, or at least that was what she liked to pretend. But it was obvious that this had truly shaken her.

Daniella opened her mouth to say something, but Mom beat her to it. "You've always been brave and daring, honey. I'm sure you were the one telling your classmates that everything would be all right, even if you were scared to the bone. If you want to talk about it, though, we're here."

Taking a sip of her coffee, Lucia grunted in agreement. For a moment, I thought she would dismiss what had happened with some silly joke, but when she set her cup down, her expression made us all pause.

A long silence stretched before us.

"Those things scare the crap out of me," Jake said as if to let Lucia know it was all right to admit it.

Lucia swallowed thickly. "What are they?"

Jake inclined his head toward me, indicating I should be the one to answer that question and reveal all the gruesome details. I would have rather spared them the knowledge, but soon, it would be all over the news, and they would find out anyway.

With everyone listening intently, I explained what I could, without breaking the vows of secrecy I'd sworn to the Pack Rule. I didn't go into specifics of how the hybrids were created, or how I'd almost been turned into one. What I shared with them was enough to scare them properly, however, and it made it easier to tell them the next bit.

"I think… it would be best if you keep a low profile."

"You mean leave the house again?" Mom asked.

I nodded.

She blinked rapidly. "But why? Are you suggesting those *things* were there to… hurt Lucia?"

"Um, no. I mean… maybe. I can't be sure, but better safe than sorry. There is this witch. She has it in for us and has control of those monsters."

"What the hell kind of mess have you gotten yourself into?!" Daniella exclaimed.

"Language!" Mom said.

Daniella ignored her. "We can't keep abandoning our lives every other day."

"I'm sorry, Dani. It's not my fault."

"Is it not?"

I peered toward Mom, at a loss. Was it my fault that they had such screwed-up people in the world?

"Whether or not it's Antonietta's fault," Mom said, "the most important thing is to be safe. We can't ignore her warning, can we?"

Daniella crossed her arms, looking angry, but she didn't argue.

"We'll pack up and go to a hotel," Mom said with finality.

"Can you make sure it has a pool this time?" Lucia put in, lightening the mood a bit. "And a Jacuzzi. Maybe I can invite Noah."

"No! You're not inviting Noah or anybody else, young lady!" Mom wagged her finger at her. "That would defeat the purpose of keeping a low profile, I'd say."

I doubted it was the *low profile* thing Mom was worried about exactly. And I had to admit that the idea of my *baby sister* in a hot tub with some guy didn't sit well with me either.

As they hurried about packing a few things, I breathed a lot easier. I couldn't do what needed to be done if I was constantly worrying about my family.

Jake and I had a pact to break.

CHAPTER 13

"No way, but I'm not going to Wolfskeep," I protested for the *nth* time.

"I second that," Eric said. "Besides, I quit the Pack Rule, remember? And not only that, your dear ally doesn't want me there."

Ulfen Erickson stood in the middle of Eric's study, looking extremely frustrated at us. His red hair and beard were unkempt, and his tie hung loosely around a crumpled shirt. He had the appearance of a shaggy stray dog on the run from animal control. Eric and I were the only ones here. Rosalina was resting since the situation at the high school earlier today had exhausted her. And Jake and Damien had left—Jake to take care of pack business and Damien to ponder about the best way to break the blood pact. He said he did his best thinking alone.

"You must come tomorrow," Ulfen insisted.

Eric scoffed. "Nope."

"So you're washing your hands of things. Is that what you're saying?" Ulfen demanded.

"Yep," Eric replied at the same time that I said. "Not exactly."

Ulfen glanced between us, anger beginning to show in his features.

"Look, I have my own problems," I said. "I have my family to worry about and—"

"That only means it's in your best interest to take that damn witch down. Unless you expect your family to hide for the rest of their lives."

It turned out, Ulfen had seen Eric and me on the news as we ran out of the high school, which was the reason he was here. He'd wanted to learn what happened. Now, I wished we hadn't given him the scoop—not if he was going to use it against me.

After we told him what happened, he'd proceeded to talk about the upcoming Pack Rule meeting, and when we said we weren't going, he'd cranked up his engines to convince us.

Ulfen turned to Eric. "You can't let your pride get in the way of this city's well-being."

"Of course I can," Eric shot back, nonchalantly. He reclined in his desk chair, practically fanning himself with indifference.

I was standing by the fireplace about to turn on my heel to walk out the door. I had too much on my mind to take up a vendetta against Mekare Graves. I had tried that before, and it hadn't gone so well. It'd been my desire for revenge that had resulted in Rosalina's kidnapping, the destruction of the agency, and the attack on Lucia's school. If I'd just stayed out of it, my life would be in much better shape. I'd already decided that others could take care of that deranged Midnight Witch: the police, the packs, the vampire covens… she had pissed them all off, after all. I was nobody, just a lone wolf without the backing of a pack. Ulfen could risk his life and everything else if he wanted to avenge his son's death. I'd already lost too much, and I didn't have a hefty bank account, like he did, to make everything right once this was all over.

"We could use someone of your abilities to stop her," Ulfen told Eric, raising his voice.

Slowly, Eric stood from his chair, placing the tips of his fingers on the desk and slightly leaning forward. "I would suggest you control yourself. You are in *my* home, and I won't tolerate you disrespecting me or my guests." His alpha command carried such intensity that the hairs on the back of my arms stood on end. Red bristled, even though the menace wasn't directed at me.

A flash of fury sparked in Ulfen's blue eyes. His jaw clenched and fists tightened. It took him a few beats and noticeable effort to gather his temper, but the next time he spoke it was with measured calm.

He turned to me. "Jacob Knight will be there," he said.

"I know." I tried to put on an indifferent expression, but I failed miserably.

I wanted Jake to be free of that burden, but he was a pack leader now, and he was compelled to make sure the members of the Knight pack weren't set adrift now that Walter was dead. With the title came many responsibilities. The Knight legacy included a substantial fortune and many businesses that served as a livelihood for a lot of people, including the majority of his pack members. Decisions had to be made. Actions needed to be taken. As the inheritor, it all fell upon Jake's shoulders, including attending Pack Rule meetings.

I held Ulfen's probing gaze. He knew there was something between Jake and me, but he didn't seem willing to come out and say it. After all, to everyone's knowledge, Jake was going to marry Allison Blackridge in three days. Not that I would let that happen. I'd invite Mekare for tacos before I allowed that wedding to take place.

"We can't allow that witch to destroy our way of life," Ulfen said, changing tactics. "We have enjoyed peace for a long time and look at what she's done in such a short time. How do you think things will look in a year if we don't stop her? You do hope to maintain your residence in St. Louis, don't you?"

Our silence was his answer.

"Then you *must* care about what happens," he continued. "You have fought the hybrids successfully. You even rescued all those kids at the high school and all the cops were able to do was get themselves killed."

"That's not true. They rescued the rest of the kids and took down a few hybrids."

He made a dismissive gesture.

"We are only two people," Eric said.

"Two powerful alphas, with extraordinary abilities." At this, his blue gaze focused entirely on me.

I shuffled from foot to foot, feeling self-conscious. "Don't look at me. I'm just a newbie alpha without the pack. What little I know, Eric has taught me, and I'm far from competent at any of it."

Ulfen huffed, whirled, and stomped toward the door. Before exiting, he stopped, his large hand on the handle, his chest rising and falling in an agitated manner. After a long moment, he glanced over his shoulder and said, "If you sit idle and she destroys our city, you will deserve the guilt that'll haunt you for the rest of your lives."

Sheesh, easy with the foreboding, dude! I was trying to be positive, and he wasn't helping.

Turning away from us, he opened the door and marched out of the room, leaving his severe admonishment hanging in the air like a noose that, with time, would wrap itself around our necks to suffocate us slowly. I could almost feel it tightening around my neck already.

"God damn that righteous asshole!" Eric spat, making his way around the desk and sending a reproachful glower in my direction as if it were my fault.

I pondered his expression for a moment—my thoughts doing uncomfortable twisty things—and arrived at a feeling of lousy realization.

Shit!

It *was* my fault. Just like with my family, Eric was in this situation because of me. If he had never agreed to help me, he would have…

"No!" I exclaimed, startling Eric. "This is *not* my fault."

"Who said it was?"

"You did."

"You must be imagining things."

"Uh-uh," I shook my finger at him. "Your eyes don't lie. You were throwing all kinds of shade my way."

"Get over yourself. This fucking mess is my own fault, and no one else's."

My mouth opened and closed in a perfect impersonation of a Pac-Man figure.

Rubbing his forehead and looking as tired as a two-hundred-year-old man, he walked toward the sofa and collapsed on it. He was silent for a long minute, then his face acquired a slack quality as if he'd fallen into some sort of trance.

I could sense a story coming as he got lost inside his own mind. I dared not to move for fear he wouldn't speak, so I stayed frozen by the fireplace, barely blinking.

"This started fifteen years ago, and I guess it was bound to catch up with me at some point. I was happy then. You wouldn't have recognized me. I loved my wife and daughter. I didn't know it then, but they were my everything. I thought the pack mattered more, but in the end, they didn't. I should have never been born an alpha. If I hadn't, they would still be alive."

He glanced up at the portrait of his family that hung above the mantle. The sadness that swam in his eyes was murky and deep, a load that I could barely begin to comprehend.

"The Cross Pack was one the most powerful in the city," he continued. "I had ten strong betas under my command. They were loyal and helped me run the pack like a well-oiled machine. We controlled the trade up and down the Mississippi River. We owned factories, restaurants, stores. Other pack members managed things. It was a big community. Productive and strong.

"Of course no one gets that successful without making a few enemies. We didn't exercise ruthless business practices. We were fair and our decisions were never personal. Business is business. There was a small pack in the Murphy area. They owned a growing brewery business. They had a big order of barley coming down the river, but their payment fell through. You see… their alpha had a gambling problem and had drained their accounts. In the end, many lost their livelihood. He came to me, begged me to give him a break, promised he would pay. But he had steadily gained a bad reputation, and although he might have straightened his path, I couldn't take the risk. Besides, if I offered him lenience, I would have to do the same for others. I turned him away. His pack members blamed him, not me. They understood it was his job to look after them and make the right calls, but he was humiliated. I saw it in his eyes. As an alpha, myself, I understood very well how he felt.

"What I saw in him should have served me as a warning. I should have known to be wary of him, to watch my back. But I'd grown overconfident. I was so high on my pedestal that I felt unreachable. And not only that, I was full of myself and only thought of me. And maybe *I* was untouchable, but my family…

"That coward. He had no honor. He was a beast without scruples, without decency. He had a friend, a vampire he'd known since before he was turned. They broke into my house and…" Eric swallowed thickly, a muscle twitching in his jaw, his breathing restrained as if it pained him. "At first, I wanted to die. I almost killed myself, but one of my betas stopped me. With my wife and my daughter gone, I found out that the pack didn't matter to me. I lost my sanity, and I don't think I've ever regained it completely. I made him and that vampire pay, made them suffer. A simple death wasn't enough. I tortured the alpha for days. Then I asked Damien to make a poison that would slowly kill a vampire. I fed it to him and taunted him every day as he withered away. So you see… it's my fault."

He paused. I tried to find words that could help, but I was struck mute.

"Sometimes," he went on, "I fear what I may do if anything happens to any of you. When I thought Damien had died…" He let the words hang, and in the silence, I felt his pent-up anger like a bomb that could explode at any moment.

I stood there with a knot in my throat. The entire time Eric had talked, he hadn't glanced in my direction, and I was afraid he'd forgotten I was here. If I moved, would he realize he'd said more than he'd meant to? Would he decide I was not worthy of that glimpse into his dark past?

I fear what I may do if anything happens to any of you.

We had all mourned in our own way when we'd thought Damien was gone. I didn't want to go through that again, and it seemed Eric didn't either. The mage's "death" had surely taken a greater toll on Eric than I'd imagined. He was afraid of what would happen if this war cost one of us our lives.

Was it possible that without meaning to Eric had formed a new pack?

We were nothing but a mismatched bunch. Two too many alphas, a prima donna mage, and a Stale. No one would have put together such an unlikely, fragile group, and yet, here we were. And we cared about each other. Deeply.

Slowly, I let the knowledge sink in. He wanted to wash his hands of Mekare not because he didn't think Ulfen was right about the future of St. Louis, but because of the risk it posed to our lives. He was afraid one of us would truly die, and he wasn't sure if he could handle that.

Tentatively, I approached him and sat at his side on the sofa. If he'd been anyone else, I would've wrapped my arms around him, but even after this confession, I wasn't sure he'd let me.

I thought about what to say and realized there was only one thing he would appreciate, and it had to be a tit for tat.

"I want to end that witch," I said. "I don't think I will ever feel safe knowing she's alive, but getting involved in this mess wrecked my life. And Rosalina's. My mom and sisters are also suffering the consequences. If I don't get out now, I'm afraid I'll lose more than just the agency. If it's just my business, I can live with that. Maybe it's still salvageable, and if it isn't, I'll get a job doing something, and it'll be fine. But if I lose any of you…" I shook my head. Just the thought of it made my heart ache.

"So yeah, I need to stay out of it. There's a lot I could do without, but I couldn't live without my family, Jake, Rosalina, Damien… and you."

When I finished, Eric was as stiff as a statue, staring straight ahead at the floor. After a moment, he let out a long exhale and shook his head.

"How the hell did I let myself get into this situation?" he said in a half-amused tone meant to diffuse our stern mood. He glanced over at me sideways, one eyebrow raised, and nudged me with his shoulder. It was a companionable gesture that was nothing like the Eric I was used to. "It's better when you don't care, Sunder. Did no one ever give you that piece of advice?"

I shook my head. "Even if they had, clearly," I looked him up and down, "the advice doesn't take 'cause you're a hot mess."

"No shit." He stood up, stretched, and cracked his neck as if he'd just finished doing something strenuous, which I figured he had. "So we have our reasons to allow that fucking witch to get away with the unspeakable, and they amount to the same. We want the people we care about to be safe."

That was it, in so very few words.

"I guess that makes us selfish," I said.

Eric blew a puff of air through his nose. "In my book, that's a good thing to be. Problem is…" He paused and turned to face me, "as much as we want to, I'm afraid we won't be able to stay out of it."

I had a feeling he was right.

"I know you may be tired, but what do you say we go downstairs for some training. You've got the hang of fleeting. How about we try to figure out that sensory thing you've got going? You never know when it might come in handy again."

I sighed. Here we were refusing to get involved but knowing deep inside that we could run, we could even fleet, but we could never hide.

CHAPTER 14

Eric and I faced each other in the training room. His blue eyes assessed me as if he were looking at me anew. After a long minute, he blinked and shook his head.

"Honestly, I don't know what to tell you, Sunder. Where to start. I have no idea how these powers of yours work." He rubbed his chin. "How about you try to explain?"

"Okay, I'll do my best." I thought carefully, then began. "My tracking abilities rely on all my senses. When I track someone in a trance, I can activate my senses one at a time. I normally start with my nose. My hearing and sight follow. I've never used my taste or touch. It would be impractical, really.

"Anyway, when I activate my sense of smell, the scents that surround my mark hit me full-on, and at first, it's confusing as hell when the onslaught comes. It took a lot of practice to not let them overwhelm me. I learned how to sift through them, how to identify them, then discard them one by one. They're still there but in the background. It's the same with my hearing and sight."

"So what happened when you used these skills on that hybrid?"

"It's hard to explain exactly, but it was like I was able to push a sensory overload into him all at once. All the senses, though, even touch and taste."

He considered. "But how? You weren't tracking anyone, so where did the shit you sent into them come from?"

Good question. I hadn't stopped to think about that. "Hmm, I guess it must have come from me. Maybe all the stuff I've experienced throughout my life..."

That was the only thing that made sense.

Eric frowned, uncertain. In truth, he was just helping me explain this to myself, and trying to put it into words for someone else was actually working.

"In that case, maybe..." he started tentatively, "would it help to focus on a particularly… *busy* moment of your life? Not sure if that's the right word, but maybe you know what I mean."

I nodded slowly. "Yeah, maybe it would."

"Can you think of such a time?"

I cringed as one instance immediately came to me.

He waved his hands in the air. "Don't worry, you don't have to tell me what it is."

I narrowed my eyes at him, wondering if he was trying to spare me or himself. Either way, I preferred not telling him. The time of my life I'd thought of wasn't one that made me proud. It was actually the *suckiest*, that wallowing nightmare after Jake left me when I fell off the deep end.

During the time I was homeless, I experienced so much. Bitter cold, hunger, thirst, insults. It had been pure misery, and at times, before Rosalina helped me get my shit together, it felt inescapable, like hell.

"So… keeping that in mind," he said, "try to shock me."

"No! What? Are you crazy?! I could kill you."

He shrugged. "I doubt it."

Gah, such a male!

"I killed a fucking vampire and a hybrid." I reached my hands toward him, wiggling my fingers.

He took a step back. "On second thought. Hmm," he considered for a moment, "you do glow when you channel your tracker skills, right?"

"Yeah, so I guess we will know if it's working when I do my Christmas tree impersonation."

He nodded and gestured with a hand, inviting me to start.

I took a deep breath, shook my arms, and closed my eyes. Focusing, I thought of that shimmering limbo where I went after taking a tracking potion. Nothing came. The back of my eyelids just glowed orange with the overhead lights.

"Take deep breaths," Eric said, his voice low and suggestive.

I did as he said, focusing on the way my chest rose and fell, imagining particles of air filling my lungs.

The world around me went dark, and slowly, tiny glimmers appeared in the black expanse. For a few beats, I let my mind settle, trying to become familiar with the feeling to make sure I'd be able to recall it. Once I had it, I invited in the shameful memories of my past. They came one by one, then all at once. So many of them that I couldn't have named them if my life depended on it.

My heart started beating out of control, pounding against my ribs like fist blows. Fear rippled through me as I imagined myself stuck in here like the last time, the time I'd been trying to track the Midnight Witch's supposed mate.

I broke my focus. My eyes sprang open, and I staggered forward. Eric made as if to steady me, but I waved him off.

"I'm fine," I said.

"I don't think that worked."

"No shit."

I tried again. The second time, the fear returned, so I attempted to release all my sensory memories at once.

"Did it work?" I asked, eyes shooting open.

Eric twisted his mouth to one side. "There was no glow, so I don't think so."

I flexed my fingers. They felt restless and tight at the tips. "It's like I need to sink my claws into something."

Without a word, he ran upstairs and returned with a few cushions from his many sofas. "Try with these."

I did. In fact, I shredded the poor things to bits, but nothing worked. After about twenty tries, I sank to the floor and sat cross-legged. "This is useless."

"It's only our first try. We'll figure something out. We always do."

Pushing away my frustration, I jumped to my feet. He was right. We would figure it out. "How about we do some regular training?"

His answer was to shift, and for the next hour, we ran in the woods behind his house and did wolf things.

CHAPTER 15

Damien arrived only a few minutes after Eric and I finished training. He had a few large leather-bound books with him, which he set on the study's coffee table.

He removed his cloak and top hat and glanced around with a frown.

"Rosalina took a nap," I said. "She's showering right now and then she'll get online to file a claim with the insurance company, but she'll join us after that."

He huffed as if he was indifferent to the information, but I knew better. Whenever he was here, he cut glances in her direction every chance he got, especially when he thought she wasn't looking. Funny enough, she did the same.

I approached the coffee table and examined the books he'd brought. "What are these?"

"Some *light* reading material about blood demons. That one," he pointed to a tome with gold scroll on the cover, "is a Demonology Register and it lists the names of several demons we might be able to conjure."

"Demon names?" I frowned up at him.

Eric abandoned his desk and came closer, a deep line between his eyebrows.

"Yes," Damien said, "you need a name in order to call upon a demon, that among other things."

"What other things?" I asked.

Eric sat in an armchair and threw the front cover open. The book was as long as my arm and as thick as my hand. He leafed through it, giving me a glimpse of yellowed pages, tiny print, and a few black-and-white illustrations.

"Well," Damien began, "we'll need chalk, a sigil, trammel heads…"

Trammel heads? What were those?

"I tried to contact a friend for help. She works at the League of Demon Hunters in New York City, but she can't come, so I'll have to do it myself. I'm not an expert by any means. I've never dabbled in the arts too deeply, but I can manage. Now, where is your beau?"

"He'll be here in another thirty minutes," I said. "He has some pack business to tend to."

Damien's face suddenly lit up. "Oh, you won't believe the surprise delivery I received this morning."

Eric looked up from the book, his curious expression matching mine. "Well, don't leave us in suspense."

"It came from the Dark Donna herself."

Eric and I made similar faces of disgust.

The mage paced toward the sofa and sat, luxuriously crossing his legs and making himself comfortable. "She received *my* special delivery and sent a lovely thank you note with an invitation to go to dinner."

So Bernadetta had gotten what she wanted. The day I gave the Prince the cure to hide it, I would've never imagined she would end up being the recipient.

"You would think that after hundreds of years walking this

earth, she would be sick of it," Eric said.

"I hate that she was the one to get the last bit of cure," I said.

"Not me," Damien put in. "Bernadetta finally called back her bloodthirsty minions. They'd been breathing down my neck for a while. I was starting to get nervous."

"Nervous?" Eric said with a frown. "You? The mage who is capable of resurrection."

The mage made a dismissive flourish with his hand. "Though I assure you there was no luck and muck skill involved in my *resurrection,* as you call it, I'd rather not take that risk again. Being an earthworm was very unpleasant and although a cat was a nice upgrade, I much prefer my current state."

"I do, too," Rosalina said from the door, shooting Damien a warm smile.

After some rest and good food, she seemed to have returned to her usual vivacity. She was dressed in a tank top and a pair of workout shorts. Her tanned legs were smooth and shone with the light from the many lamps in the room. She was barefoot, and as she padded across the layered rugs, Damien's copper gaze slowly admired her from head to toe.

"Good evening," she said, taking a seat on the arm of the sofa and crossing her legs.

Damien's eyes nearly popped out as he admired her legs. All his bluster seemed to sputter out of him, and he had the look of someone who'd forgotten all his words.

"Are you ready to start?" Rosalina asked, gesturing toward the books.

"Yes, we're just waiting for Jake," I said.

At that moment, Eric's cell phone buzzed. He took it out of his jeans pocket and looked at the screen. "Speak of the devil." He pressed a button to let Jake in.

A couple of minutes later, Jake walked into the study. I welcomed him with a smile that quickly fell as I noticed how frazzled he looked. His handsome face spoke of little rest. Since this morning, his eyes had become bloodshot and his skin sallow. His stubble was longer, which meant he hadn't even had time for his personal care. He glanced around the room with impatience as if he wanted or needed to be elsewhere.

"Everything all right?" I asked.

"Hmm, yeah, just a lot on my mind. I got here as soon as I could. Are we ready to start?" He shook himself and made a visible effort to focus on the moment.

"We were only waiting for you," Damien said, reluctantly tearing his attention away from Rosalina.

Eric stood and moved to a spot in front of the fireplace. "You two sit there," he said, offering Jake and me the twin armchairs. Once we were all situated, Damien pushed to the edge of the sofa and began explaining his plan to undo the unbreakable pact. We all listened, transfixed.

"So, like I said, I read *Blood Treaties: My life in France* in detail," Damien said. "Alodar Rune's account of how he witnessed the dissolution of an unbreakable pact sworn by a werewolf peasant to his landowner seems quite legitimate, and it makes me hopeful that the method will work for us. We know it won't be easy, and not only that, but it will also be dangerous. Jake could die," he said plainly and let that sink in a little deeper as if the awful idea wasn't already a thorn in my eyeball.

He went on, wearing a stern expression. "The magic of the pact runs in Jake's veins. His blood and Allison's were used to craft the treaty between them. Blood magic is the most powerful, the most binding. If Jake were to break his vow, the curse in his system would strike," he pointed at his heart, "right here. His heart would stop." Another brutal pause to annihilate any remaining doubt about the seriousness of what we intended to do.

I gulped and avoided looking at Jake. If I did, I would just get angry at him all over again for putting himself in this situation, and

I didn't need to do that. I'd been angry at him long enough, and the time for reproach had passed.

Instead, it was time to fight for our future. Together.

Rosalina put a hand up. "If Jake breaks his vow, as you said, would Allison also… die?"

"No," Damien shook his head. "Only the person who breaks the vow would."

"So… what if Allison was… say… struck by a train?" Rosalina vaguely waved her hand in the air.

"The magic makes provisions for that," Jake said, looking like someone who had imagined Allison's death a thousand times. I knew Jake wouldn't be capable of hurting her, but we weren't innocent little angels, and I would be lying if I hadn't had similar thoughts.

"Blood magic used for this purpose is so powerful and intricate," Damien said with a reverent tone, "that it can distinguish between accidental death and one caused by the counterpart involved in the pact. If Allison were to die and Jake was involved in any way—even if someone else committed the crime—he would die along with his victim. If she was generally struck by a train without Jake's knowledge in any shape or form, then he would be spared."

"Damn, if only trains were on my side," I joked, then immediately felt callous. I didn't wish any ill on Allison. She was in the same boat as Jake and me. In love with somebody else.

"So what does the blood demon do exactly?" Rosalina asked. "How does it get rid of the curse in Jake's veins?"

"That's the dangerous part," the mage said. "The blood demon needs to enter Jake's body to be able to eat away the magic that binds him."

"Enter his body?!" Rosalina exclaimed in horror. Her green eyes flicked in my direction loaded with an implicit question. *Are you crazy?* she seemed to ask.

Jake reached across the small table between our armchairs and rested his hand on mine. "I'm willing to do what it takes to be with Toni," he said. "I had to convince her to agree, but she understands why I must do this."

Rosalina's expression grew sad, but she nodded. If she disapproved, I knew she wouldn't say anything else. She always respected everyone's decisions and knew how to be supportive, even in the face of adversity.

"So how do I let the demon in?" Jake asked next. "Will it be like a possession? Do I invite it in?"

We had been wondering about this since Alodar Rune's book didn't go into detail about this part of the spell. I tensed, though my heart beat a thousand miles per hour as I waited for the answer.

Damien shook his head. "No, it is not like a possession, and you don't invite the demon in either." He stopped, looking reluctant to continue.

"Then what?" I pressed.

"The demon has to enter Jake's… bloodstream."

"His bloodstream?!" Rosalina and I exclaimed at the same time.

"Yes, it will be necessary to make a deep cut, which will serve as a door into Jake's circulatory system."

Jake's circulatory system! I shuddered. That was so clinical, so cold. If Damien was trying to dissuade us, he was certainly outdoing himself.

"All right," Jake said, swallowing thickly. "It sounds… positively terrifying."

"I'm glad you realize that," Damien said, nearly glowering at Jake.

It was this pointed look that made me realize he really was trying to scare us.

"I want to impress upon you the enormous risk you'd be undertaking. You need to go into this with your eyes wide open."

What Damien didn't know was that Jake and I had rehashed

this a thousand times. The mage didn't know how determined Jake was or how resigned I was to his decision. Still, I appreciated Damien's effort, his concern for Jake's life.

"I'm no demon expert," Eric said, standing under the portrait of his wife and daughter, "but how do you keep *the thing* from devouring Jake's life force?"

"Good question," Damien said. "That's the tricky part."

"*That's* the tricky part," Rosalina huffed. "It all sounds tricky to me."

"As it would to most Stales," Damien said in a tone that suggested he was glad Rosalina knew nothing about this sort of thing, at least until this point. "But really, summoning the demon won't be difficult. I've summoned one or two in the past, and my LDH friend in New York can give me some pointers if I have questions."

Rosalina frowned. "LDH?"

"Short for the League of Demon Hunters," Damien clarified. "Anyway, as far as directing the creature into Jake… well… blood demons are called that for a reason. As soon as it senses the blood, it will go straight for it. Blood demons are always hungry. Vampires, even new ones, pale in comparison. Left unchecked, the demon would *ravage* Jake in a matter of minutes. First, it would devour his blood, but not only that. The cherry on top is the victim's life force, the heart."

Cold fingers raked up my spine, and I had to bite my tongue not gasp in despair and knock Jake unconscious right where he sat. I could keep him KO'd until Saturday. I might even be able to deliver him in his tux to the church steps. It wouldn't be easy, but the alternative was way worse.

"How do you stop it from going that far?" Jake asked, looking too cool for someone who was planning to serve himself on a platter.

Damien paused and acquired a pensive expression. He rubbed

his chin, lost in thought. Watching him made my stomach tumble. He hadn't figured out how. Why were we even talking about this if he didn't know how to prevent the heart-munching part of the cleansing?

"The key," he finally said, "is to not let the demon reach your heart."

Well, duh!

"And… do you know how to do that?" Jake asked.

"In theory, yes."

"That's not very reassuring," Rosalina put in.

Damien inhaled and gave a slow nod. "I know, but I still have two days to figure it out and to practice."

That made me feel better. A little.

"Good," I said. "You should practice. A lot. I'll be there, of course. For moral support and whatever else you need. Anything. All you have to do is ask. More tacos, a stiff cocktail, a back massage." I was rambling.

"Hey!" Jake complained, not happy about that last one.

"I think you'd better leave the back massages to Rosalina," Eric suggested.

I sputtered a laugh and had to bite my lower lip to stop it. Damien became very interested in the ceiling, and Rosalina blushed deeply, though she recovered quickly with a clever comment.

"That might be more *your* department, Eric," she said. "I'm sure it won't be the first in you all's long bromance."

This time, I let the laughter roll out of me, making no attempt to stop it. Eric's grimace of disgust was priceless as was Damien's raised eyebrow at his friend. He seemed to be saying *excuse me, but you could only wish we really had a bromance.*

"As if!" Eric exclaimed, not missing a beat. He knew Damien too well not to read the commentary in his expression.

This lightened the mood considerably. The tension across my shoulders eased a bit, especially when I took in the amusement in

Jake's features. Despite everything, he didn't look as frazzled as when he'd first come in. After I stopped laughing, he circled back to what we all wanted to know.

"So when do you start practicing?"

Damien turned his attention to Jake. "Right away."

"Good."

The mage had one more question. "The wedding is still scheduled for Saturday, correct?"

Jake nodded.

"So if we do the cleansing on Friday night that gives a few days to perfect my technique. It involves powerful telekinetic control. I possess a wide range of skills, but telekinesis is not one of them. I can certainly move things using my magical abilities." He wiggled his fingers at one of the heavy books on the coffee table and made it slide a few inches to the left. "But… I don't have the finesse that years of practice or an innate ability can give someone. As you might imagine, a demon's essence is different from that of an inanimate object like that book. They're made of matter, of course, though not like this sofa or that table. No, their makeup is more like that of light or air. Those things are harder to control."

"So what you're saying," I started, carefully putting my thoughts into words, "is that you'll need to control the demon's essence while it's inside of Jake so that it can't reach his heart."

"Precisely!" Damien exclaimed, holding a finger up for emphasis. "Once the demon enters Jake's bloodstream, it needs to be held in place for several minutes while Jake's heart does its job and pumps blood. However, the creature cannot be allowed to get anywhere near the heart. The idea is that each beat will deliver more blood until… it's all gone."

I almost choked. "But that will kill him."

"If he were a Stale, yes," Damien said. "But he's a werewolf, a strong one at that. Once I pull the demon back out, we will do a transfusion and hydrate him really well."

The hell?! I grabbed my head and glanced at Jake, a plea in my expression.

"I'm sure I can get through that," he said with conviction.

What did he think he was? A sea cucumber?

Jake turned to Damien. "So do you think you have enough time to learn how to control the demon?"

"I hope. I will certainly do my best. Now," he reached for the Demonology Register, "I'll let you read about a couple of blood demons I found. I think either one of them could do the job, but I figured I would let you choose.

Jake threw a squeamish glance toward the book as the mage pushed it across the table. "What difference does it make?"

"None, really," Damien said, "if it makes no difference to you whether I use a demon that is said to have created hemophilia or the one who convinced physicians that bloodletting was a good idea."

Rosalina gasped in horror. "Are those the only choices?"

"We're talking about demons, not unicorns," Damien put in.

At the thought of such filthy creatures entering Jake, I shuddered. The possibility that he might die was terrifying, but something I hadn't considered was the likelihood of something else going wrong.

"Damien," I pressed a hand to my chest, feeling my heart speed up as a host of horrible thoughts rushed into my mind, "could there be any side effects? I mean… if you manage to keep the demon from killing Jake, could going through the cleansing affect him in any other way?"

The mage thought for a moment, then said, "To be honest, I have no idea. I've never done anything like this and don't know anyone who has either."

Jake huffed. "Well, if I lose my mind or anything like that, just throw me in the nuthouse, and don't bother to visit. I'm sure I won't mind."

I gave him a pointed glare.

He put both hands up in the air in apology for the crude joke. "Honestly, I don't want to worry about any of that right now. One thing at a time, okay? If I've survived and there are side effects, I'll deal with those later."

"And what if you can't?" Eric offered.

"I guess that would mean I ended up brain-dead or something, in which case I won't be worried about anything."

I jumped to my feet. "Can you stop talking like that? This is no joke."

He hung his head, looking chastised. "I'm sorry, Toni. It's just too much to worry about, and there's no use. Why don't we just let Damien practice and see? Can we do it here?" Jake glanced around the room, looking unsure.

"No, not here," Damien said. "Perhaps in the garage. The large one."

The large one? There was more than one? Apparently, I'd only seen the small one.

"Well, what are we waiting for?" Eric stood, then led the way out of the study.

I had no idea what kind of day we were in for, but I sure wasn't looking forward to it.

CHAPTER 16

"Toni, wait." Jake placed a hand on my shoulder as the others made their way downstairs. "Can we talk?"

I struck a pose, a hand on my waist and eyebrows as high as they would go. "Is this about you being an insensitive ass?"

"No, not about that. I'm sorry if I upset you with my stupid comments. I didn't mean to."

"It's like you don't care what happens to you."

"You know that's not true. It's just my way of… coping. That's all."

His clear eyes told me he was speaking the truth. He was dealing with a lot, and sometimes laughter was the best medicine in these situations—even if you were laughing at your expense and others didn't think it was the least bit funny.

"Are you going to the Pack Rule meeting later tomorrow tonight?" he asked.

I shook my head. There was a certain tightening around his eyes. It came and went quickly, but I noticed it. He'd been expecting me to go, and he was disappointed, maybe even hurt. But going there might just bring me more trouble, and I had enough of that already.

"I want to focus on us," I said. "And on building things back up with Rosalina, if we can, if there's any hope left for our agency."

"As you should." There was no trace of disappointment left in him as he offered me a genuine smile. Whatever he'd expected from me, he'd renounced it, putting me and my needs first. A strange niggling stirred in the pit of my stomach. By focusing on doing what it took to break the pact, I thought I was doing what was best for our relationship. But was I? Maybe he needed my support more than he let on.

"You want me to come?" I asked.

He shook his head. "No, it's fine. You're focusing on the right things. Besides, it's best if you're out of this mess."

I could sense his relief at the thought that I would be safe and away from the comings and goings of the Pack Rule and, by default, that psychopathic Midnight Witch. And yet, now I was second-guessing myself, thinking that I should be with him, that he needed me, that if we broke this pact and I joined him, he would need me by his side in all his affairs—the same way that I would need him.

I opened my mouth to say something as I reconsidered my earlier decision, but his mood flipped on a dime. His hand slid slowly from my shoulder all the way to my hand, his light touch making me shiver. He took a step closer, wrapped an arm around my waist, and pulled me against him. His solidity was delicious, and I immediately became aware of every peak and valley in his body.

"It wasn't the Pack Rule meeting I wanted to talk to you about. It was something else," he said, his voice a low rumble, that did unspeakable things to my insides.

"Yeah?" I said, a little breathless, finding it hard to concentrate when every cell in my body seemed to riot and demand that I focus on the sensation of his closeness.

"I was wondering…" He tilted his head to one side, his player charm full-on with the same intensity it had been the first night he noticed me. "Would you go out with me tonight? On a date?"

My mouth opened and closed as I processed my surprise. *A date?* Did we have time for that? There had been so much on my mind lately, and none of those things resembled anything as normal as the date.

"Aren't… we too busy for that?" I asked.

He smiled a little sadly, then opened his mouth to say something but seemed to change his mind. He thought for a moment and finally spoke, leaving me with the distinct impression that this was not what he'd been about to say.

"Not *that* busy. We can make time."

Then it hit me how obtuse I was being.

Yes, we were *that* busy. We only had two days to ensure Damien's plan would work, and even though I would be nothing but a spectator during the cleansing, I was the one leading the charge, keeping everyone to a schedule and committed to doing what it took. So in truth, there was no time for a date.

Except… we *had* to make time because it was possible this would be our last chance to be together in that way.

My breath caught as I realized how insensitive I'd been, how doggedly focused on succeeding that I wasn't truly considering the possibility of failure.

"So what do you say, Toni? Do you want to be my date tonight? I promise you a good time, the best of your life. You won't be disappointed." His voice was sexually charged, and I understood his promise of a good time would mean ecstasy. My skin rippled at the thought.

I leaned closer, let my fingers caress his hard pec, teasingly. "I would love to be your date. Where are we going?"

"It's a surprise, but you'll want to wear something girly and elegant."

"Girly and elegant, huh?"

He nodded. "I can't wait to see you. You clean up well."

I laughed. "You clean up well yourself. Though I like this stubble." I rubbed his jaw, enjoying the sandpapery feel of his scruff against my fingers.

"You do?"

"Hmm. I love it." I closed my eyes, remembering how perfectly rough it felt against my thighs as he kissed his way to private places.

"I'll make sure to keep it then."

"You do that."

He leaned forward and kissed me, his tongue penetrating my mouth, promising so much more.

"Are you two coming or what?" Eric screamed from somewhere down the hall.

We broke apart. Regret washed over me as I wished I could zip our world closed, leaving us in our own cocoon where no one else could enter. But we didn't have that option. We couldn't run away or hide. The unbreakable pact would get to Jake no matter what.

"Yeah, coming," I yelled back and reluctantly took a step away from Jake.

"We'll finish this tonight." He smiled wickedly and just that simple gesture made heat pull in my belly.

CHAPTER 17

The larger garage was L-A-R-G-E.

It was in the back of the house, at basement level. It was the size of two basketball courts and had three wide automatic doors instead of one like the smaller one. Better yet, seven different ah-mazing cars took residence under its roof.

My jaw hung open as I walked around admiring their perfection. There were three classics and two modern cars.

"You've had these all along, and you didn't tell me?" I asked Eric. I felt betrayed.

He shrugged as if the cars were an afterthought to him. It must really sucked to be thatfilthy rich.

He had a 1960's Jaguar E-Type, a Mercedes Gullwing with the cool doors that lift up, a Lincoln Continental convertible, and an Aston Martin. Add to that a Lamborghini Aventador and a freaking Czinger. He did love sports cars! I gravitated toward the last one, and admired its aerodynamic lines.

"What's this baby's top speed?" I asked, caressing the car's slick top. It was platinum with black accents.

"About 250," Eric said.

"That's a dope spoiler," I said.

"You'd better quit or you're going to make Jake jealous," Rosalina said.

I shook my head. "Doubt it." I pointed at Jake who was salivating over the Lamborghini.

"Let's clear all this clutter." Damien waved a hand at the cars.

Eric flipped him the bird but walked toward a set of hooks on the wall to retrieve the keys and press a set of buttons that opened the garage doors. All three rose smoothly to reveal a narrow wooded road I'd never noticed before—not even during our outside training sessions.

"I'll drive the Czinger," I said, wiggling my finger for the keys.

Eric handed me all the keys and fobs. "You can drive all of them."

I squealed like a kid.

"You'll have to park them in a line."

"Okay." I turned toward the cars, pondering. "Which one first?"

"You've had these all along, and you didn't tell me?!" Rosalina exclaimed from the back of the garage, repeating my words.

I glanced back and found her standing in front of a large array of weapons inside up-lit glass displays. There were pistols, automatic rifles, crossbows, swords, knives, you name it.

"How could you?" she said, opening one of the displays to caress a particularly sharp-looking sword.

"It's Eric's turn to get jealous," Jake said, getting Rosalina back for her earlier joke.

Ten minutes later, all the cars were parked outside and the ample floor cleared. Damien knelt in the middle of the floor and set a case the size of a carry-on suitcase in front of him. I hadn't noticed it before. I'd been too dazzled by the cars, it seemed.

He opened the case to reveal a variety of things lying inside. Candles, matches, several boxes of chalk, a jar of salt, and a wooden instrument I had no name for. He grabbed the latter and used it to make a large circle on the concrete floor. A piece of chalk was attached to one end while the other one was anchored to the center of the shape.

"It's like a drawing compass," Rosalina said.

"Exactly," Damien said. "Though it's called trammel heads."

"What are all those other things?" I asked, pointing toward the case.

"It's just the summoning kit—common to demon hunters."

"Interesting," Rosalina said. "The tools of the trade, I suppose."

"Precisely." Damien finished crafting the circle. It was about eight feet in diameter and perfect. Next, he pulled out a long ruler from the case and began drawing a 5-pointed star to complete the pentagram. After that, he drew four small pentagrams at each cardinal point and placed lit candles on them. Lastly, he stepped carefully inside the pentagram and drew a strange, intricate circle.

"This is the demon's sigil," he said. "Its name is Dregnar, and this sigil represents it."

When he was done, he stretched to his full height and walked around the finished product. "Help me make sure there aren't any gaps in the lines. I haven't summoned a demon in some time, and I'd like to practice without worrying about the imp breaking free."

"So, the pentagram keeps it… bound?" Rosalina asked, her tone carrying an edge of fear.

Damien took a step toward Rosalina and pressed a hand to the side of her arm. "That is correct, and as long as the pentagram is satisfactory, we'll be safe. I assure you."

My friend glanced up at the mage, her green eyes wide in surprise at his sudden proximity. Damien's hand lingered for a moment too long, and when he pulled it away, he took the opportunity to briefly caress her skin.

As he moved away, Rosalina's shoulders trembled with an obvious shiver. I met her gaze and mouth, "Oooh, hot!"

She sent death rays in my direction and shook her head. I snickered and so did Jake. Eric, for his part, crossed his arms over his chest and looked annoyed. Only Damien hadn't noticed, lost in his worry about the pentagram.

Shaking myself, I abandoned all silliness and walked around the chalk drawing, checking each line, placing special care at the points of intersection.

"I think it looks good," I said.

"I think so, too," Damien agreed. "What does everyone else think?"

The others took time to inspect the pentagram as well. Everyone agreed that Damien had done a proper job.

"All right," the mage said, cracking his neck and standing a few paces away from the candle located on the south cardinal point. "Everyone stay a safe distance away from the pentagram and remain quiet during the entire process. Keep in mind that demons are tricky creatures and nothing you see or hear can be fully trusted."

An uneasy feeling settled in the pit of my stomach. I had no idea what we were about to see, what type of being we would allow to enter Jake's body.

Before I had any more time to worry, Damien began the summoning. "From the depths of hell, I command you to come forth. The circle will bind you. The flames will charm you. Dregnar, you are summoned."

At first, there was nothing, then a thick cloud of smoke materialized in the center of the pentagram. It was small, not any taller than my knees. Its edges undulated as if it would dissipate, but it remained in place.

I frowned. Was that the demon? Or was it hiding under the haze? I had expected some sort of monster with long, clawed fingers and bulging eyes, but this was nothing like that. I threw a quick glance toward Damien. He was squinting at the thing as if trying to see something behind the smoke. I wanted to ask if this was it, but he'd said not to talk, so I just waited.

Across from me, on the west cardinal point, Jake's silver eyes were also intent on the smoky mass. His jaw was set, and I thought I detected a slight trembling in his lower lip. I regarded him with surprise. I'd never seen Jake scared, but he was scared now—even if what lay in front of us appeared like little more than a patch of fog on a chilly morning.

As he stared, his chest rose visibly, and his fists clenched at his sides. Soon, his breaths became audible, attracting everyone's attention. Damien scanned him with a frown, then his gaze flicked to mine in question.

I gave a slight shrug, then abandoned my spot and slowly walked in a wide circle, and approached Jake from the side. I placed a hand on his tense biceps and shook him a little. He continued staring at the dense cloud.

"Do you hear it?" Jake asked in a barely audible whisper.

I exchanged a glance with Damien, searching for answers in his expression, but there were none.

"It says… Neil is there."

I gasped. Neil was Jake's brother. He had disappeared several years back. If he was dead or alive, nobody knew. A body had never been found, even if Jake's father had spent many hard months searching for him, then drank himself to death in despair when he couldn't find him. Even if Jake's mother had followed her husband to the grave shortly after.

"Reveal yourself!" Damien commanded in a booming voice, sending my heart into a wild rhythm. The cloud shivered slightly but didn't dissipate. Maybe this *was* the demon, after all.

"REVEAL YOURSELF!" Damien shouted.

This time the cloud shivered violently, and finally, the haze dissipated, leaving behind a nasty, slithering *thing* that made my bones turn to water.

If I had to compare the demon to an animal, I would've said it resembled something like a snake combined with one of those hideous deep, deep water fish with huge eyes and a mouth full of sharp little fangs.

Dregnar was no more than two feet long and no thicker than a roll of quarters. Its brown, slimy body tapered to a tail that ended in what looked like a stinger. Half of its length hovered in the air, keeping its big head high and off the floor. The body undulated, making the head swing from side to side in a hypnotizing fashion. The huge eyes were round and all black, and the top of the mouth was lined with what looked like several nostrils. The many teeth snapped together, and separated, letting a forked tongue slide out to taste the air.

An insidious voice that seemed to crawl into my ears like an oil spill, slowly advancing and coating me with its cloying slickness, spoke as if revealing a secret.

"He hates you," the voice said.

What?

"He already knows, and he hates you."

I shook my head and glanced at the others. Rosalina looked terrified, and Eric's face was practically twisted into a ferocious snarl.

"Stop your games. I command you to be quiet!" Damien spoke with a fierce edge.

The slithery feeling inside my head ceased immediately.

Jake shook his head and so did I. He blew out a shaking breath. I rolled my neck and reminded myself of what Damien had said.

Keep in mind that demons are tricky creatures and nothing you see or hear can be fully trusted.

The demon continued to undulate, its attention devoted entirely to Damien. With its sharp tail, the imp seemed to test the boundaries of the pentagram as if it could somehow see or sense the chalk lines.

I peered at Rosalina and mouth, *are you okay?*

She nodded doubtfully while she hugged her shoulders and rubbed her arms as if in need of warmth.

Damien blinked hard and continued staring at the demon straight in its creepy eyes. It was as if a battle of wills was taking place between them. I twitched my nose at all the scents riding the air, fear and aggression the prevailing ones.

Sweat appeared on Damien's forehead. He hissed as he took in a breath through clenched teeth. With an abrupt growl of frustration, he spoke, "Dregnar, to the depths of hell, I command you to return."

The tension left the room, and all of a sudden, I could breathe easily again. Damien staggered backward, his face pale. In an instant, Rosalina was at his side, wrapping an arm around his slender waist, offering her support.

The mage let out a self-deprecating laugh. "I'm… more out of practice than I thought."

"You should sit." Rosalina glanced around and seemed to spot something in a corner of the garage. "Toni, can you get a folding chair?"

I followed her gaze to a pile of lawn chairs stacked on top of each other.

"I'll get it." Eric snatched the chair that rested on top, unfolded it, and set it behind Damien.

The mage allowed Rosalina to help him as he lowered himself and sat. Slowly, the color returned to his cheeks, and his blotchy pupils shrank back to normal.

We remained quiet for several beats. Finally, Jake broke the silence.

"So… we're not supposed to trust anything that thing said, right?"

Damien swallowed thickly and nodded. Eric strode toward the back of the garage again, opened what looked like a shelf but turned out to be a mini-refrigerator. He pulled out a cold one.

"This might help," he said, offering Damien the can.

"Thank you." The mage popped the top and drank a couple of greedy gulps. "Much better."

Witchlights, this isn't good!

Damien had done nothing more than conjure the demon, and he looked as if he'd lost a match against an MMA champion. How was he going to be able to accomplish the rest? Were two days enough for him to practice and build up his strength?

Something told me it wasn't. Not at all.

"Neil wasn't there, was he?" Jake asked, sounding as if he didn't really want an answer.

Damien blinked and glanced up, his eyes wandering for a bit before they alighted on Jake. "Neil?"

Jake nodded but didn't offer an explanation as to Neil's identity.

I jumped in to help, knowing how hard it was for him to talk about his brother. "Neil is Jake's brother. He went missing a while back."

Damien rubbed his forehead and said, "That was more than just the blood demon. The damn book must be out of date. I should have realized."

We all stared at Damien at a loss. No one here knew anything about demons. We had enough troubles as it was to mess with creatures from that realm. Therefore, no idea of what he was talking about.

When he took in our confused expressions, he explained, "I think the demon must have also been a fearmonger. Witchlights, do I know how to pick them?" He shook his head, looking disappointed in himself.

It was surprising to see him fail at something. He was always so overconfident, arrogant even. It made him appear more human and less godlike, which after he pulled a resurrection was hard to do.

"Fearmonger?" Eric asked. "What does that mean exactly?"

Damien peered up at everyone in turn. "I'm sure you can guess."

When no one volunteered anything, the mage explained what I'd, indeed, guessed.

"It digs deep," Damien made a claw and raised it to his chest, "roots out your biggest fear, and makes you believe it has come true."

Jake exhaled and lowered his head, looking relieved. I reached over and interlaced my fingers with his, an awful pressure squeezing my heart. I never imagined that he was still holding on to the hope that his brother was still alive. Neil had disappeared so long ago without leaving a trace or a word behind that, in my mind, his death was almost a certainty. But if Jake didn't believe he was dead, what other possibilities were on his mind? Did he think Neil had just abandoned them? Did he think someone was holding his brother against his will? And if he believed those options were likely, weren't they harder to live with than the knowledge of his departure from this earth?

Oh, Jake!

Why hadn't he ever mentioned this? *God*, there was so much more we needed to learn about each other. I only prayed we would have time.

Rosalina cleared her throat. "It's close to dinnertime, why don't we order something and rest? Damien looks like he could use a bit of downtime."

"Great idea!" Eric exclaimed, rushing out of the garage as if he couldn't get out of there fast enough. Undoubtedly, the fearmonger had told him something about his family, and he needed to clear his head.

CHAPTER 18

To my dismay, on second inspection, Damien found out that his Demonology Register was almost two years out of date. It didn't seem like an awful long time, but he explained that demonology records were updated constantly. Apparently, there was a sort of wiki—though it wasn't really online because… who would publish sensitive information about summoning demons and make it available to the masses?! *Duh!*—which the LDHs across the world kept up-to-date with the latest information. Demon hunters everywhere turned in their findings, and the data was compiled and curated by a dedicated body of people.

To avoid more complications like the one we had today, the mage contacted his friend in New York, who promised to email the relevant information on the second blood demon on Damien's short list.

"I'll be back at eight for our date," Jake said with a kiss. He had a couple of things to take care of *and* he had to change.

I was concerned about us going out and being attacked by Mekare—she was a vengeful bitch, and I wouldn't put it past her to be planning something against us—but Jake assured me it would be all right. Wherever we were going, he said we didn't have to worry about the Midnight Witch.

It was hard to clear my mind from all my worries and get in a date mood. I felt it would be impossible to have any fun with all the worries weighing me down, but once I told Rosalina about the date, my outlook started changing.

"Oh, gosh, what are you going to wear?" she asked. We were in my bedroom. "All you have here are ratty jeans, sweats, and T-shirts."

"I was hoping I could borrow something from you. You're always prepared for this type of emergency."

"I have a few pieces that are better than what you've been calling your wardrobe lately, but nothing like what Jake suggested. I do have my makeup kit on hand, so in that department, you're safe." She gasped, her eyes going huge. "And what about… your undies."

"Huh?"

"You know…"

"Shit!" I pressed a hand to my mouth, realizing I didn't have anything nice to wear except for drab cotton panties and functional bras. I collapsed on the bed, suddenly stressed out about very different things than this morning.

"We have to go shopping." Rosalina placed her hands on her hips, her expression suggesting she thought this was a matter of life and death, and by the way my hands had gone clammy, it seemed that my instincts agreed with her.

I rubbed the back of my neck. "But it wouldn't be sensible. I mean… we're at war, and there is this nutty witch bent on killing us all."

She sat next to me and started tapping her fingers on her thigh. "We have to find a way."

"I have a feeling Eric isn't going to let us walk out of here to go to the mall." I hadn't told Rosalina about the moment Eric and I had shared earlier. Had the fearmonger demon made him believe one of us was dead when it reached into his soul? I felt pretty certain it had.

I glanced sideways at Rosalina, wondering what the demon had shown her, but I was afraid to ask and find out it had something to do with the agency.

"Maybe we can order something online." I reached for my phone.

"Who's going to deliver in a few hours?"

"I don't know," I said as I pulled up one of the major stores that had same-day deliveries.

Rosalina leaned her head into mine, and we spent the better part of an hour trying to find something suitable that could be delivered in time. Nothing satisfied my friend.

"No way you're going on this date wearing that bathrobe!" she exclaimed, snatching my phone and throwing it across the bed. "It's useless."

"It's better than what I have."

"It's cheap and the measurements are dubious. The dress needs to fit you like a glove or it's not worth it."

"Cheap and dubious are my middle names." Thirty bucks was about all I could afford to spend anyways, so I couldn't get picky.

"C'mon, Toni, you need to stop saying things like that about yourself. Self-esteem, remember?"

I hadn't heard that from her in a while. In the beginning, the words self-esteem had come out of her mouth every two seconds. When Jake left me, he'd destroyed more than my heart. The number he did on my confidence was epic.

Suddenly, Rosalina jumped to her feet. "Wait here!"

"Where you going?"

"To talk to Damien, if anyone can figure out a way to get what we need. It's him."

Of course, why hadn't I thought of him? He was a powerful Copper Mage, after all.

ꙮ

"It's gorgeous!" Rosalina exclaimed, pressing my brand-new dress to her torso and twirling around. "And those shoes. Oh my God, I'm so jealous." It was two hours later, and we were in my room again where Damien had delivered two packages. With a knowing grin, he'd placed the boxes on the bed and left the room without a word. Rosalina had immediately opened the bigger box and pulled out the dress and shoes.

It was a lapis blue gown with an a-line silhouette and layers of tulle in its skirt. It had a sweetheart neckline with off-the-shoulder straps and a jeweled bodice that sparkled with the light.

"You're jealous? *I'm* jealous," I said.

She frowned.

"Your boyfriend is able to procure shit like this in a matter of hours."

Rosalina made a face. "He's not my boyfriend."

"Maybe not yet, but he will be."

"You think?" Her green eyes lit up at the thought, and I was glad to see her experience with that fucking witch hadn't stolen her zest and joy for life and its simple pleasures.

Though, there was nothing simple about the dress and accompanying shoes. They were simply amazing.

"Let's open this," she said, wiggling her eyebrows and pulling the smallest box closer. Delicate tissue paper covered its contents. She unfolded it carefully to reveal the sexiest, skimpiest, lace lingerie I'd ever seen.

"Holy shit!" My friend's jaw literally fell open. The panties were little more than a triangle of lace with two little straps. The bra was see-through and would, for sure, leave my nipples on full display.

"Wow," I whispered, gently running my fingers over the delicate lace. "I wonder how much all of these things cost. This is all designer shit."

"Damien said not to worry about it," Rosalina chided me.

"But I mean—"

She cut me off. "*Shh*, he said he owes you for taking him in when he was nothing but a stray cat. He also said the kibble was delicious… some of the time."

We both busted out laughing. During his time as a feline, Damien had lapses in which he forgot he was supposed to be a human mage. I imagined that was when he didn't mind eating his dry food. The rest of the time he enjoyed pizza much better.

The next order of business was to take a shower and go to town with my razor. I took my time, enjoying the feel of the hot water on my skin and the floral smell of the shampoo and body wash. Every time I thought of where the night would lead, an electric jolt traveled down my belly. I both wanted the time to slow down and fly by. I couldn't wait to be alone with Jake, but the wait and anticipation were delicious.

I stepped out of the shower and rubbed my wet hair with a towel. When I'd gotten rid of the excess moisture, I wrapped myself in a bathroom towel and padded on bare feet toward Rosalina's room next door. She was waiting for me, her makeup implements lined up perfectly on the bathroom counter. She had maneuvered the chair into the small space and extended a hand in its direction as soon as I walked in.

"Let's begin with your hair," she said, and I submitted myself to her care. "I wish we were at my place, but I'll make do."

Pursing her lips with a disappointed frown, she perused her stash of cosmetics and beautifying contraptions. I blinked at everything in surprise. To me, it looked like we had enough stuff to put on a Broadway show, but I didn't say anything. She was the expert, not to me.

She dried my hair with practiced ease, dividing it into sections and using a round brush to create smooth, silky waves. When that was done, she began on the makeup while she quizzed me for the name of everything she was applying.

"The first thing is the…?" she prompted.

I narrowed my eyes, trying to remember. "Mmm, the foundation?"

"No, silly. You have to begin with a primer."

"What am I? A wall?"

"Kind of."

"Hey!"

Her hands fluttered over my face as she used sponges, brushes, pencils, and who knew what else to beautify me.

"Falsies?" she asked when the eyeshadow was done. "I have different kinds." She pulled out a thin plastic case with a clear top, presenting me with an array of fake eyelashes. She read the different labels on the box. "Prima donna, little flirt, debutante, pin-up girl."

"No, I think I'd rather not." I'd use them once before, and I'd felt weird and self-conscious the entire night.

"That's fine," Rosalina put in. "Your natural eyelashes are very pretty. Mascara will do." She proceeded to curl my *very pretty* eyelashes with her tiny torture device and to put three coats of mascara on them.

The girl really had a thing for makeup. The most interesting thing about it was that, even though everything she did seemed excessive, in the end, the final result looked nothing but subtle and natural.

"You look absolutely gorgeous," she said a moment later when I was fully dressed and pacing the room as I waited for Jake to arrive. "He's going to flip out."

I smiled nervously, wringing my hands.

"You should make him wait for a few minutes after he gets

here." She let out a little evil laugh.

"Is that supposed to torture him? Or me?"

My phone buzzed. It was a text from Eric saying that Jake had arrived and was waiting for me by the main entrance.

"He's here!" I exclaimed, my heart jumping into my throat.

Rosalina bit her lower lip and gave me a quick hug. "Have fun. Think of nothing but you and Jake. Don't let anything spoil your night."

"I won't."

I took a deep, nervous breath and walked out of the room.

When I entered the large living room with its many sitting areas, Jake was standing by the glass wall, looking out. He held a casual stance, resting heavily on one leg, a hand stuffed in his pocket. He wore a dark gray suit that made his wide back look even wider. When he heard me approaching, he seemed to hold his breath before turning slowly.

His silver eyes were nearly iridescent in the evening light. They focused first on my face and smiled at me. After he drank in my features, he allowed his gaze to travel downward. I stopped a few paces in front of him and allowed him to admire me at the same time I admired him.

I felt his scrutiny like a caress, like foreplay to what was to come. I drank him in, too, making no effort to conceal my desire for him.

As promised, he hadn't shaved his sexy stubble, not entirely anyway. He *had* used a razor to create sharp lines at the edges, making him look polished. His body and his face were to die for, but it was his unique eyes that captured me. From day one, it had always been his eyes with their clear irises and pupils that seemed to invite me into a bottomless universe where I would keep falling and falling and falling for him.

He approached me and took my hand in his. "You are, without a doubt, the most beautiful woman I've ever seen."

In any normal book that had to be an exaggeration, but not in Jake's. He truly believed it, just like I believed he was the most attractive man ever born. No one else had ever captured me the way he had, and no one ever would. I was sure of it.

He leaned closer and pressed his lips to mine. It was a light, quick brush, a simple greeting that had no business igniting my blood.

Witchlights, this is going to be a long night!

"Are you ready?" he asked.

"You have no idea."

We shared a complicit smile.

"Where are we going?" I asked, my curiosity about ready to blow a gasket.

Jake reached in his pocket and pulled out a wooden token that looked a lot like Damien's.

I blinked, confused. "Elf-hame?"

He nodded.

"Where did you get that?"

"From a friend of yours."

I frowned. "A friend of mine? Do you mean… Prince Kalyll?"

"The very same."

"How? When?"

"I have to confess something. The token is yours. I was going to give it to you right away, but then I had this… genius idea, so I decided to hold on to it for a bit."

"What do you mean it's mine?" He was making no sense.

"Kalyll gave me the token when we got here after rescuing Rosalina and the others when you ran upstairs and left us behind. He said he wanted you to have it. He wanted you to always be able to get to Elyndell should you need to. He said he and his family owe you a debt they'll never be able to repay."

I shook my head. "He doesn't owe me anything. We exchanged favors. Besides, I didn't even track Gonira."

Jake shrugged. "Fae are weird. They don't see things the way we do." He held the token up and rotated it in his fingers. "Pretty, isn't it?"

It really was. The carvings on its surface were intricate. The piece was shaped like a sunflower, and every minute petal and seed was absolutely perfect. I couldn't imagine how someone could carve something so delicate. Maybe it hadn't been done by hand. Maybe magic had been involved. Though something told me it wasn't. The Fae put a lot of value in the different crafts they practiced. Some people could paint scenes on tiny pieces of rice, so it wasn't so far-fetched to imagine someone carving this.

"So our date is in Elf-hame?" It felt a little bit ridiculous to wear a cocktail dress and a suit to a place where people dressed as if they were in a fairytale. We were going to stand out like two giant sore thumbs.

"It is," he answered with a twinkle in his eye. "I was there earlier… arranging everything. I think you'll love it."

"Whoa, I don't know what to say." I was truly at a loss for words. Sometimes it was hard to reconcile the romantic man who planned special dates with the idiot who made the wrong promises and got himself into engagements involving unbreakable pacts.

Was this even the same person?

"Men grow up in spurts," Mom told me once. *"One day they're incredibly mature and sensible, and the next they run headfirst into a wall to see if it hurts."*

Honestly, I didn't think she was too far from the truth. But whatever the case, Jake was turning out to be a very fine man. I only hoped he was done growing up. I wouldn't be able to survive another screw-up.

"Ready?" he asked.

If he'd said he was taking me to the end of the world, I would've said yes. The man owned my heart and soul. I nodded, and we vanished into Elf-hame.

CHAPTER 19

We materialized in Elf-hame a moment later. I expected to see the edge of the forest where Damien's token took us every time we used it, but this time we materialized much closer to the Elyndell. A massive tree with a girth as wide as a compact car stood to my right, its thick branches spreading above us, completely blotting out the sky.

The sweet scent of flowers rode in the air. Grass tickled my toes through my strappy shoes, and the sound of loud crickets filled my ears. We were draped in shadows, but gentle light glowed a short distance away, flowing out of round windows, hanging lanterns, and honest-to-god candle lamp posts. We stood about fifty yards away from a cluster of Fae homes, their natural walls twisting out of the ground, and their roofs topped with leaves and moss. Through a window, I made out a family of four, sitting at a table, enjoying their dinner together.

"This place is like a dream," I said under my breath, afraid that I might break the spell.

"It is." Jake interlaced his fingers in mine and led me in the opposite direction of the homes. We turned away and walked down a narrow dirt path, lined by ankle-high grass and flowers.

"Where are we going?"

"You'll see," Jake said, a smile in his voice.

He walked next to me, tall and proud, casting glances in my direction every few seconds, his silver gaze twinkling with mischief and true happiness.

"These trees are massive." I gestured towards a row of trees to our left. They followed the path at a distance, though after a short, lovely walk under a purple-blue sky dotted with brilliant stars, the path twisted into the trees, leading us toward the biggest one of them.

"Witchlights, that tree is thick as Eric's skull!" I said.

Jake laughed. "I'm glad you didn't compare it to *my* skull."

"Oh, yours is not that bad. It's more like…" I scanned the trees until I found one that wasn't as wide, "… that one."

"I guess it takes one to know one." He chuckled.

When we were almost to the huge tree, he tugged on my hand and made me stop. He then pulled a folded piece of cloth from the inside pocket of his jacket and stood behind me.

"What are you doing?" I glanced back over my shoulder, eyes narrowed.

"Blindfolding you."

"Oh, I like this."

"Me too." He reached around me and tied the silk handkerchief over my eyes. When he was done, his fingers traveled down the length of my neck, then slowly slid over my shoulders, the touch so light it made me quiver.

He kissed the crook of my neck and inhaled my scent. "You smell delicious. I can't wait to taste every inch of you."

The purr of his voice seemed to get under my skin like a shiver intent on reaching my very bones. The thought of his tongue on my skin almost undid me. This was exactly what he'd done to me the night we made love for the first time, the night he claimed my virginity. He seduced me all night, driving my desire into a tailspin that plunged into indescribable depths once we were finally alone.

At the time, I'd been completely inexperienced and at his mercy. Now, however, I knew how to play the game, and I didn't intend to let him be the only participant.

Throwing my head back, I stepped into him, pressing my body against his solidity. I seized his hand, which rested at my waist, and pulled it over my stomach until his arm encircled me. I moaned in pleasure.

"I can't wait to do the same to you," I said as I pressed further into him, my backside rubbing against his front.

"Be careful," he warned. "I have to last the night, and it won't be easy."

Last the night? I hoped he wasn't expecting that from me. I wanted him so much that I was sure the sight of his naked body would be enough to drive me to ecstasy.

He pulled away from me, took my hand again, and led me forward. "Small steps. Good. We're almost there."

My nose twitched as a host of delicious scents reached me. Dinner was served, apparently. I detected the aroma of roasted meat more strongly than any other. There was also the tang of wine and the pleasant smell of honey.

"Okay." Jake made me stop, stood in front of me, and undid the knot in my blindfold.

I gazed into his handsome face, my curiosity forgotten as I admired his chiseled features. He was so beautiful it made me ache, but what was more astounding was the love brimming in his eyes.

Oh, Jake, what will I ever do if I lose you?

I stiffened and shoved the thought aside. I would not let this night be ruined by fear.

"You okay?"

"Perfect." I gave him my best smile. It worked, immediately wiping away the worry that had momentarily entered his expression.

Inhaling deeply and looking like a kid ready to present his final project to the teacher, he stepped aside to reveal what he'd prepared for us.

My breath caught at the sight of the most romantic display I'd ever witnessed. We were standing at the edge of a small clearing surrounded by trees. In the middle, there was a small table for two, set with a white tablecloth, fine china, silver dinnerware, crystal wine glasses, and ornate candelabra topped with six candles and their dancing flames. Next to the small table, there was a second one, narrow and long. It was laid with a feast fit for ten kings and their extended families.

The centerpiece was a large roast set on a silver platter and adorned with fruit and green garnish. Next to that, there were other delicacies. Blackened fish, stewed vegetables, roasted plums, and five different desserts. Several loaves of freshly baked bread sat next to a bowl with creamy butter sprinkled with herbs. At the corner of the table, there were several bottles of wine that I was sure had come from our realm.

And the food was only the beginning. There were rugs underfoot and flowering vines hanging like garlands from the tree branches. The clearing was illuminated by tiny glowing lights that seemed to hang from nothing at all. I peered up at them, trying to figure out what they were. Christmas lights on very thin cables? Lightning bugs? Magic sparkles? I had no idea, all I knew was that they were magical and created an inviting, gentle atmosphere that inspired nothing but baby-making thoughts.

Jake had, indeed, been busy these past couple of hours. How in the witchlights had he accomplished all of this?

"Do you like it?" he asked, his deep voice trembling a little.

"I love it," I whispered. "It's absolutely perfect."

He puffed his cheeks and blew air out. "Now what I'll be worried about is how to ever top this."

"Yeah, that will be tough."

"I'll think of something. If not, I'm pretty good at heating up Chef Boyardees."

I made a face. "I'm half Italian, remember?"

He laughed, then extended a hand toward the table. He pulled the chair out and, like a perfect gentleman, scooted it into place as I sat.

With an affected air, he picked up a cloth napkin from the table and draped it over his forearm. "What would you like to drink, mademoiselle?" When I gave him a questioning glance, he said, "I wanted it to be only you and me, so I'll be your date *and* your waiter."

I shook my head and sighed. "How far I've fallen. Now, I'm dating the help." I made a flourish with my hand. "I will take some white wine."

"My pleasure." He poured wine in the crystal glasses for both of us, then sat across from me.

He drank me in as if he were seeing me for the first time. We were silent for a long moment, just enjoying each other's company and the beautiful space he'd created for us, so we could share a moment that would be unforgettable.

"When you were in ninth grade," he said, "your brother told me you had a crush on me."

I almost choked on my wine. Squirming in my seat, I felt blood rush up my neck. "He did?" I croaked. Jake and my brother were classmates throughout school and graduated at the same time.

"Yes, in fact, he said that you had a crush on me since you were in kindergarten."

"That bastard, I'm gonna kill him."

"So it's true?"

"Of course it's not true."

Jake raised his eyebrows, looking doubtful.

"You can't believe anything Leo says. He said he would come

for Christmas last year, and he didn't. He said he would write often, and we haven't heard from him in almost two months. So there."

He fought to repress a smile, then went on. "I can't say that I had a crush on you when you were in kindergarten. Second-grade was kicking my butt, to be honest. I had trouble with the concept of sitting still for six hours. Actually, I struggled with that concept for a while, also with the idea that girls had cooties. But once I got over all of that, I did notice."

I swallowed, feeling breathless.

"You were in sixth grade. You had cut your hair up to here." He touched a finger to his jaw.

"I remember that haircut." I had actually wanted a buzz cut, but Mom convinced me to try a bob first. She said that if after a month I still wanted to look like a boy, she would take me to the barber.

Jake reached over and took a strand of my pink-tipped hair between his fingers. Except for that one time, my hair had always been the same length, about five inches below my shoulders. Needless to say, I never went for that buzz cut. Even with the bob, I'd missed the weight and feel of my hair too much.

"I remember thinking that you looked cute in that haircut, but that I much preferred you with longer hair." He smiled to himself. "The thought shocked the hell out of me. It was the first time I'd noticed a girl that way."

And all this time I'd thought he'd never realized I existed until that spring break party, during my senior year. *Damn!*

"After that," Jake continued, "I found myself looking for you in the halls, the gym, the cafeteria. I did my best to hide my interest, though, 'cause of Leo, you know. He made sure to let everyone know his sisters were off-limits to the likes of us. He assured us he would beat the crap out of anyone he caught looking their way, and he wasn't joking. One time, he beat the crap out of Joe Manzo for making a comment about Daniella. The dude was on the football team and twice as heavy as Leo, but he never saw it coming."

My jaw just kept falling lower and lower as the story went on. I'd never known Leo had done that. *What a jerk!*

"Besides, he was my friend. I thought if I had a sister, I would hate it if any of my friends hooked up with her. I was pretty obsessed with you my entire eighth grade. Then I got the impression that Leo had noticed. Hell, I thought the entire world had noticed. You were all I could think about. So… to throw your brother off the scent, I started dating anyone who'd look my way."

"Which was pretty much everybody." My mouth twisted to one side disapprovingly. "Even some of the guys."

Jake put his hands up. "I never hooked up with any of them."

"Not that I would think any less of you."

"I know. Just saying. Anyway, it went on that way up to graduation. I got better at pretending you weren't there, thinking of you like this unattainable person… *the one I would never get.* Then we graduated and I thought I'd moved on, but then I saw you at that party." He sighed, his gaze wistfully rolled over me as if he couldn't believe I was actually here. His unattainable crush. God, if I had known that. I couldn't even begin to imagine how things might have turned out.

My heart fluttered like an idiot. Really, the stupid thing practically turned into a butterfly and forgot its job.

"I knew your brother was gone, and I realized how stupid I'd been to be afraid of making him angry. I thought of all the wasted time and figured I would make up for it. By then, I thought of myself as some worldly dude. I thought it would be amazing to have a little fling with you. I never imagined that I would… fall in love.

"I freaked out, Toni. Big time. Then I lied to myself, thinking that if I put some distance between us, those feelings would go away. I was so wrong. They just got stronger, and when I saw you again, all the emotions I'd been trying to ignore just came to a head." He paused and regarded me for a moment, finally he said,

"Can you ever forgive me for being such an idiot?"

"There's nothing to forgive, Jake."

Despite everything, the words felt true. A few months back, I would have thought forgiveness impossible. A few months back, I was sure I hated him. I'd worked for over a year making myself believe he meant nothing to me, but it only took one look at him to realize I'd turned into a very good liar.

I doubted few had ever deceived themselves so thoroughly.

He cocked his head to one side. "I still would like to hear you say it, that you forgive me."

"It was an impossible situation, Jake. It wasn't until I found out that I'm a werewolf that everything became clear. Our love was inevitable, and I bet you were confused as hell that you'd fallen so hard for a tracker."

"That might be an understatement."

"I don't blame you. I understand why you wanted to keep that promise to your dad. I can't fault you for trying to be honorable, and for trusting your grandfather."

"I did grow smarter in the last couple of months," he said matter-of-factly.

I laughed. "I believe that. Just promise me not to wig out again. Oops, sorry, wrong word. Forget I asked you to promise anything."

He put three fingers up, while his thumb held his pinky down. "Scout's honor. It's as good as a promise but a bit different," he explained.

"Okay, I'll buy that."

"You haven't said it yet." He cocked his head to one side.

"I forgive you."

He let out a big exhale as if he'd perform a very difficult task and was satisfied by a job well done. And I had to agree, he'd done a heckuva job. He had me the moment he mentioned that silly haircut.

"Hungry?" he asked, gesturing toward the food.

"I could eat." I had other things in mind, but I didn't need to get ahead of myself. Did I? Besides, I was enjoying this way too much.

Everything was absolutely delicious, and the desserts were arguably the best I'd ever had. Without a doubt, the food was from this realm, and I had to wonder how Jake had pulled this off. I decided not to ask, however, and to believe that he was as magical as the setting would have me believe.

I was savoring my last bite of cream tart when Jake set his spoon down, stood up, and offered me a hand. "Would you like to dance?"

"Dance?" I glanced around to indicate there was no music.

He smiled, retrieved his cell phone from his pocket, and brandished it in the air.

"Oh, that should do just fine."

"There's no signal, but the battery is charged up, and I downloaded our song."

"Our song." I frowned. "We have a song?"

He scrunched his face in exaggerated disappointment. "Of course, we have a song. You wound me."

"I'm sorry."

"It's okay. I did decide this was our song without consulting you, but I hope you'll approve." His fingers moved quickly over the screen and *Shape of You* by Ed Sheeran began to play. He slipped the phone back in his pocket and reached out a hand as the song played.

"Do you remember?" he asked, squeezing my fingers as he helped me out of my chair.

"I do." At that spring break party two years ago, it was one of the songs we'd danced to.

He pulled me close, wrapping one hand around my waist, while, with the other, he held my left hand and brought it to his chest. We began swaying gently, following the music's rhythm. The melody seemed to fill the clearing, encapsulating us in a bubble that no one else could pierce. I inhaled his fresh scent of pine and rain and rested my head on his firm chest. His heart was beating hard and fast, and his breath was agitated, tickling my hair as it blew past his lips. The song had an upbeat rhythm, but we kept our dance slow and quiet.

As we moved in circles, I forgot everything else and pretended there was nothing else outside this space, outside of us. If any troubles lay beyond this clearing, they disappeared.

When the song ended, Jake gestured toward a cobbled path that lay to the right.

"What is that way?" I asked.

"You'll see."

Hand in hand, we walked under the cover of trees down the meandering path. The stroll was idyllic, the beauty that surrounded us, unlike anything we could experience back in our realm. Around a sharp bend, we crossed in front of a tall hedge, and when we came out on the other side, a small cottage built of stone and illuminated from within in the warm glow welcomed us.

The place was small, no bigger than a garden shed, but it was absolutely sublime. It had a cedar-shingled roof with a circular door in the middle and matching windows to either side of it. Flowerbeds overflowed with beautiful plants I had no name for.

We walked closer, and I had to remind myself to breathe. My heart was beating so fast that I might as well have been running at full speed on a treadmill.

Jake threw the door open and, without preamble, lifted me off my feet and cradled me against his chest. He crossed the threshold with me in his arms. He had to duck and be careful not to knock his head on the door frame. Once inside, he used his foot to shut the door and stood in the middle of the space without putting me down.

I glanced around at the simple, yet beautiful, space. There was a fireplace to the left and a few logs burning to embers—not a full fire, it wasn't cold enough for that—but just the perfect amount to create a warm atmosphere. Candles burned in different corners, resting on rocks that protruded from the walls like specially-made ledges for that very purpose.

Across from the fireplace was a sitting area with two armchairs and a table topped by a bouquet of aromatic, purple flowers. And in the back of the room, right in the middle, there was a bed with a headboard carved in rough wood and a cover of the purest white.

At last, Jake set me down. He seemed to quiver as he deposited my feet gently on the stone floor. I turned to face him, searching his face, drinking in every emotion that swam in his clear eyes. Everything I was feeling was reflected back at me. Incredulity that we were finally here, fear for what was to come, unbound desire, but most of all… love.

His large hand reached for my face. He caressed my cheekbone with his thumb, never breaking eye contact. His lips parted and he leaned forward. That first kiss was gentle, tentative. Slowly, it deepened, his movements becoming more insistent, his breaths coming faster. His tongue slipped into my mouth. I moaned and threw my head back as a jolt of want shot to my center. His lips abandoned mine and traveled down the column of my neck, trailing kisses, biting slightly, licking a feverish path to my collarbone.

My hands felt clumsy as I pushed the jacket off his shoulder and helped him remove it without ever breaking apart. When it fell to the floor, I removed his tie, then started on the buttons of his shirt. Likewise, he found the zipper at my back and lowered it, his hands slipping under the fabric, caressing my back, his fingers digging into my skin possessively.

I pushed the shirt off his shoulder, same as his jacket, but this time we had to stop and break apart to remove his cufflinks. I fumbled with one of them, and as I got it undone, it slipped from my fingers and clinked to the floor. Jake undid the other one and tossed the shirt on top of his jacket.

My eyes roved over the smooth expanse of his chest, over the arrow tattoo around his left biceps that he said represented me.

"*You pierced my heart through and through like the Cupid that you are,*" he'd told me.

My hands trembled as I laid them on his pecs. He sucked in a breath as I caressed him, my hands sliding down his rock-hard abs, my thumbs tracing the waist of his pants, and my eyes feasting on his magnificence.

"My turn." He took both dress straps on my shoulders and slid them down my arms, making me quiver.

I had to wiggle a bit for the dress to finally come loose and slide down my legs. As it pooled around my feet, Jake took a step back to better look at me. He bit his lower lip, eyes traveling slowly down the length of my body. He lingered on my breasts for several beats, then my abdomen, then that secret spot between my legs.

"You are as breathtaking as ever," he said. "And this…" He raised a hand and, with one finger, followed the edge of my bra, simultaneously caressing the top of my left breast. "This looks so hot on you."

I took his hand, stepped out of my dress, and slowly twirled, letting him admire me.

"What did I do to deserve this?" he asked no one in particular.

"I ask myself the same question about you," I said as I followed the trail of light hairs down his belly button to his tented pants. "I seem to be at a disadvantage again."

I reached for his belt and pulled it loose. I made quick work of the button and zipper next. It was his pants' turn to drop to the floor to leave him in tight boxer shorts that left very little to the imagination. His erection pressed against the stretchy fabric, threatening to rip it open. We drank each other in for a long moment, reveling in the splendor of our young bodies.

In one swift motion, he picked me up again, cradled me against his bare chest, and carried me to the bed. He placed me in the middle of it, then settled himself between my legs, his sex pressing against mine, making me arch back to feel it better.

"Toni," he said as he began kissing me hungrily, his tongue lapping my lower lip, his teeth biting gently.

His hips rocked against mine, teasing me, driving my desire to irrational levels.

Oh, God!

I dug my fingernails into his back as if to urge him to go faster, though the pleasure of the anticipation was too much to relinquish.

One of his hands slipped behind my back and expertly undid my bra. Abruptly, he tore it off me and threw it aside. He pushed up on one arm to look at me, then dived down, his mouth alighting at the top of my breast and slowly kissing his way to its peak. His tongue made lazy circles, then he sucked briefly, leaving to bestow the same attention on the other side.

I tugged at the waistband of his underwear, trying to pull it down. His lips traveled to my abdomen, canceling my mission to remove that piece of fabric that stood between us. As it turned out, he was on a similar mission. He grabbed the thin straps of my panties at either side and slid them slowly, taking his time to caress my legs on the way down. He knelt between my legs, a look of absolute sexual yearning in his eyes, then pressed a kiss to one knee and then the other.

Slowly, he continued kissing up the length of my inner thigh.

"Oh, Jake!"

He found my core and focused his attention there, tongue lapping and swirling, rendering me his possession. His hands slid under my butt. He tilted my hips up, took me fully into his mouth, and sucked. I moaned in pleasure, my skin pebbling, my eyes rolling backward.

My ecstasy climbed and climbed, taking me to the cusp. I

teetered at the edge, ready to fall.

Jake stopped.

The waves of my desire blissfully ebbed, rolling through me, keeping me on that cutting edge. He stood as I wriggled on the bed ready to curse him to hell for leaving me. Slowly, he removed his boxer shorts.

He fell free in all his glorious manhood. He was hard, long and thick. He let me admire him for a moment, then reached for my ankles and pulled me to him, rotating me on the bed. Holding himself, he climbed on the bed, settled between my legs, and guided his shaft to my middle.

Our gazes held for an eternity, then he thrust forward.

I clenched the covers in pleasure as he filled me so deep and so thoroughly that I nearly cried out. Then he began to move, quickly returning me to that edge where he kept me swaying between solid ground and a precipice of my climax. He was careful not to lose me until he was there, too, and together, we gave in to the utter delight of our release, shivering and panting in each other's arms.

Spent, he lay on top of me, utterly at my mercy. Then it was my turn to drive him out of his mind.

CHAPTER 20

If before, I'd been determined to break Jake's pact, now I was utterly resolute. No one would take my mate from me—not now that he had been fully mine once more. Not ever!

After our perfect night together, I was certain I wouldn't be able to live without him.

We got back from Elf-hame in the early hours of the next morning. It had been difficult to say goodbye as he left to go back to his pack, to serve as their leader while they continued preparing for Mekare's threat. All the packs had been getting ready, training, taking guidance, passing information down the chain of command from alphas to betas to everyone else.

I was in my room, trying to catch some shuteye. It was three in the morning, and I was deliciously tired but didn't fall asleep right away. Instead, I lay in bed, recalling every detail of my date with Jake, and everything he'd done to make it perfect. Slowly, blissfully, I drifted into a deep sleep, free of nightmares and worries.

At 6 AM, I awoke. The restlessness I'd been dealing with for the last couple of weeks returned in full force. I showered and dressed in under ten minutes, a record for my lazy ass. I'd missed my training session with Eric, and it wouldn't be the last one this week.

He said nothing about my absence when I walked into the kitchen in search of coffee. Instead, he informed me that Damien had the new Demonology Register in his possession, and he would arrive shortly. Rosalina joined us shortly, made herself some jelly toast, and sat across from me, expectant.

When I didn't say anything, she sat straighter and said, "Sooo?"

My eyes flicked in Eric's direction She rolled her eyes.

"Do you want me to leave?" he asked, then added, "my own kitchen?"

"No," I said. "Of course not. In fact, I don't mind if you hear all about it."

His blue eyes went wide as he stood in one swift motion, grabbed his cup of coffee, and headed out. "I just remembered there's something I need to finish in my study. I'll text you when Damien gets here."

Rosalina and I snickered, watching him leave as if his tail was on fire.

"That worked better than I thought it would," I said.

"Priceless." She bit into her toast. "So how did it go?"

I told her all about our dinner and dance in every detail, then glossed over the rest of the night. When I was done, she sighed deeply.

"God, that man really knows how to show a woman a good time," she said, looking wistful.

"You must be talking about me," Damien said, strolling into the room, the folds of his cloak billowing behind him.

He removed it and bowed, his copper eyes connecting with Rosalina's for a long time before flicking to me. The mage certainly appeared to be in an upbeat mood, judging by his playfulness and the huge smile on his face.

"Nope," Rosalina said with a deadpan stare. "I was talking

about Jake."

Damien blinked and appeared taken aback.

"However," Rosalina went on, "the judge is still out on you."

Damien cleared his throat and raised an eyebrow. "Challenge accepted."

The sexual tension between the two was almost palpable. Turning back on Rosalina, I winked to indicate I fully approved of her open approach. If there was anything this last couple of months had taught me it was that the best approach to life was to take it by the balls. You never know when your existence and its very fragile contents could be blown to pieces by black magic.

"Where's Eric?" Damien glanced around the kitchen.

"His study," Rosalina responded.

"We should get started. I think I found the right demon to summon in this new book my friend let me borrow." He cracked his fingers, appearing excited about the prospect of summoning another demon despite the fact that the last one had whooped his ass.

I jumped to my feet, catching his excitement. "Let's do it! We only have two more days."

Damien headed out. "Is Knight here?"

"No, he said to go on without him. This pack business is keeping him busy. He is still signing documents with the estate lawyers, stuff to do with his inheritance, and learning the ropes about running the pack and the businesses they own."

"I see."

The three of us marched down the hall, our steps perfectly synchronized. Eric came out of his studio as he heard us pass.

"You look like three people with a mission," he said, then joined us, and we all marched to the garage, where Damien refreshed the lines of the pentagram to ensure they all connected properly. Next, he erased Dregnar's sigil and drew a new one.

"Light the candles, will you, Toni?"

I did as I was told, and in no time, he was ready to summon a demon named Velthgrek.

ஐ

"This one is *only* a blood demon," Damien said as he took his position at the south end of the pentagram. He inhaled a few deep breaths while Eric stood opposite him, I planted my feet on the east end, and Rosalina stepped up to the west cardinal point.

Damien cleared his throat and began. "From the depths of hell, I command you to come forth. The circle will bind you. The flames will charm you. Velthgrek, you are summoned."

As soon as he finished the conjuration, the demon appeared in the middle of the pentagram. Velthgrek presented itself with six legs, one huge eye, shaggy hair, and a stubby tail that tried to wag but just looked pathetic. The thing resembled a dog but was the size of a bear. It didn't give us any weird feelings or seem threatening in the least. It was strange-looking, but somewhat… adorable.

"Again, don't let appearances fool you," Damien warned.

A long, purple tongue rolled out of the creature as it began panting. Its saucer-sized eye blinked, giving it a goofy air.

"This is only what it wants you to see," Damien said. "Isn't it, Velthgrek?"

The creature nodded its big head, still panting.

Well, at least it wasn't trying to deceive us or mess with our minds. A few moments passed. We all watched Damien carefully for any signs of strain. There were none. He nodded, pleased. Standing straighter and firmly planting his feet on the concrete floor, he said. "Toni, the box."

I handed over the cube-shaped box he'd asked me to hold. It was just a regular cardboard box, taped shut from both sides and a hole carved on one side. It was only big enough to hold a coffee mug.

Damien took the box from my hand and immediately let go of it. It started to drop, but he twirled his fingers and stopped it in midair. Slowly, he moved his hand, guiding forward until it crossed above the lines of the pentagram.

Velthgrek's legs shuffled in excitement as his eye followed the box's trajectory.

"Stay," Damien ordered as the demon made as if to jump towards it.

The creature whined like a sad puppy but obeyed.

Gently, the mage deposited the box in front of the Velthgrek. Its legs marched in place as it stared fixedly at the container as if it wanted to play.

"Velthgrek," Damien's commanding voice instructed, "get inside the box."

The demon's head snapped in the mage's direction. Ours did likewise. He hadn't explained what the box was all about. How was the huge thing going to get inside that tiny box?

"Do it NOW!" The mage's order was unequivocal.

Velthgrek bared sharp fangs, but the grimace lasted only a flash, then the creature dissolved, turning into dark smoke, reminding me of that trick Mekare had pulled when she'd escaped us.

Taking the shape of a floating snake, the demon dived into the box through the hole, quickly disappearing like a hose being reeled in.

As I watched its tail-end vanish, I realized the box represented Jake. My stomach twisted into a knot at the thought of a deceitful creature from hell slithering into him. Did we really want to do this? Were we making a big mistake? What if this craziness became the biggest mistake of my life?

Damien cracked his neck, appearing satisfied but also a little tired. I held my breath expectantly. This was progress, I guessed. Though I still couldn't make up my mind whether it was for better or for worse. Maybe the sane alternative would be to fail. Maybe fate should make the decision for us, so we could be spared from a huge screw-up.

The mage blew air through his pursed lips, then shook his arms loose and pointed his hands toward the box again. His fingers twirling in an intricate pattern.

"Now, I have to try to hold it in place. I'll have to release it in order for it to eat out the curse. Also, once it gets its first taste of blood, it'll be impossible to control it through verbal commands," Damien explained.

I watched on pins and needles, a little confused about what was happening, then Damien spoke again, issuing another command for the demon.

"Velthgrek, get out of the box!"

Sweat broke out on the mage's brow as he stared intently at the box. A moment later, it began to shake in place. Damien crouched and leaned into his weaving hands, concentration pinching his features.

As I watched, another realization hit me. Damien had said that the demon would try to go for Jake's heart and that he would have to use telekinesis to hold it back. If Velthgrek got out of the box, it would represent Jake's heart being devoured.

The box continued shaking, at first subtly, then quickly. Soon, the container was bucking, its corners coming off the floor. Damien's arms and hands were stiff and shaking as he held them out. Suddenly, the box jumped as if it had a frog trapped inside, moving dangerously close to the edge of the pentagram.

Rosalina gasped and took a step back.

"It can't get out," Damien said between clenched teeth as he continued struggling to hold the demon in.

Did he mean the box couldn't get out of the pentagram? Or the demon couldn't get out of the box? Either way, I figured that was good news, and we—

The box exploded, sending bits of cardboard flying everywhere. The black cloud that was the demon expanded into something that looked like a mushroom cloud. Bits of box rained all around the pentagram.

"Shit!" Eric cursed under his breath.

In a few beats, the cloud coalesced into the shaggy creature it had been moments ago. It glanced happily around, panting and marching in place as if eager to play another game.

I stared at the fragments of cardboard, my lower lip trembling and tears pooling in my eyes. I barely noticed when Rosalina and Eric rushed to Damien's side and caught him before he collapsed to the floor. I was too busy worrying about one question.

If Velthgrek getting out of the box represented Jake's heart being devoured, what the hell did it mean that the box had exploded?

CHAPTER 21

"Did that mean that Jake would've… exploded?" I asked in a trembling voice as we sat in Eric's study half an hour later.

No one said anything. Damien had one hand pressed to his forehead while in the other one he held a tumbler full of Scotch.

At last, the mage answered, "Maybe not literally exploded, but… it wouldn't have been pretty."

I stood from the armchair where I'd been sitting and began pacing in front of the fireplace. We only had two days left, and though Damien had made some progress, it didn't feel like enough, especially considering he was exhausted and didn't look as if he could have another go at Velthgrek.

As if she'd read my thoughts, Rosalina asked, "Do you think you'll have enough time to learn what it takes by Friday?"

Damien's copper eyes went to Eric. There was a certain quality in them that seemed to hold the answer to Rosalina's question. Eric knew Damien better than we did and read the response right away. He winced, and we didn't need more than that.

The mage didn't think he could do it.

He took a sip of his Scotch, then set the tumbler down on the side table. "I'm sorry, Toni, but two days is simply not enough time for me to be ready. Commanding the demon is a draining task in itself. Add to that using additional energy for telekinesis, and the whole thing... it's just too much right now. It would take me weeks to build the necessary stamina." He said that last bit between clenched teeth as if it pained him to accept defeat.

I stammered. "M-maybe one of your mage friends can help."

Damien shook his head. "I don't know anyone who specializes in telekinesis."

Tentatively, Rosalina put a hand up, a careful expression on her face as if she were a kid trying to ask a question to the meanest person they knew.

"Um," she began, "this is probably a terrible idea, but… what about your sister, Toni? Lucia has telekinetic powers, doesn't she?"

I shook my head and stopped my pacing. Of course, this same idea had been taking root in the back of my head, but it was something I'd been resisting since it first occurred to me. I didn't want to bring my little sister into this. Everyone who'd gotten involved in this mess was at risk. She had already been under the threat of Mekare's hybrids. I didn't need to put her under the threat of demons.

One of Damien's white eyebrows went up. "Your sister has telekinetic powers?"

Eric nodded several times, remembering. "Yeah, she hurled basketballs at the hybrids, kept them from eating me, really. I never thanked her."

"A natural telekinetic with innate abilities?" Damien persisted.

"Yes," I reluctantly admitted.

"Why didn't you say so?" the mage peered up at me as if I were as dense as a brick.

"I'm not dragging her into this!" I said, adamant. "Besides, my mom would kill me. There's no way she'd let her anywhere near a demon. Mom would have an aneurysm, a stroke, and a heart attack all at once."

"Isn't that a bit exaggerated?" Eric asked.

Damien moved his head from side to side very deliberately. "No, I think that's a pretty accurate assessment. Amalia is a bit… melodramatic."

"If only telekinetics weren't so rare. I don't know any of them. Or if the skill wasn't so hard to master for mages," Damien mused. "Anyway, if it's any help, your sister won't be in any danger. You've seen how it is. The demon is confined to the pentagram to begin with. Then I let it out for a bit to do its thing, and when it's done done, I command it back. I can certainly handle that. Lucia would be perfectly safe."

I frowned, considering. Looking at it like this *did* help. A little. If there would be no possibility of the demon breaking free and taking possession of my sister, maybe it would be all right to let her help. She would enjoy the opportunity, for sure. Lucia loved doing shit she wasn't supposed to do. Still, I doubted I could convince Mom to let her be part of our scheme.

Damien sank further into the sofa, closing his eyes and throwing his head back. "You think about it," he said in a tired tone. "But don't take too long. If you decide to bring her in, she'll have to practice, too."

I sank back into the armchair, raking stiff fingers into my hair, feeling as if our problems just kept getting more and more complicated every day.

"Maybe I'll—" My phone vibrating in my pocket stopped me mid-sentence. I pulled it out and read the name on the caller ID.

"It's Tom," I said.

Rosalina's eyes widened. Eric frowned. Damien sighed, sounding as if he was on the brink of falling asleep.

"Your detective friend?" Eric asked.

I nodded and pressed the *answer* button. "Hey, Tom."

"Hello, kiddo. How's it going?"

I grunted noncommittally.

"That good, huh?" He paused for a beat, then continued. "Listen, I'm sorry to bother you, it's about that girl you brought here last time."

"Em? What about her? Is she all right?"

"Yeah, she's all right, but she just had a very interesting story to tell me about being kidnapped by a witch and being rescued by you."

Oh, shit!

"She claims," Tom continued, "that she was held in a dark room and her only clue was Bach playing faintly beyond the walls."

Silence stretched between us, and I was tempted to act as if we had a bad connection, as if I hadn't heard what he'd said, but that wasn't going to solve anything.

"Are you still there?" he asked.

"Y-yeah."

"So, is this something you'd like to talk to me about?"

"Not really."

He huffed.

"Well, you asked."

"Toni, I think this game has lasted long enough, and it's time for you to come clean with me."

Em's kidnapping and rescue had to do with the cure and the dead vampires and hybrids in front of my agency. Two things I couldn't discuss.

I sighed. "I would like to but, like I said before, there's stuff I'm not at liberty to discuss."

"The werewolf stuff?"

"Uh-huh."

"More illegal stuff?"

"Some of it," I admitted reluctantly, then hurried to add, "but it was all in the interest of defending innocent people."

He hummed doubtfully.

"See, that's what I'm afraid of, Tom. If I tell you everything I know, I—"

He cut me off. "I already told you, as wrong as it is, I would never snitch on you or betray your trust."

That shut me up.

"If that's what you're worried about," he added.

Silence.

"You can trust me."

Eric, who I knew could hear the conversation with his enhanced werewolf senses, glowered, seeming to disapprove of the idea of sharing anything with the detective.

Tom let out a sigh. "I can't force you to tell me anything, but if there's anything that could help us stop this mess, I hope you'll consider sharing it. You will probably get a visit from the detective Em talked to. They will want to question you about the kidnapping claim."

Crap! As if I didn't have enough on my plate already.

"Okay, I'll talk to you later," he said.

I disconnected the call and absently stuffed the phone back in my pocket.

"Do you trust him?" Eric asked.

I met his gaze and nodded. "I do."

He shrugged. "I wouldn't tell him anything if I was you, but then again, I'm *not* you."

"Did something happen to Em?" Rosalina asked, looking worried.

"No. She was just there *tattletaling* about her kidnapping." It was stupid for me to say that. She was well within her rights to raise the issue with the authorities. I was just upset because I didn't need any more problems, and she'd just outed me to a detective that wasn't Tom.

We were quiet for a moment, then I remembered something

that had struck me as odd.

"Em said something weird about Bach playing beyond the walls of wherever Mekare was keeping her."

Rosalina sat up straight, her eyes showing white all around the irises, her hands gripping the armchair, nails digging in.

"What is it?" I asked.

She blinked at the floor several times. "I remember…" She nodded. "Yes, I remember that music, classical music." She pressed her fingers to her temples as if trying to recall more.

Eric and I sat still, not moving a muscle, afraid of distracting her train of thought.

"There was something else," she went on, "other sounds like planes? And fire engines?"

I perked up, my mind whirling with the information and what it could mean. "Maybe she was keeping you near an airport?" I asked suggestively.

"And a fire station?" Eric added a bit sarcastically.

"Don't they have fire stations in airports?" I asked. It made sense. Planes crashed.

"Dunno," Eric said.

I pulled up my phone and did a quick search. "Yeah, both STL and Lambert have a fire department nearby."

Eric's initial skepticism washed away. He pushed to the edge of his chair.

"There are lots of warehouses around Lambert," Damien said, sitting up and blinking. "Perfect places for a rhabo operation."

I thought he'd been asleep, but it looked as if he'd been listening the entire time.

"Eric," I pointed toward his desk. "Can I use your computer?"

"Have at it."

I jumped on it and ran a quick search. Just like Damien had said… there *were* a lot of warehouses around Lambert International Airport. It was an industrial-looking area just like where Pulse Inc.

had been located. In fact, there were a load of similar structures in the vicinity.

"Anything?" Eric asked.

"Yeah, it's like Damien said." I shook my head. "Do you remember anything else, Rosalina?"

She frowned and squeezed her eyes shut. After a moment, she just blew air through her nose, frustrated. "I… I don't…"

"*Shh.*" Damien took her hands in his. "Relax. Close your eyes." He made circles over the top of her hands with his thumbs and spoke soothingly. "Breathe deeply. For just an instant, you're there again and you hear the classical music, the planes, the sirens. And perhaps there's something else."

Rosalina started nodding. "When they were taking me there, I was groggy, but I saw lights flashing and a bell was ringing because a train was coming." Her eyes sprang open, her pupils reduced to pinpricks, the green irises looking sharp, almost iridescent. "It was a railroad crossing." Then, under her breath, she added, "Frost."

"Frost?" I echoed. "What do you mean Frost?"

She looked at a loss. "I don't know. It just popped into my head." Suddenly, she seemed to realize that Damien was still holding her hands. Their gazes met. I expected him to withdraw and act nonchalant as he always did, but he continued to trace circles on her skin, looking concerned.

"What?" Rosalina asked.

He narrowed his eyes but said nothing.

I pulled up a map of Lambert international Airport and zoomed in and out of it without any real idea of what I was doing, then something caught my eye.

"Frost Avenue," I whispered.

Quickly, I clicked the mouse and held it down, grabbing the little yellow man in the corner of the screen. I dragged the figure and dropped it on top of the digital representation of Frost Avenue. The screen immediately changed to a real street view. I followed the road, pressing on the forward arrow and paying close attention to the many warehouses that lined either side. After a bit of clicking, I reached…

A railroad crossing!

I closed the laptop and stood up from the desk. "There is a Frost Avenue close to the airport and it dead-ends at a railroad crossing."

We were all silent for a moment, then Damien shook his head.

"Something not sitting well with you?" Eric asked.

The mage shrugged. "I don't know that witch well, but it seems to me that allowing her hostages to remember these details is a bit sloppy."

"Do you mean she could have erased my memories?" Rosalina asked, sounding afraid of the answer.

I had no idea if Midnight Witches and Mages had that kind of power. If they did, that was terrifying, and from the look of panic on Rosalina's face, she felt exactly the same way.

"Like telekinesis," Damien said, "that sort of skill takes a lot of practice and dedication. She may or may not be capable of manipulating people's memories. I don't know her well enough. Maybe her knowledge and control of the subject are minimal, hence the sloppy nature of it. But… I don't know. I just don't like it."

"But what if she's hiding in that area?" I asked. We couldn't waste that knowledge. This could be the chance to finally put a stop to the Midnight Witch.

"And what if it's a trap?" Damien shot back, and in the same breath he shakily got to his feet and answered his own question, "I guess we'll have to be ready for that."

"We?" Rosalina asked, but not in fear or hesitation. No, there was a glint of eagerness in her eyes, that fierce darkness that came to her whenever Mekare came up, as if she couldn't wait to discharge an entire magazine into the witch's body, as if there was nothing else in the world she'd rather do. His protest had to do more with Damien. She just didn't seem sure he should go since he was weak.

"Maybe we should stay out of it, tell Tom about it instead," I offered since our call was still fresh in my mind.

"And risk the cops screwing it up?" Eric said. "Don't forget that *we* had to go in and rescue your sister. Don't forget those dead men on the floor."

"Maybe we can give them some hints, work with them," I suggested.

Judging by the way Eric crossed his arms and twisted his mouth, he didn't seem to think much of that idea either. Damien, for his part, appeared indifferent to the suggestion, like either way would be fine by him. And Rosalina… she just looked disappointed. I read her expression and interpreted it as *I should be the only one allowed to put a bullet between her eyes*. I honestly hoped I was reading her wrong. I still couldn't reconcile her two very different personalities, no matter how hard I tried.

Witchlights, what should we do?

I had resolved not to get involved anymore and to focus on breaking Jake's pact. I couldn't jump back into the fray. A very bothersome pang in my chest shot back an argument I didn't want to contemplate.

As much as I wanted to wash my hands of the witch, I couldn't leave my city at Mekare Graves's mercy. I couldn't just sit here and do nothing while there was a possibility of stopping her. Only the witchlights knew how far she intended to go with her attacks on the city and with the use of those hybrid monsters.

If I didn't fight against her and rid us of her threat, how could I expect our home, our way of life, to come out unscathed on the other end? What kind of chaos would those I loved have to live in if we didn't stop her? Ulfen was right.

I *had* to do something. I was still thinking when Rosalina shot to her feet and quickly dialed a number.

"Who are you calling?" I asked.

"Jake."

Huh?

Rosalina explained. "He's been doing all that research on his fancy computers, maybe if we tell him about this something will click."

Shit! Everything was getting derailed. I shook myself realizing that by *everything* I meant *my goals.*

Hello, the world doesn't revolve around you, Toni Sunder.

If others wanted to run around chasing mad witches to exert revenge, who was I to stop them? Especially when they were all about helping me when *I* needed them. I only hoped that, by getting involved, those plans of mine didn't get totally trashed.

CHAPTER 22

Damn it all to hell!

I didn't want to attend another Pack Rule meeting, but that was where I was headed. There was one huge difference from last time, though. I was alone in the back of the windowless delivery van while Eric drove, and Jake headed there on his own.

It was 9 PM. We'd wasted an entire day without getting closer to a solution for Jake's curse, and now this!

Rosalina had immediately regretted taking matters into her hands and calling Jake. He had derailed us into this. Quite unexpectedly. She hadn't been happy about it or about being left behind since only werewolves were allowed in Wolfskeep.

She'd been right, though. Mentioning the airport to Jake had jogged his memory. There was something in his research of empty warehouses around St. Louis that suggested Rosalina's recollections might be right. He had been looking for another place from which Mekare could be distributing rhabo—the flow of the drug into the city hadn't stopped despite the fact that Stephen Erickson was dead, so it was safe to assume the Midnight Witch had taken over the operation—and among the many potential places on his list that fit the profile, there was a large warehouse on Frost Avenue.

The van rocked. I sighed, trying to figure out Mekare's endgame.

Though the Dark Donna's plan of starting a war between vampires and werewolves had failed now that all the packs knew the truth, whatever Mekare's schemes, they still involved killing vamps with rhabo. Was that only about making money? It seemed unlikely.

Either way, the war was now between her hybrids and everyone else instead. The creatures had made another appearance. This time at a mall. I'd caught the news before we left, and it hadn't been pretty. Fifteen people had died, Stales and Skews alike. They moved on before the police arrived. Lucia's school had only been the beginning. Soon, no one would be safe anymore.

Jake had also shared that small packs were becoming targets for the witch, and she seemed to be very busy making new members for a growing army. He'd heard the news through the werewolf grapevine. Two packs in the Green Park area had been decimated. Only their young had been left behind, orphaned and traumatized by the attack and how their parents had been taken from them.

The van lurched and started on an unpaved road.

Damn Jake! I wouldn't be in this van if it wasn't for him.

On the phone, he had refused to share the location of Mekare's warehouse. Instead, he'd, wisely and responsibly, told us that, this time, we shouldn't go at it alone.

Since his grandfather's death, he hadn't only been taking care of the financial side of things, he'd also been spending time with the Knight pack members, getting to know everyone, especially his leading betas. Regardless of how he felt about being their alpha, he was taking his responsibility seriously and seemed to be gaining a sense of belonging and loyalty towards them. This had also resulted in a flow of communication between him and the other packs, which all along had been training together, preparing to defend their own against the hybrid threat. No doubt, this was the reason he'd decided to make this a pack-wide issue.

Jake was changing. I wrangled with this knowledge. Could this affect our relationship at some point? It had certainly rubbed Rosalina and Eric the wrong way. Rosalina because she seemed bent on being the one to teach Mekare a lesson, and Eric because he wanted nothing to do with the Pack Rule or any of the packs. That he'd let us into his life was amazing, but it was clear he didn't intend to allow anyone else in.

The van finally lurched to a stop. I held on to my metal bench to stop my body from sliding forward. A moment later, Eric threw the doors open. I squinted in his direction to learn he was just as pissed as he'd been when we left his house. He didn't want to be here, but since I didn't know the location of the entrance to Wolfskeep, he had to drive me.

"Fine!" he had told me, "I'll take you, but I'm not going in. In fact, I'm not staying at all. You'll need to catch a ride back with someone else."

"Thank you," I said as he helped me out.

He huffed, slammed the van door shut, got back in the driver's seat, and tore out of there, the back tires slinging rocks left and right. For a moment, I panicked, thinking I was alone, but when I turned to face the back of the cave, I noticed a silver BMW parked there, shining under the torchlight.

Travis Hillworth reclined against it, smoking a cigarette.

Shit!

I checked my watch. I was fifteen minutes early. I whirled toward the entrance, thinking maybe I could wait outside. Moving from foot to foot, I debated what to do. I didn't want to talk to this man. And where was Jake?

God, please hurry up!

"I don't bite, Ms. Sunder," Travis's voice echoed through the cave.

My wolf got prickly at the sound of his voice, taking it as a challenge. Red wasn't scared of anyone. Turning on my heel, I approached him. The light from the torches made my shadow dance on the uneven terrain of the cave.

I stopped a few paces away from him and watched him suck on his cigarette, its tip growing brighter. He blew smoke out of the corner of his mouth, then threw it to the ground and stepped on it, his dark eyes intent on what he was doing. Slowly, he raised his gaze to mine. I held steady, showing him I wasn't intimidated.

He considered for a moment before shocking me with his next words. "A long time ago, I met someone by your same last name... *Sun-der.*" He pronounced it carefully, enunciating the syllables. "Last time we were here, it made me curious, so I had someone look into it."

My gut clenched.

He knows. He knows.

God, I didn't want him to know. Whatever he found out, I would deny it.

"Imagine how much my interest piqued," he went on, "after I discovered that the person I knew is related to you."

I stood still, giving nothing away despite the turmoil of emotions twisting in my chest.

"Amalia Sunder is your mother," Travis said. His eyes narrowed, examining my face as if looking for a resemblance between us. "And you are, how old, Ms. Sunder?"

I didn't reply. If he had someone *look into* me, I was sure he already knew my exact age.

He blew air through his nose, half-amused by my silence. I lifted my chin, daring him to say more, to voice what he seemed to be itching to throw out in the open. What I couldn't understand was why? Why would he want to open this Pandora's box? I sure as hell wanted to leave it closed, put a chain around it with a big ass padlock, and throw it in the depths of the Pacific Ocean.

"She never told me," was what he said next, and the edge of regret in his tone was like a punch to the gut that I hadn't expected. He was supposed to hate me just like I hated him. I took a step back and glanced away.

"But I guess I should've known," he said.

I peered back at him, confused. What did he mean by that?

Seeing my questioning expression, he answered, "I was taken by Amalia as soon as I laid eyes on her. I met her at a public function and was drawn to her like a magnet. I could tell it was the same for her."

Gah, I didn't want to hear any of it. I wanted to tell him to shut up, but I was struck mute.

"I was surprised by the attraction because she's not a werewolf. I'd never cheated on my wife, never thought I would. I loved her. Still do. But it wasn't something I could resist. It was a compulsion."

I gasped, realizing what he was saying. "Cravedark," I said under my breath.

Travis nodded. "It didn't occur to me at the time because, like I said, your mother is not a werewolf. I thought Cravedark was only possible between members of our kind, but recently, I've learned that is not the case."

I clenched my fists, fighting the host of new emotions rising in my chest.

Cravedark.

If their attraction has been due to Cravedark, could I blame either of them for what had happened? Had they had a choice?

There was no choice, a voice said inside of me. It was Red, who understood these things better than my human side ever could.

She did have a choice when she decided to lie to me, another voice said. The anger I'd been feeling toward my mother redoubled.

I glanced at Travis, expecting a similar torrent of feelings to crowd my chest at the sight of him, but they didn't come. He hadn't known. My mother had never told him. Instead, she had chosen to lie to everyone. My father, Travis, me, my siblings.

"Now," he said, "I understand why my interest in her died so suddenly." His eyes scanned me from head to toe as if to say I was the proof, the cause for that abrupt end to his infatuation. "You… came along."

Cravedark created a compulsion between people who would make strong offspring, and it ended the moment that goal was achieved. So when my mother had gotten pregnant with me, Travis's desire to mate with her went away.

As if to leave nothing to interpretation, he added, "You're my daughter."

I wanted to tell him it wasn't true. I wanted to tell him that Peter Sunder was my father, but the anger I'd harbored toward him seemed to have disappeared. When he spoke next, whatever remnants of animosity I still had toward him went up in smoke.

"If I had known, if Amalia had told me, I would have been there."

Part of me wanted this to be a lie, but I realized that he had no reason to lie. Admitting that he was my father would still bring chaos into his life. His wife would be mad. His kids would be mad. Wouldn't they? Why would he bring that on himself unless he meant to take responsibility? Red stirred with her own emotions.

A pack. I would've had a pack, she seemed to say. It was true. My entire life would have been so different. I would never know all the things Mom had deprived me of.

I struggled to find something to say, but I had no idea what.

He spoke first. "Perhaps, you and I could—"

High beams pierced through the dim light, and a Land Rover drove in, filling the cave with the stench of its exhaust. Ulfen Erickson stepped out of the SUV and joined us. He looked more put together than the last time I'd seen him. His red hair and beard were trimmed to perfection, and he wore an expensive suit, a matching tie in place.

He nodded in greeting as he approached us. "Craig is right behind me, I think."

"And the Knight boy?" Travis asked.

The idea that he thought of Jake as a boy struck me as funny.

Ulfen glanced toward me, expecting me to answer the question.

"He'll be here," I said.

Travis frowned and seemed to consider the small interaction between Ulfen and me. These two had an alliance, one that also represented a rivalry against the Knights and the Blackridges. Was he wondering whether his newfound daughter had a thing going with the alpha of an enemy pack? Did he care? I knew I didn't.

A moment later another car pulled into the cave. This one a BMW much like Travis's. Craig got out of the driver's side, and to my surprise, Jake came out of the other door. I didn't like the sight of the two together. Craig would not be happy if he found out what we'd been doing in Eric's garage.

Jake's gaze bore into mine, and memories of last night filled my mind. A blush heated my face. He smiled wickedly, deliciously. I wanted him between my legs all over again, but I had to stamp my urge down. *So inopportune. Seriously!*

"We're all here," Ulfen said without preamble and walked toward the back of the cave, where he pressed his hand to the wall.

The others did the same.

CHAPTER 23

The wall disappeared like last time, and a moment later, a figure appeared inside the dark tunnel. I brightened up at the thought of seeing Yura again. A moment later, the keeper of Wolfskeep stepped out of the shadows and welcomed us with a smile.

"Greetings. Please, say your vows and enter," she said in her melodious voice. She wore the same braids at either side of her dark hair, like last time, except now she had feathers and beads adorning them. They matched the colorful embroidery of her outfit perfectly.

Ulfen went first. "At this sacred juncture, I vow to a moratorium with all the alpha members of this and any other Pack Rule. I vow to uphold our values and make every decision for the protection of our kind."

The others followed. Jake went last and vouched for me before I was allowed to pass.

As we entered the passage, Jake and I hung back, letting the others get ahead. He brushed the back of my hand with his and gave me a bedroom smile that brought back more memories of last night and sent a thrill of excitement down my belly. I returned his smile.

"So not the place, Jake," I whispered.

He leaned forward and spoke in my ear. "You unleashed something," he purred.

Images of his fine, naked body flashed before me.

Someone get me a bucket of ice water!

I needed to walk into Wolfskeep with Jake's mouthwatering physique out of my mind. For what was to come next, we needed to sober up and leave all our hormones outside the door.

As we reached the end of the tunnel, and we entered the meeting area, Jake shook himself, also seeming aware that our time for games of any kind was over.

Everyone took a moment to walk around the room. The banners hanging on the stone walls, and the inlaid table held a beauty that could be admired every day.

Yura stood at the window, peering at the faraway mountains. I wondered again about Wolfskeep's location. It seemed like another world, at least another continent. She sensed me as I approached and smiled over her shoulder.

"Beautiful, huh?" she said.

I nodded.

"How do you fare among all these male alphas?"

"Not too bad." They could be a pain in the ass, but they weren't my real problem.

"It all changes when you try to lead," she said, a certain bitterness in her tone.

"Are you a pack leader?"

"That, I am."

Red seemed to tremble with a mixture of awe sprinkled with jealousy, which surprised me. Did she want to lead a pack?

"It can't be easy," I said both for Yura and Red's benefit.

"It is not, but sometimes, it's very rewarding."

I sensed wisdom in her but also the sense that whatever rewards she enjoyed didn't come without pain.

"You should know," she continued. "You're a pack leader, Toni."

"What? No." I shook my head, chuckling ruefully.

She raised an eyebrow. "Are you sure about that?"

I blinked, considering. I didn't know if I was a leader or not, but she was right about one thing. We *were* a pack. Rosalina, Eric, Damien, me, and maybe… Jake? Could someone belong to two packs? I had no idea.

A genuine smile stretched my lips. Yura returned it and nodded, pleased she'd made me realize something important.

I was about to thank her when Travis spoke.

"Do we start?" he said behind us.

We took our seats around the table, and after a beam of moonlight shone through the hole in the wall and illuminated the eyes of the wolf inlaid on the table, the Keeper spoke.

Yura began. "I want to let you know that the Supreme Pack Rule has been kept abreast of the latest developments, and we are following your situation with great interest. It seems to us that things are spiraling out of control, and we would like to ascertain if our assistance is needed in the matter."

Everyone seemed to tense at that last bit. Even Red bristled. St. Louis was *our* territory. I liked Yura, but we didn't need anyone's help. We could take care of our own problems. *Dammit!*

Yura inclined her head, wearing an amused smile. I imagined she knew well what everyone thought about receiving help from the Supreme Pack Rule.

"Just like you allow their help with *your* problems," Travis shot back.

Yura's smile disappeared. She and her people practically lived in a different world, constantly fighting religious zealots that believed Skews were an abomination. It was a wonder things like that went on in the world, but the Maliseet—the first nation folk Yura belonged to—were still fighting for their rights. The border between Maine and Canada was a vast wilderness dotted with small cities occupied by Stales who wanted to live away from Skews and wished to eradicate them from their own territory. It was a constant war, one in which the government didn't get involved, claiming they respected everyone's rights and taking a side would be in violation of religious freedom. *Such bullshit!*

"Our situation is entirely different," Yura said, her powerful gaze drilling into Travis's.

He shrugged and pretended nonchalance, but I sensed his respect for her authority.

After a loaded pause, Yura made a sweeping gesture over the table. "You may begin."

Like last time, Travis took the reins. "I understand we have a possible location for the witch responsible for our latest problems, is that correct?" He directed the question toward Jake.

"That is correct," he answered, sitting straighter, his silver gaze going around the table.

"How did you come about this information?"

"Through very careful detective work," Jake offered. "Toni can explain."

I started by relating Rosalina's kidnapping and ended with how we'd come up with a location.

Travis huffed. "And are we certain this is the correct place?"

"Yes, we are," Jake said, surprising me. "I had someone do some reconnaissance earlier today. They didn't get too close, but they noticed suspicious activity, and workers that looked like little more than automatons."

"The hybrids," I said.

Jake nodded. It seemed he had been busy before coming here. A burst of adrenaline coursed through my body as I realized we had the correct location. Was Mekare there? It seemed unlikely, but maybe we would get lucky. Maybe that was her base of operations. And if that was the case, and we played our cards right, we might be able to end things soon.

"Yes, the hybrids," Jake said. "It seems that at times, they do manual labor in their human form, pushing rhabo around. And at others, they terrorize the city in their grotesque animal shapes. All of this following Mekare Graves orders. She is a Midnight Witch," he elaborated. "In the beginning, she was working with Bernadetta Fiore and Stephen Erickson, but she betrayed them. She stole the Unholy Vessel, and from the looks of it, also the control of the rhabo trade."

"She sounds like a piece of work," Travis said.

"Do we have any idea how many hybrids she has created?" Craig asked.

"A rough estimate based on the number of small packs she has decimated. We think it's around a hundred, and every day that passes, the number threatens to become larger. So far, she has focused on targeting small packs that control territories around the city, but I suspect soon she'll get bolder, and we'll have to worry about members of our packs."

I shuddered at the thought of more and more innocent werewolves being turned into those mindless, awful creatures.

"This means we should act quickly," Craig said.

Travis leaned back in his chair, looking frustrated. "Sometimes I think we've become too complacent. Things were going well for too long for our packs. If we would have kept a tighter hold on… certain individuals, we wouldn't be in this situation."

By *certain individuals*, I guessed he was referring to Stephen Erickson and Walter Knight. As much as I hated it, I had to agree with him. Those two had screwed up. Royally.

"At this point," Yura offered, "playing the blame game will not help anyone."

Travis waved a hand in the air. "I know. I know. It's just

infuriating to think that two of our own played such a big role in creating this mess."

"I take responsibility for my grandfather's actions," Jake said, which was more than Ulfen had ever done for his son. "And I assure you, I will do everything within my power to put a stop to that witch."

It was surprising to see Jake in this role, to witness his poise and leadership despite everything else he was dealing with and despite the fact that being a pack alpha had never been his preferred choice. But he had never done anything in half measures, and he wasn't shying away from his responsibilities. On the contrary, he was taking full charge, stepping to the forefront with uncanny authority. I couldn't help but admire him.

"So what's the plan?" Travis asked. "I assume we need to move quickly and—"

"Tonight," Jake interrupted.

"Tonight?" I said, fearing the delays a confrontation could pose on our other plans. What if we ended up in the hospital? Or arrested? Or kidnapped by Mekare? Not that I wasn't confident in our ability to fight her, but shit happened, and we couldn't afford any delays.

"Yes, tonight," he said. "We spotted several trucks there earlier today, and men loading heavy boxes on them. I worry that this may be a sign they're changing locations. I could be wrong, but I feel we should act."

Craig leaned forward. "I would hate to miss our opportunity, so I vote we go in tonight. Anyone else?" he asked, putting a hand up in the air.

Ulfen put his hand up immediately. Travis took a moment to consider, then did the same.

"We should send our best people in," Craig offered. "Our strongest betas and a strong alpha to lead them."

"I will go," Jake said without hesitation.

"Me, too," I said right on his heels.

I expected someone to protest, to say that I didn't belong to any pack so I shouldn't be part of the mission, but no one did.

Travis met my eyes across the table. There was a strange expression on his face that made me wonder. It looked like a mixture of concern and protectiveness as if he didn't want me to get involved in any type of danger.

"I will join you," he said.

"I will go as well," Ulfen put in. "Like Alpha Jake Knight, I take responsibility for my son's actions."

"Perhaps, that is too many alphas," Yura offered.

"I concede leadership to Alpha Jake Knight," Travis said. "He knows the situation better. I go only out of concern for my… pack. My strongest betas happen to be my son and daughter."

Yura inclined her head in understanding. "I see. If this is all, I will report the proceedings to the Supreme Pack Rule. I will report back and inform them you're taking measures toward correcting the situation and recovering the Unholy Vessel, which should be a top priority. No one wants to see more of our kind be turned into mindless monsters. I feel this is still something the local packs can accomplish, so I will tell them that. As of right now, our involvement doesn't need to go beyond moderating these meetings."

"As it should be," Ulfen said.

"I'm all for everyone solving their own problems," the Keeper said.

Jake stood. "Let's discuss how to go about this, then."

CHAPTER 24

Two hours later, after the Pack Rule meeting was over, I was stuffed in the van again, but this time I wasn't alone. Rosalina and Damien were there with me while Eric drove us toward our rendezvous place—an empty lot several blocks away from our target and the place where we would meet the others. A small ball of light floated above us, a bit of magic Damien was using to illuminate the dark interior.

Jake had gone with Craig, and I hated that. I wanted him to be here with me, part of our team.

I shook my head. In this operation, the team was larger than just us. The team would have other werewolves, including my biological father and siblings. I didn't like the idea very much, but I understood we couldn't do this alone. A bigger force was needed if we were to encounter hybrids. We knew little of what to expect. It was possible Mekare had entirely moved out of the warehouse, and we would find nothing there. Or we might encounter the witch's monstrous army. It could go either way, and it was best to have more people with us.

The van came to a rolling stop. Damien doused his light. After a few beats, Eric opened the back door and let us out. He had stopped next to what looked like an abandoned building. A parking lot riddled with cracks and weeds stretched before us. One lonely lamppost shone a distance away, flickering on and off. The night sky was covered by a blanket of clouds that hid the stars. A plane engine whirred in the distance.

Next to me, Rosalina patted her trench coat, checking her weapons. It seemed to be a nervous habit she was developing. She'd done it four times already since we'd left Eric's place. She was quiet and took deep breaths every once in a while as if to center herself.

We hadn't talked much about our agency and its future. The claim was with the insurance company, but there would be a lot of paperwork and back and forth before we heard a definite answer. I bet the assholes were making sure the destruction of our beloved agency wasn't due to some sort of insurance fraud.

But even if I hadn't made an effort to talk to her about it, it was on my mind, and I was sure it was on hers, too. With everything that was going on, however, it was impossible to make any decisions. Until this was all over, and we could see past our current problems, it was best to wait. I just hoped that when we came out on the other end, there would be enough left of our dream, of us, to build everything back up.

We waited for several long minutes before three more vehicles arrived. One was a big Ford Expedition, another one a Lincoln Navigator, the last one a Hummer. All three were black and new.

Ulfen and three guys I recognized stepped out of the Expedition. I had met his betas at Packmind when I went to tell them about the hybrids. They were the wiry guy and the giant whose fight had caught my attention when I first walked into the training room. They walked on either side of Ulfen. All three of them wore black military fatigues, guns holstered at their sides, and swords at their backs. Clearly, they remember the hybrids didn't tend to stay dead for very long.

Travis and his son and daughter stepped out of the Hummer. They were dressed the same as Ulfen and the others, down to their boots and the weapons they carried. No doubt, they shopped at the same mall.

Jake got out of the third car. When he came back from New Orleans, he only drove his Harley, but apparently, he also owned a truck and who knew what else? A man of average height accompanied him. He had dark skin, black hair, and a hooked nose. He appeared to be of Middle Eastern descent. They also wore fatigues, guns, and swords of their own.

Man! I was starting to feel left out.

But really I shouldn't. Before long, I'd probably be tearing what I was wearing to bits. I was decent with a gun and useless with a sword, so trusting my teeth and claws was the sensible thing to do. Eric didn't have any weapons either and Damien, well, he didn't need any—not even fangs. He had his twirling fingers.

Jake glanced around, his eyes pausing on me for a long moment before he spoke. "All right, everyone's here. Any questions before we go?"

Olivia, my half-sister, watched Jake with interest. Red perked up, growing restless. I took deep breaths to control the alpha vibes that were trying to pour out of me.

"This is Jacob Knight," Travis said, noticing his daughter's interest.

"Nice to meet you," she said as the interest that had sparked in her eyes died. I figured she knew about Jake's engagement to Allison Blackridge, which, in her mind, put him in the *unavailable* category—even if that wasn't the real reason Jake wasn't on the market.

"I'm Marcus Hillworth." My half-brother introduced himself. His shoulder-length blonde hair was pulled back into a ponytail like Olivia's, which made him look like her twin.

A few more introductions went around. The wiry guy with Ulfen was called Patrick, and the big guy, Ben. The alpha with Jake introduced himself as Khal. Then it was our turn to share our names.

"Aren't you the Copper Mage who died?" Marcus asked after Damien introduced himself with a flourish of his top hat.

The mage rolled his eyes. It seemed he was getting tired of being recognized as *the Copper Mage who died.*

"I am," he said with a smile that didn't reach his eyes. "But I resurrected."

Marcus laughed, not believing a word of it.

I shook my head. Clearly, Damien was working on being known as *the Copper of Mage who resurrected*, instead—even if that wasn't exactly what he'd done.

I scanned every face, wondering how much we could rely on these people. I trusted my team. We'd been through enough together, but could we trust these newcomers? We were twelve in total. We had discussed attacking with bigger numbers, but in the end, we decided that stealth and the element of surprise would be to our advantage. If we approached with a full-on army, Mekare would likely spot it and flee.

Olivia caught me looking at her. As our gazes connected, I noticed a certain gravity in her expression. When I first met her, she had seemed haughty and intent on letting me know she was better than me. But now, I detected something else in her manner, something tentative and curious. Had Travis told her who I was? I glanced away, pushing those worries aside. I had to get my head in the game. I couldn't let anything distract me.

One thing at a time, Toni.

"Ready?" Jake asked.

Everyone nodded.

"Groups of at least two, all right? No one should fight by themselves. These hybrids are incredibly hard to take down. It's not smart to go at it alone." He looked at his wristwatch. "We storm the place at oh-one-hundred."

Damien checked his watch, a silver piece with a wide band, very expensive-looking, then inclined his wrist in my direction, so I could read the time. We had a little more than twenty minutes to make it to the warehouse. We would all approach from different directions under the protection of one of Damien's spells, while Eric Rosalina, Patrick, and Ben created at distraction.

"Be careful, Rosalina," I said.

"You, too. Make her suffer if you find her before I do." She winked, leaving me wondering whether or not she was serious.

Her team got in Eric's van, while the rest of us scattered, slinking under the shadows of the abandoned building and making our way toward the warehouse.

"You don't need to walk crouching," Damien said as he strolled as if he were in a park. "My spell is keeping you hidden."

I straightened, feeling foolish. "Are you sure?"

"Positive. Last time, she didn't detect Bernadetta's vampires, which means my concealment spells are effective against whatever surveillance magic she's using."

"Yes, but we're not dead."

"I made some modifications to account for that. I suspect she uses the Wozniak variation. Nothing fancy or of her own creation, so in this area, I'm certain I'm better than her."

"The what variation?" I had no idea what he was talking about.

"Wozniak, a German mage came up with it. There are certain standards when it comes to magic. At first, mages and witches learn the basics in a variety of subjects in order to be capable, kind of like… learning to play chess. After that, depending on our inclinations, we delve deeper into certain topics. In my case, I was always interested in potions. They simply fascinate me. If you're really good, you come up with unique techniques."

That explained how he'd been able to create rhabo *and* the cure.

"What do you think Mekare specializes in?" I asked.

Damien thought for a moment. "I've been trying to figure that out for some time. You know that trick where she turns to smoke?"

I nodded. "She's really good at that."

"Yes, she is. I will admit it's not something I care to master since it involves… dealing with branches of magic too dark for my taste. There is more than one way to accomplish what she does, and I haven't figured out which way she's using. It is a common trait for my kind to keep this sort of thing secret from others. It gives us an edge. Plus, we like an air of mystery about us."

"I can tell." I gave his cloak a sidelong glance. After a moment of silence, I said, "I hope Jake and Rosalina are all right."

"They'll be fine. They know how to take care of themselves."

We reached the corner and stopped to glance both ways. The streets were deserted, no cars in sight, and only the sound of a train rolling slowly down its tracks could be heard.

"I'm still not used to seeing Rosalina with all those weapons," I said. "It worries me."

"Why?"

"I don't know. She's changed a lot, and I fear she's becoming someone else, someone she was never meant to be." It was the first time I voiced my fears to anyone.

"You think it's your fault."

My head snapped in his direction. How had he deduced that so quickly?

"Toni, you can't expect to be part of someone's life and not have an effect on it."

I blinked at that.

"Everyone you meet will teach you something. Good or bad. Right or wrong. Some people teach you to love, others to hate. There are those who open your eyes to cruelty and the many levels of evil. Many push you away with their simple presence, while others attract you like magnets. And when you have collided with someone who becomes a fixture in your life, they're almost guaranteed to throw you off your axis. So yes, you *have* played a part in changing who she is, but have you considered the part she has played in changing you? And do you think she should feel guilty about that?"

"She has only changed me for the better?"

"And why are you so sure you haven't done the same for her?"

My head started spinning as I tried to process that concept. "Has she said anything to you? Is that what she thinks?"

Damien shrugged. "She has not. Perhaps, you should talk openly to her about your worries. Personally, I think it's damn sexy."

What?!

I opened my mouth to say something, but he put a finger to his lips. We had reached Frost Avenue, and we were standing across from the warehouse.

He checked his watch. In the distance, I heard a car engine. It got louder and louder, then tires screeched, and Eric came around the opposite corner, the van going at full speed. He headed straight for the warehouse.

The van climbed the sidewalk, bucking wildly as the tires hit the curb. When he was only a few feet away from the building's main door, the driver's side door sprang open, and Eric jumped out. He shifted in midair. His tawny wolf hit the ground running. Patrick and Ben jumped out of the back, just seconds before the van crashed. They landed almost as gracefully as Eric, despite the fact that they were in their human forms. The sound of crunching metal filled the night as the van rammed through the front door.

I reminded myself that Rosalina had been dropped off so she could take a sniper position in the building across from the warehouse.

Almost immediately, a second door burst open and a couple of confused-looking men came out. They blinked at the scene and spent a moment taking it all in. Once they added two and two together, their bodies shifted, muscles expanding and bones elongating. Their clothes fell to the ground in tatters as sinew ridden with black, bulging veins tripled in size. The beasts lifted their short snouts skyward, roared their displeasure, and bounded toward Eric and the others.

Patrick and Ben pulled out their guns and started unloading wolfsbane bullets on the pair. The smaller hybrid zigzagged out of the way, leaping forward, avoiding injury, his front limbs barely touching the ground as he hurdled forward like a freight train.

The second one was much bigger and slower. A couple of bullets hit him, but they barely slowed him down. Eric ran between Patrick and Eric, lunging toward the hybrids to serve as a distraction. About six more men came out of the warehouse and wasted no time shifting. My skin itched to do the same. Red wanted to leap forward to help Eric, but that was not the plan.

Shots rang from above, and two of the new hybrids thudded to the ground. The others slowed, giving Eric, Patrick, and Ben time to regroup. Rosalina was at it with her rifle already, and she was a damn good shot.

Damien put a hand up in the air, holding five fingers up. Mouthing down the seconds, he started lowering his fingers. I pulled out my handgun and held it by my side.

Five, four, three, two, one.

He stepped into the street with a confident air and began walking toward the warehouse. I stayed frozen for a beat but quickly joined him. I glanced around, searching for the others, but of course, I couldn't see them. They were concealed under Damien's spell, just like we were.

The *pop, pop, pop* of bullets echoed through the night as Rosalina, Patrick, and Ben unloaded full magazines into the hybrids' misshapen bodies. They had retreated a few yards to put some distance between them and the monsters. Eric continued to run in the periphery of the creatures, weaving in and out to distract them.

Damien and I reached the side of the building without notice, just as we'd hoped. The mage was concealing our scent and any sounds our steps would produce. There was no door for us to enter through on this side, which was the reason Damien was with me. The others didn't need a mage. They would have doors to burst through.

With an elegant flourish, Damien weaved his hands and pointed them at the wall. A blast of energy sprang from his fingers. There was a crack and an explosion of light that his concealment spell made sure to obscure. A hole just wide enough for us to squeeze through formed as the corrugated metal wall melted away.

Damien turned to me. "I would say ladies first, but in this instance, that wouldn't be gentleman-like."

Cautiously, he stepped in first, hands held in front of him. I waited for a second, then followed after him, my heart pounding out of control and Red nearly breaking through. All around us was darkness. My eyes took a moment to adjust before I was able to make out the shapes of some sort of large equipment.

I couldn't tell what the machines were for, but certainly something industrial. Conveyor belts stretched from one machine to the next. Did they use the equipment for the production of rhabo? I had no idea what was needed to make the drug, but it seemed unlikely. Maybe the equipment was left over from whatever the place was used for before Mekare took over.

Damien walked further in, while I follow behind him at a crouch, my eyes darting in every direction, searching for more hybrids and for any sign off that fucking Midnight Witch. The mage threw a sidelong glance in my direction. He was standing erect as if parading in his own house. There was nothing furtive or defensive about his stance. I huffed. Did he think that made him braver? I sure felt more ready than him to lunge toward any attacker. Or maybe, with magic constantly at his fingertips, he thought of himself as untouchable. Maybe he'd forgotten about his stint as a worm and a cat.

We kept moving toward the center of the building. When we reached a door, Damien opened it a crack, peered out, then let it swing open. An expansive room illuminated by sparse fluorescent lights stretched before us. The concrete floor was pitted and stained by oil and paint spots. Narrow, overhead windows hung high on the walls. Besides that, there was nothing else to see. It was empty. *Damn!* We were too late.

My eyes narrowed as I scanned the space. A slimy feeling of foreboding slid down my back. A door opened across from us, then another one to the side. I crouched lower, a rumbling sound building in my chest.

Damien moved his hand up and down in a pacifying gesture. "It's just the others."

I squinted harder trying to make out their shapes behind Damien's magic, but I saw nothing. I imagined Jake's silver eyes scanning the area, sweeping right past us.

The mage cocked his head to one side as if listening for something, then he uttered a spell under his breath.

After a moment, his expression changed, and his next words froze me in place, "Oh, no!"

CHAPTER 25

The lights above us went out. I blinked repeatedly, willing my eyes to adjust to the poor light that broke through the windows. After a moment that felt like an eternity with nothing but the sound of my heart pounding in my ears, I made out Damien's cloaked figure, standing a few paces to my left.

"What's going on?" I murmured in a voice that trembled as much as my taut nerves.

Damien didn't answer. Instead, the next time I blinked, he was gone. I batted my arms in his direction, trying to touch him, but he was no longer there.

"Damien, where did you go?"

No answer.

I crouched lower. Red begged me to let her out. Instead, I held tighter to my gun. A bullet in the right place could take a hybrid down from a distance. If I shifted, I would need to get close to attack, and there was no way I could win against one of those beasts—not unless I used a blast of my tracker energy against them, and I still wasn't so good at making that happen on command—not to mention that it left me exhausted, and I had a feeling there was more than one hybrid waiting to pounce on each of us.

"Jake," I projected my alpha thoughts forward. *"Can you hear me?"*

No answer either.

It was as if everyone had truly disappeared.

Or maybe *I* had.

Maybe Mekare had used her magic to somehow… what? Teleport me out of the warehouse? I shook my head. No, that wasn't possible. Mages and witches couldn't teleport themselves or anyone else. That wasn't something anyone could do.

But then what?

My panic roared in my ears. I took a deep breath, trying to keep my cool.

There's nothing scary here, I told myself. *It's just dark. And empty.*

"Jake?!"

I took a step forward.

"Ulfen?!"

Another one.

"Marcus? Olivia? Travis?!"

Nothing. No one was here.

I whirled around and retraced my steps, searching for the door, but it wasn't there either. Swallowing thickly and gun at the ready, I whirled, searching for signs of… anything.

He will die, an oily voice spoke all around me. Or was it only inside my head? I couldn't tell.

Pain. So much pain before he finally goes.

I shook my head.

No. No. No.

"Get out of my head!"

And it will be your *fault.*

I clenched my teeth, willing whatever this was out of my head.

He's doing this for you. And he will die because you don't love him enough to let him go.

A piercing pain shot through my temples. I threw my head back as the jolt of agony slid down my spine, dropping me to my knees. The gun slipped from my hand and clattered to the floor. Shrinking from the pain, I patted all around me until I found it and gripped it tightly again.

The pain receded slowly, its ebbing waves making me rock back and forth.

Selfish. You're so selfish. You take and you take and you take.

"It's not true. Not true!"

This time I let go of the gun so I could dig my fingernails into my head. My claws snapped into place, and I cried out as they pierced into my scalp.

"None of it is true. None of it!" I hissed between clenched teeth and, without thinking, released a short blast of energy straight into my head.

My body spasmed with the load of sensory signals. The deafening cacophony of multitudes. Flashes of color and light on psychedelic strobes. The scent of death over lilacs and roses. The taste of sweet chocolate and rot. The touch of a thousand clammy hands and the caress of a feather. Back and forth sensations yanked my system up and down, left and right, to and fro, like a fish on a hook.

Insanity brushed its bony fingers down my back.

I threw my hands to the sides and screamed, lost in the agony of too much *everything*. For the first time, I knew what the others had felt when I'd used my singular power on them.

The quality of so much awareness was maddening and painful. My eyes and ears felt as if needles had pierced through them, and my skin seemed raw, all of its nerve endings exposed.

It seemed an eternity before the effects of the violent onslaught passed. I came to, blinking and lying on my back on the floor. I tried to sit, but my arms and legs trembled. Instead, I rolled onto my stomach and slowly got on all fours. I glanced around and spotted my gun. With trembling fingers, I picked it up, drew it toward my chest, and sat back on my heels, panting. It was still dark all around me, but my eyes had somehow adjusted. I was still in the warehouse.

After a long moment of centering my mind, I felt stronger and rose to my feet. A dark figure startled me as I turned. Quickly, I realized it was Damien. He was standing as still as a statue, his eyes fixed on a faraway point. His face was twisted in pain and a tear was sliding down his cheek. I approached cautiously and waved a hand in front of his face.

"Damien."

No reaction.

"Damien, wake up!" I shook him, wrapping a hand tightly around his upper arm.

I thought of sinking my claws into him and shocking him, but I wasn't sure if that would be a good idea. What if I overdid it? What if I killed him?

I stepped away from him and turned to look for the others. Across the large space, I made out two dark shapes standing as still as a Damien. One of them was Jake. I could tell despite the darkness. I would recognize his silhouette anywhere. The two next to him were Ulfen and Khal. They seem to be okay, though probably lost in the agony of their own thoughts.

I searched for Travis, Olivia, and Marcus next. I spotted them at the back of the building, three dark shapes clustered together, unmoving. I pondered what to do.

Undoubtedly, Mekare was doing this, but where was she? Did she know I'd broken out of her torturous stupor? The pain I'd felt had been similar to what she'd put me through while interrogating me about the cure, except this time, there had been a voice, and it had slipped into my mind, same as the fearmonger demon's voice.

A loud clunk startled me back into the moment. The sound had come from outside where Eric and the others were still fighting the hybrids. I shook myself. We had to get out of here before the monsters turned their attack toward the warehouse again. Clearly, this had been a trap. There was no rhabo here. No witch.

I turned to go to Jake. He was strong. He would be able to stand a sensory jolt from me. He would help me figure out how to wake the others up. I rushed toward him, but a groan from Damien made me stop and whirl around. He was on his knees, clasping his head. As I hesitated, he fell flat on his face and started convulsing.

"Damien!" I turned and dashed toward him.

I knelt at his side and pressed his shoulders down, trying to keep him still, but his body continued writhing even as I did my best to hold him down.

"Damien!" I shook him. "Wake up!"

He continued convulsing. Foam bubbled out of his mouth. I had to wake him up before his brain turned into a fried nugget. I let my claws spring out. They broke through his cloak, jacket, and shirt and sank into him. I tried to release my tracker energy into him, but it didn't work. I was about to try again when his convulsions stopped, and he went as stiff as a board. I pulled back, withdrawing my claws and wiping bloody fingertips on my jeans.

The mage wheezed, every breath a struggle, but he seemed to be free from whatever had held him.

I pressed a hand to his cheek. "C'mon, you have to—"

A shot rang out, echoing through the empty warehouse. My head snapped toward the sound, in the direction of Travis and his kids. Grunts and the rustling of a scuffle followed. I squinted in the dark and saw they weren't standing frozen anymore. Instead, they seemed to be fighting each other.

What the hell?!

After a last glance at Damien, I sprinted toward the three struggling figures. When I got closer, I could see Travis had a gun in his hand, and Marcus and Olivia were fighting him back, holding his arm up and trying to disarm him.

Another shot exploded. I shrank back as the bullet whizzed a few feet away from my head.

"Dammit!" I cursed. "What are you doing? Stop it!"

It was as if I wasn't even there.

They continued fighting, Travis slowly bending the gun in Marcus's direction.

God, he's trying to kill him!

I acted without thinking. Like a linebacker, I rushed Travis and slammed my shoulder into his side, wrapped my arms around his waist, and took him down with me. The gun went off again. My ears rang with the shot. We fell to the floor, Travis crashing with a *humph* as the air was forced from his body.

I bounced off of him and fell to the side, jamming my shoulder. I groaned as I scrambled to a sitting position. Travis sat up like a Jack-in-the-Box, pointing his gun at Marcus. In the blink of an eye, he took aim and pulled the trigger.

The gun discharged.

Before I even realized what I was doing, I was on my feet, fleeting toward Marcus and knocking him down. We hit the floor with bone-breaking force. Marcus bared his teeth in pain and blinked at me, confused, strands of his blond, long hair framing his face.

"What… what's going on?" he asked, shaking his head.

I scrambled away, glancing around. From the looks of it the mental attack had stopped. Jake was sitting up, shaking his head. My shoulders slumped with relief.

"No! Noooo!" A cry of absolute pain rent the air. It was guttural, primal.

My attention snapped to Travis as he knelt on the floor, his face disfigured in despair, his neck corded as he screamed with all his might.

I was confused for an instant until I followed his gaze and *saw.*

Olivia was sprawled on the floor, a puddle of blood building around her head. My spine turned to ice as I stared, unable to blink, unable to process.

Travis crawled toward his daughter, the gun still in his hand, clanking with every move. When he got there, he seemed to realize he was still holding it. With a disgusted growl, he flung it aside then used that same hand to tentatively caress Olivia's face.

"Baby? Baby girl?"

I blinked, and a lone tear slid down my face. She wasn't going to answer. The bullet had hit her right between the eyes. No werewolf could survive that—even if the bullet hadn't been laced with wolfsbane.

"O?" Marcus whispered as he sat up and took in the sight. "No. Not you, O."

Travis broke down and began sobbing out of control, picking up Olivia's hand and pressing it to his lips as he wept.

"My baby girl. My sweet baby girl," he sobbed.

I pressed tight fists to my temples and squeezed, hoping to erase the horror, to wake up from the awful dreamscape.

A hand squeezed my shoulder, startling me. I glanced up to find Jake standing there, his clear eyes scanning every inch of me to make sure I was all right. His attention slowly drifted to Travis and his daughter. Ulfen and Khal stood to the side, looking confused. It seemed everyone was free of the trance now.

Marcus got to his feet, his entire body trembling, his face shining with tears under the dim light trickling in through the windows. He moved closer to his sister, grief making him sway like a drunkard.

When Travis noticed his son's approach, he glanced up. For an instant, his expression revealed the ravaging pain tearing through his soul, then his face morphed, first going slack, then tensing into a grimace of unadulterated fury. He dropped Olivia's hand and rose to his full height, glowering at his son. Marcus took a step back, looking stricken.

Travis opened his mouth then closed it again. His dark eyes darted left and right until they came to rest on me. Baring his teeth, he stepped over Olivia's body as if she weren't even there anymore, as if she'd already vanished from his mind.

"*You*, you did this!" He came at me, charging like a bull.

Jake took a quick step forward and blocked Travis's line toward me. "Heel," he ordered, the brunt of his alpha strength pouring forth.

As if he'd hit a wall, Travis came to an abrupt stop. He bore his fangs, growling. Dark fur sprang in streaks over his face, while his ears grew pointed.

I didn't know why—the sudden fury toward me shouldn't have mattered—but my heart shriveled, struck by pain and regret. Whatever could have been had simply died tonight.

Travis tried to come at me again, leaning his weight forward and raising his hands as if to strangle Jake.

"HEEL!" Jake commanded again.

"Get. Out. Of. The. Way!" Travis ordered.

Marcus stepped into his father's field of vision. "And then what?!"

A frown appeared on Travis's forehead and, reluctantly, he glanced sideways at his son.

"What are you going to do to her, father?" Marcus demanded.

Travis shook his head, his frown deepening, his fur and ears retreating back into place, but not his fangs or claws. He appeared bewildered, lost.

"You're going to kill her for *saving* your son?" There was so much hurt in Marcus's words that I felt the raw ache in my own chest. He thought his father would've preferred it if *he* had died.

Travis pulled back and whirled, muttering something between a sob and cry. Pulling at his hair, he disappeared in the shadows while Marcus went to his sister, knelt by her side, and wept inconsolably.

I tried to understand what'd just happened and found myself unable to cope with the emotional upheaval. I shook my head and closed my heart and soul to all the pain.

Jake faced me. "Are you all right?"

I buried my face in his chest. He wrapped his arms around me and held me tight.

Damien approached, limping and looking dazed. "What happened?"

On the heels of his question, half a dozen hybrids rushed into the building.

They were hungry for blood.

CHAPTER 26

"We have to get out of here!" Jake said.

Taking my hand and intertwining his fingers with mine, he started running.

"Wait!" I pulled him back and gestured toward Marcus, who was desperately trying to pick his sister up off the floor.

Jake understood, and we faced the incoming hybrids to give Marcus time to get Olivia out. Jake started shooting and so did Ulfen and Khal. I picked up Travis's discarded gun and squeezed the trigger.

One, two, three times.

My bullets struck two different hybrids, slowing them down. The others hit a few more. One of the monsters—a huge one, his entire body stained with blood already—broke from the rest and came at us. I re-aimed and took several shots. Jake did the same. The beast kept coming. Red rose to the surface, ready to take over.

A storm of crackling magic hit the hybrid in the back. The beast went stiff, then his arms and legs twitched uncontrollably, and finally, it collapsed to the floor. Coming from the side, Damien teetered past us, taking careful steps, doing his best to appear nonchalant.

Marcus was already running the way he'd come in, cradling his sister in his arms. We followed him and got out of the warehouse through the back door.

For a moment, I hesitated. What about Travis?

Reading my mind, Jake said, "Leave him. He knows how to take care of himself."

Outside, Marcus was already turning the corner, not a single concern over his father. I guessed if he wasn't worried, I shouldn't worry either. He had tried to… to what? Hit me? Kill me? I wasn't sure, but that probably meant I didn't owe him any concern. Pushing thoughts of him aside, I focused on those who really mattered.

Damien was hot on Marcus's heels, running this time, if a little drunkenly.

"Eric, are you all right?" I pushed my alpha thoughts forward as we kept running, headed toward the front.

No answer came. My legs weakened from worry, but I powered forward, trusting that nothing had happened to him.

A crashing sound came from behind us. I glanced over my shoulder to find the hybrid Damien had shocked coming after us. The creature was staggering, his legs weaving from side to side, his massive shoulders hitting the metal walls as he tried to catch up with us.

At the front, we found a mess of blood and body parts. Patrick was hacking at a fallen hybrid's neck with his sword. His face was so splattered with blood, he was practically unrecognizable. He swayed to his feet, looking dazed. When he spotted movement, he raised his sword threateningly but lowered it as soon as he recognized us.

"We have to get out of here. NOW!" Jake ordered.

Patrick didn't hesitate. Even if the order wasn't from his alpha, it still carried that undeniable power.

"Where's Eric?!" I asked.

But as we got closer to the van, I got my answer.

Rosalina was there, doing her best to drag Eric's wolf toward the back of the van. His fur was matted with blood, and there was a huge wound in his belly.

"Oh, God, no!" I exclaimed, rushing to help.

"I'll take care of him," Damien said, extending his hands toward Eric and using his magic to levitate him into the back of the van. The wolf floated slowly and unevenly. Damien grimaced with the effort, but he managed to deposit Eric inside and quickly followed after him.

"Are you guys all right?" Rosalina asked me, scanning us with concern.

"Yes, you?" I said.

She nodded in answer.

"You drive," Jake said to me. "I'll help Patrick." He pointed toward Ulfen's beta, who was now lifting Ben off the ground. One of his legs looked badly injured, and he was too dazed to know which way was up.

Rosalina started toward the passenger side door and stopped when she noticed Marcus just standing there, holding Olivia in his arms. She gasped, her gaze flying in my direction, a million questions swimming in her green eyes.

There was no time for answers. Instead, I got behind Marcus and urged him to move, pushing him toward the back doors.

"Get in. They're coming!"

He moved reluctantly at first but then hopped in just as Jake and Patrick got there with Ben. Ulfen and Khal got in next.

"Go. Go. Go!" Jake urged us.

Rosalina and I jumped in last. The front of it was badly wrecked and embedded in the building. I turned the key, praying. The engine came to life.

Unsure of whether or not I should get moving, I peered into

the side mirror. Had they closed the doors yet? Three thumps on the separating wall behind me let me know it was time to put the pedal to the metal. I grasped the wheel tightly and accelerated. We lurched backward, metal whining as the van peeled out of the building. As I whipped it around, a hybrid appeared in front of us. I shifted to first.

My heart jumped in my chest at the sight of his hideous mug. Baring my teeth, I stepped on the gas and ran over the bastard. The van jerked from side to side as the back wheels cleared the lump. We sped out of there, and I couldn't help but wonder how much I would come to regret tonight.

ꙮ

Unsure of where else to go, I drove toward Eric's house. I kept checking the side mirrors to make sure no one was following us.

When my heart finally settled, I pushed my alpha thoughts outward.

"How's everything back there?"

Jake answered right away. *"Damien healed Eric and Ben. They're going to be okay."*

I exhaled in relief. Rosalina glanced helplessly in my direction.

"Jake said that Eric and Ben are going to be okay," I shared the good news with her, wishing I didn't have to tell her about the one who hadn't made it.

"Oh, God." She buried her face in her hands and scrubbed up and down. I thought she might ask what happened inside the warehouse, but she seemed to understand, as she always did, that I was in no shape to talk about it. And maybe she wasn't either. It had been a massacre outside the warehouse, and she had witnessed it.

Twenty minutes later, I pulled into Eric's small garage. The door was closed, and I had no idea how to open it. I glanced around, looking for his phone, which he used to control the security system. I found it tucked in a nook in the dashboard. I pressed the screen. The phone came to life, but I didn't have the passcode.

"Shit!" I exclaimed in frustration, stuffing the phone back where I'd found it.

I was about to get out of the van when the garage door started to open, scrolling upward like a curtain. I figured Damien had used a spell to activate it. I drove inside as soon as there was enough room to get through. After shutting off the engine, I hopped out, ran toward the back just as Jake threw the doors open. He hopped out, then turned to help Eric out.

Eric was in his human form, his clothes perfectly clean, a sharp contrast to the skin on his face, hands, and arms, which were so caked with dry blood that he almost looked black. He was holding his middle and got down gingerly with Jake's help.

Without thinking, I crashed into him and wrapped my arms around him.

He let out an *oomph* and a groan of pain. Still, I couldn't let him go. I was too relieved he was all right. At first, he was stiff, but then he relaxed into the hug and patted my shoulder.

"I'm okay, Sunder. I've been through worse."

I pulled back, draping his arm over my shoulders, and helped him walk inside. The training room didn't have any furniture, but it was the closest to the garage, so I took Eric in there and helped him as he gingerly lowered himself to the floor, resting his back against the mirrored wall. He slumped, a hand still pressed to his stomach.

"Can I get you anything?" I asked.

He shook his head. "I'm good. I just need to rest." He closed his eyes and let his head drop to one side. Jake came in with Ben who was using him for support as he hopped on one leg. His pants' leg was torn to shreds and soaked in blood, but, from what I could see, he wasn't bleeding anymore. Damien had done a decent job healing them despite the fact we were addled as hell.

Jake deposited Ben next to Eric. The big guy let out a heavy exhale and went limp. Patrick rushed into the room and knelt by his friend.

"How you feel, man?"

"Like shit," Ben responded, without opening his eyes.

"I told you not to go head to head with that beast."

"It was the smallest one."

Patrick shook his head. "Not as small as your pea-sized brain." He pressed his index finger to the middle of his friend's forehead and pushed.

"Hey!" Ben swatted at him weakly.

I turned away from them as Damien and Rosalina walked in, the mage leaning heavily on her. His eyelids were drooping and he looked pale.

Rosalina met my gaze, a concerned expression shaping her features. "Marcus won't… leave her."

My breath hitched. "I'll go check on him."

I tried not to feel guilty about what had happened. It had been an accident. Unknowingly, I'd saved his life and condemned his sister. When the dust settled, would he hate me like Travis did? It didn't matter. For some reason, I felt responsible for him, so I had to go.

As I started to leave, Jake grabbed my hand. I glanced back.

"Are you all right? Do you need me to come with you?"

I shook my head. "Help them here. Bring them water." Eric and Ben had lost a lot of blood and, despite their healing abilities, they still needed to hydrate.

Jake walked out with me but headed in the opposite direction, presumably toward the kitchen. I went back to the garage and, taking a deep breath, I braced myself for what waited for me in the van.

Skirting around the open back door, I faced the sight of Marcus sitting cross-legged on the van's floor, Olivia's body lying in front of him. His eyes were open but unseeing. His chin rested on his chest. An air of complete despair hung around him, a noxious cloud seemed to seep into my lungs as I breathed.

"Marcus," I all but whispered.

He didn't look up but, coming to, he blinked and peered at his sister's slack face. Fresh tears slid silently down his face.

Removing my jacket, I stepped into the van. "I'm going to…" I showed him my jacket and gestured toward Olivia.

He seemed angry for an instant, like he hated me for intruding, but then he took the jacket from me and draped it over Olivia's face. The bottom of the garment halfway covered the bullet wound in her chest. My head snapped to one side as I averted my gaze.

"Why don't you come with me?" I said, offering Marcus my hand.

I thought he would turn me down, but he squeezed my fingers and let me help him out. Together we left the garage and entered the house. I didn't guide him into the training room, though. It seemed to me he wanted to be alone right now. Instead, I took him upstairs and led him to one of the sitting areas. He sank into the sofa, his movements robotic.

"Would you like anything? Some water? A drink?" I asked.

He shook his head.

I stood there for a long moment, unsure of what to do or say. Finally, I asked, "Would you mind if I sit with you?"

He was quiet for so long I thought his silence was a way to say *no*, but just as I was about to leave, he spoke.

"No, I wouldn't mind."

I sat next to him, leaving space for another person between us. I stared at the carpet, trying to think of something that might offer him comfort but coming up empty.

He surprised me by talking first. "She wanted to get to know you."

I blinked, unsure I'd heard him right.

"Dad told us about you. Olivia felt bad about the way she treated you at Packmind, the day we met. She always said she wanted a sister." A sad smile stretched his lips. "When we were little and we didn't get along, she said it was because I was a boy. I always told her the real problem was the fact that she was a girl. We were planning on inviting you out, see if you wanted to get to know us, too."

I swallowed thickly at a complete loss for words. I would've never suspected what he was saying. I always figured they would hate me. My eyes stung as I fought to keep my tears back. My emotions were unexpected. How could I feel so much for the loss of a sister I never knew?

When I got myself under control, I said, "I would've loved that." I'd never considered the possibility, but my reaction to the idea was true and warm.

Marcus sniffled, took a deep breath, and shook himself. He squared his shoulders toward me and met my gaze. I shrank a bit, fearing an accusation from him.

"You saved my life," he said, with no hint of condemnation in his expression. "When he aimed the gun at me, I froze. I know you just reacted, put yourself on the line to save me. I thank you for that." He paused. "I wish it had been me, though, and not Olivia. She had a hunger for life like no one I've ever known."

"I'm so sorry," I said in a trembling voice.

"We knew what we were doing. Every time we go out there to fight, we know there's a chance we may not return. She wouldn't blame you. She would say it was meant to be. So… don't beat yourself up about it, and I'll try to do the same. Deal?"

Holding back tears, I nodded. "Deal."

I was grateful to Marcus for his words, for his strength in the face of so much tragedy. What he'd said would make all the difference between pinning a batch of guilt on my chest and accepting that I'd done the right thing.

I hadn't meant to condemn Olivia. I had only meant to save Marcus.

CHAPTER 27

The next day, I walked into the kitchen after two hours of forced sleep. I had made myself stay in bed, tossing and turning, the events of the night replaying in my head over and over.

Stupid, stupid, stupid.

We should have never gone there. Never. We should've stayed out of it. Damien had said it might be a trap, but it seemed all the risks we'd outrun lately had made us overconfident and reckless. I honestly thought we would walk into the warehouse, destroy Mekare's drug operation, kill her hybrids, and even her while we were at it.

She had played us. She'd known we would fall for it. She had counted on our cocky behavior.

I stared at the coffeemaker's empty carafe. It seemed I was the first one up. It was only 4:30 AM after all. I set a batch to brew and sat at the kitchen table, head in my hands, wondering where Eric kept the painkillers. My head was pounding.

Sometime in the night, Marcus, Patrick, and Ben had left. They'd called some of their pack members and took off. Marcus had tenderly picked up his sister's body and transferred it to the back of the vehicle.

No one had said much as they left.

Once they were gone, we'd helped Eric and Damien upstairs. Jake took Eric to his bedroom, and Rosalina and I helped the mage in one of the spare rooms close to ours.

The coffee machine gurgled, signaling my poison was done. I poured myself a cup and drank it without milk or sugar, wincing at the bitterness. It was strong, and I hoped it would help with my headache.

I was about to sit down when my phone vibrated. The caller ID read *unknown*. My hand shook as I answered it and raised it to my ear.

"How are you feeling this morning, dear? You have a headache, I imagine. It's a common side effect to *phantasmagoria*."

My entire body trembled with rage. I set the coffee cup down on the counter, afraid I would fling it against the wall. Eric would not appreciate any attempts at redecoration.

"I wish it had been someone else," she said. "A sister you don't really know was hardly high on the list, but maybe it's better this way. Maybe I'll have more fun if I slowly work all the way up to say… Jake or your mother. Which one do you love more?"

"What in the fucking witchlights… ?!" I understood the threat, but I was having a hard time processing its magnitude. Why would she get such a hard-on for me?

"You will pay for getting in the way," Mekare said. "For ruining my revenge."

"Revenge? I don't know what you're talking about." So she wanted revenge for ruining her revenge. That was fucked up.

"Of course you don't. You're just one of those people who think all their deeds are righteous, who believe they can make no mistakes."

"*You* messed with us first," I screamed, losing it. "I didn't know you from jackwad before you tried to kill Damien. And as if that wasn't enough, you kidnapped me and Rosalina. How dare you act like this is my fault, you crazy fucking bitch!"

"Aw, so innocent," she replied calmly. "Didn't anyone ever teach you that for every action there is a *re*action?"

Gah! I was wasting my breath. She was a psychopath.

"I will tell you what you did, so you can understand," she said. "But listen carefully because I will not repeat myself."

She paused, then knowing when she had my full attention, the witch went on.

"The Dark Donna has been around for a long time. She's one of the oldest vampires in St. Louis. She got here when the city was nothing but a dirt road. By the time I was born, Bernadetta Fiore owned half the city. She also owned my mother, a Brass Witch of moderate abilities."

A Brass Witch? That was weak considering Mekare's powers. There were six levels mages and witches could advance to, and Brass was only the second.

"She forced her to have sex with a Copper Mage," she went on. "She invited him to one of her parties. My mother had never been with a man. She was only fifteen. She wasn't free to even pick who to mate with. Because that's what it was… mating. Bernadetta is always looking for mages and witches she can control. She uses them to pave her way and make things easier for her. Why should the mighty Donna have to wait for negotiations to follow their course, for laws to pass, for people to see her designs when she can have it all taken care of by magic? Oh, no! Goddesses don't stoop to such levels. As you might expect, that Copper Mage ended up impregnating my mother with me."

Shit! A Copper Mage? She wasn't talking about Damien, was she? She was older than him, at least I thought so. It was hard to tell since they used magic to alter their appearance.

Mekare huffed. "That was the first time and the last time she ever saw him. She didn't even know his name. I didn't either, but it doesn't matter. That's not the point of the story. The point is that since I can remember, I was trained to serve that damn vamp."

Mekare's voice was charged with hatred. I could feel the magnitude of it even through the airwaves. It chilled me. Though, at least I could be relieved that she wasn't Damien's daughter. That would've been all kinds of weird.

"For over one hundred and thirty years I served her, performing every little parlor trick she requested. She has many of us at her service. White, Brass, Emerald, and Azure mages and witches. All at her beck and call. Never Copper or Midnight witches or mages, though. She always makes sure to cut the training short. She wouldn't want her underlings getting too powerful, would she?

"She put fear into our bones from the time we were able to walk. She starved us, made us clean the blood of her victims, fed on us, tortured us!

"I was her slave, just like my mother, who she sent to her death on some fool's errand when I was only eight. My mother left one day, and I got nothing back but her charred remains. It was up to me to bury her."

Oh, God! I couldn't imagine how horrible that would be for a child that age. This explained why Mekare had seemed so scared of Bernadetta when the vamp helped rescue me.

The Donna was truly evil.

"For years, I'd been planning my vengeance," Mekare said. "I studied behind her back to become more powerful. It took me ten years to become a Copper Mage, and twenty more to become what I am now. Then my opportunity came. She learned about rhabo. A little bird told her about it. Then she needed me to free the Unholy Vessel from the curse that kept it protected. With those two weapons under her control, she set out to start a war. You see, she misses the old days when she was St. Louis's virtual queen. Before other Skews started encroaching on her little empire.

"I went about it carefully, afraid of being discovered. I'm not ashamed to admit that. When someone gets under your skin when you're just an innocent, it's very difficult to overcome that type of deep-seated fear. But every day I grew braver. Every day my plan developed.

"As her plans for the city progressed, Bernadetta became distracted. It was a lot to deal with. She was killing her own kind and challenging all the packs. So she began to rely more heavily on me. You see, she thought she could trust me. She thought she had broken my spirit, but she was wrong.

"And then you came in, and you ruined *everything*," she hissed like a snake, her hatred for me vibrating in her words.

In a twisted way, her logic made sense. From the sounds of it, she had suffered the unthinkable at the Dark Donna's hands. When I thought Damien was dead, I was overcome by my rage and desire for revenge, so I understood why she felt the way she did. Still, I'd just been defending my own."

The witch inhaled deeply on the other end of the line. "That's why I'm going to make you suffer. I will take everything you love from you, just like you took the only thing I cared about."

"What Bernadetta did to you is awful," I said, "but I had nothing to do with that. And if I got in your way, it was because I was defending myself and my own. If you have a beef with me, then have a beef with me, but don't you dare hurt anyone else."

"Oh, dear, but that would be too easy. I want to see you suffer."

"Easy, you say? It wasn't easy the last time. If it had been, you wouldn't have scurried away like a coward."

"*Pshaw*, have you forgotten you had a Copper Mage on your side? Before he got there, I'd almost turned you into a chunk of charred meat."

She wasn't lying about that. If Blaze/Damien hadn't jumped on her head as she was about to deliver the final blow, I would be six feet under, wondering when the next flower delivery would happen. Still, I wasn't afraid of her, and if saving everyone I loved meant my death so be it.

"You're insane," I spat. "You're not better than Bernadetta. Why would you hurt people that have done nothing to you?"

She let out a cackle that did nothing more than prove me right. She *was* crazy. All that suffering had twisted her heart and soul into darkness and evil. No matter how justified she felt in her revenge, it was nuts.

"I never said I was better than her," she said. "How could I be? I'm what she made of me. But enough of this. I just wanted to talk to you. See how you were feeling about your new sister's demise."

I said nothing. What could I tell her that would make her change her mind? There was silence on the other end, then a huff as if she was disappointed she couldn't goad me into a cursing fit—not that I wasn't tempted to call her awful things, but I knew it would be a waste of time.

She sighed. "Nothing to say then?"

I held my tongue, especially since it seemed to be bothering her.

She huffed again. "Or maybe this will just get boring, and I'll need to rip off the band-aid. Show you how it feels to have the rug pulled out from under your feet when you least expect it. That would be fun, too."

A shiver ripped down my spine as I tried to think of all my family and friends. Where were they at this very moment? Were they safe? I needed to warn everyone, tell them this bitch's crazy plans. We only had two more days to break Jake's pact. If everyone could just stay safe until then, we would go after the witch as soon as that was over.

"I guess for now," she said, sounding resigned, "I'll just get my kicks elsewhere. Ta-ta, dear. Have fun with whatever you have going on in your little life."

The call disconnected, and I stood in the middle of the kitchen, frozen, with the phone pressed to my ear.

Jake walked in a moment later. "What's the matter?"

I set the phone on the counter, took three strides in his direction, and wrapped my arms around him.

"Who was that on the phone?"

It took me several beats to answer. "Mekare."

"What?!" He held me back at arm's length. "What did she want?"

I couldn't explain. My head was pounding from lack of sleep or *phantasma-whatever-she'd-called-it.* A host of emotions crashed in my chest. Hatred, fear, frustration. God, when would this end?

I just wanted my life to go back to normal. Would I ever be able to worry about nothing more than paying my bills on time, what to wear to the office, and eating one too many donuts?

Was it too much to ask?

CHAPTER 28

Jake was holding his head, elbows on the kitchen table. Rosalina, Eric, and Damien were sitting with us, also looking at a loss.

"That crazy bitch!" Jake exclaimed, pounding a fist on the table.

"It feels like she's always a step ahead," Damien said.

Yes, he was right. She always seemed to know what we were going to do.

How?!

"So what are we going to do?" Rosalina asked.

I shook my head. Everyone was in danger because of me, so I didn't feel like I should be the one deciding our next course of action. It felt wrong.

"We still have a job to finish," Damien said, weaving his hands in a mock spell. "The clock is ticking."

Jake and I exchanged a loaded glance. I could tell he felt the same way as me. I'd had a few minutes to think more carefully and realized I couldn't expect them to help us—not when a Midnight Witch had threatened their lives and they should be heading out of St. Louis on the next flight.

"Have you decided whether or not to ask your sister for help?" Eric asked.

I shook my head and made as if to leave at the table.

Rosalina grabbed my hand and kept me from going. "I know what you're thinking," she said. "You feel bad because you think Mekare's threats are your fault, because you put us in danger. And I'm tired of telling you—and I don't think I speak only for myself—that I make my own decisions. You and I are in this together, and I'm going to help you see this thing through. After that, we can focus our attention entirely on getting rid of that witch."

She glanced toward Eric and Damien, who immediately and without hesitation assented.

"I agree with her," Damien said.

Eric shrugged. "Me, too. I mean… if we're going to take care of Mekare Graves, we're going to do it together. That means we can't have you two distracted with all this unbreakable pact stuff."

"You're always so sweet… and practical," Damien told Eric.

"Shut up," Eric shot back.

I ran a hand through my hair. "I don't know what to say."

Jake was more graceful than me and spoke with sincerity. "Thank you, everyone."

"That works!" Damien slapped a hand on the table.

I laughed nervously. "Of course, thank you. Thank you!" I felt like kissing them all. I appreciated their support, even if I still didn't know if getting Lucia involved in this plan was a good idea.

Always perceptive, Rosalina got up from the table, giving her head a quick jerk to signal Eric and Damien. "I'm going to go call the insurance company to see how our claim is going."

Damien stood up next. "And I have to make a few phone calls."

"Hurry up and decide," Eric said, as subtle as ever.

A moment later, Jake and I were alone.

"We don't deserve such an amazing group of friends, do we?" I asked.

"I certainly don't." Jake left his chair and took the one Rosalina had vacated. "Toni, I know this is hard for you, so let me make it easier. We need to leave Lucia out of this. Maybe Damien can try again, and if he can't get better, then at least we gave it a shot."

"You'll marry her then," I said, aware that was not his plan, but hoping something had made him change his mind.

"No, I won't. We've already talked about this. My decision hasn't changed."

"Please, Jake!"

"I can't lose you." The tears that had pooled in my eyes slid down my cheeks.

He wiped them away with his thumb. "I won't do that to either of us. You may feel that way right now, but as time goes by your feelings will change."

"No, they won't."

He ignored my protest and went on, "and I will hate myself and be miserable from day one. It would not be living, and you know it."

Damien's words played in my mind, *"Your sister won't be in any danger. You've seen how it is. The demon is confined to the pentagram to begin. Then I let it out for a bit to do its thing, and when it's done, I command it back. I can certainly handle that. Lucia would be perfectly safe."*

"I'll ask her," I said out without thinking. "If she doesn't want to do it, I'll understand, but I can't let you die without doing something."

"You know your sister. She won't say *no*."

I felt the truth of Jake's words as soon as they left his lips. Lucia would be delighted to be involved in something like this. She had always been the risk-taker, the wild child. Ever since she realized the nature of her powers, she wasn't shy about using them. She was an amazing telekinetic and had received several offers from different colleges and companies now that she was close to graduating high school. Her innate power was off the scales, and controlling the demon would probably be nothing for her.

"You're right," I said. "She won't say *no*." Which meant I had to be extra sure about this. I thought for a long while, trying to weigh everything, but it was overwhelming. In the end—even though I wanted to protect my sister—it came down to the difference between Jake dying and Lucia being exposed to demons. The former was unthinkable, and the latter. Well…

It will be a controlled environment.

Damien said she'll be safe.

I can't lose Jake.

It all came down to this last one.

"I'll ask her," I blurted out.

Selfish. You're so selfish. You take and you take and you take, the thought that had echoed in my head at the warehouse came back to me.

"Are you certain?"

I swallowed, fighting against my *selfish* desire to save Jake, my fear of what my life would become without him. Pain seared through me as my mate's pale face materialized before my eyes, death rendering his silver eyes flat, empty.

No! A scream tore through my mind.

"I'm certain!" I exclaimed, startling Jake.

Hands trembling, I reached for my phone and dialed.

Selfish. You're so selfish. You take and you take and you take.

ഇൽ

An hour later, Lucia stood in Eric's study, running her fingers over the Demonology Register's spine. Her pretty face was scrunched up with interest as she picked it up and leafed through it.

I had just finished explaining why I called her here. Jake and I had picked her up from the hotel where she was staying. I'd lied to Mom, telling her I wanted to take my little sister off her hands for a bit since being cooped up together in a hotel room was starting to drive them up the wall. Mom had been glad to be rid of her youngest daughter, her big sigh as she peered longingly at the novel on the nightstand left me no doubt of that.

Guilt about my lies had started roosting in my chest, its huge wings flapping around every time I thought about it.

"This is really cool," Lucia commented as she found a particularly gruesome illustration of a goat-like demon with something that looked like pus leaking from its bulging eyes.

"Yeah, cool," I said under my breath.

She was dressed in her favorite attire, a baggy hoodie, a pair of ripped jeans, and high-top Converse. Her wavy brown hair was up in a ponytail. She wore no makeup, jewelry, or anything most girls her age did, and her simplicity was pure unadulterated beauty.

She set the book down. "You know… I haven't told you, but I got a scholarship offer from the League of Demon Hunters."

"You did?" I asked, surprised.

Being a demon hunter was a very rare *and* exclusive profession. They also made a ton of money.

"Yep, full ride, too," she said as if it didn't mean anything that one of the most exclusive higher education institutions wanted to recruit her.

"That's awesome, Luce!"

She shrugged dismissively.

I bit the inside of my cheek, doing my best not to blurt out something that would put her in a bad mood. Trackers were far more common than telekinetics, which meant I never got any offers for scholarships to go anywhere, not even the community college. If I had, my life might've been completely different. I wrinkled my nose at the thought. Despite the mess I was in, that could have meant never meeting Rosalina, Damien, or Eric. Nope,

I wouldn't like that alternate universe.

I refocused my attention on Lucia, who was now checking out the portrait of Eric's wife and daughter by the fireplace.

She hooked a finger toward it. "Is that his family?"

I nodded, pressing a finger to my lips and pointing at my ear.

"Right," she said, "werewolf hearing."

I let a few beats pass and finally couldn't wait anymore. "So… do you think you'd be up to helping us?"

She didn't reply right away but kept me in suspense. At last, she shrugged. "Yeah, why not? Can't let your hot boyfriend die, and it might help me decide if demon hunting is for me. Mom wants me to stay nearby, but heck no! The League of Demon Hunters is in New York, so you'd better believe it's on the *yes* pile." She winked and walked closer. "So when do we start, big sis?"

ꕤ

Lucia walked around the pentagram, evaluating it carefully. There was a sparkle in her eyes that betrayed her excitement. She was trying to act cool, but I could tell she was itching to give this a try.

Once again, guilt about not telling mom washed over me. If Lucia decided that demon hunting was for her and she went to New York City, it would be my fault. Mom had cried for days after Leo left, and that had been with three daughters still at home. I could only imagine what losing her last baby would do to her. She would definitely blame me when she found out I'd had a hand in exposing Lucia to nothing less than dwellers from hell.

Damien approached Lucia, holding a box in each hand. They were exactly like the one that had exploded. I guess he'd brought spares just in case.

"What are those?" my sister asked.

The mage handed her one to examine. She turned it around in

her hands and frowned at the hole.

"She looks so calm and collected," Rosalina whispered in my ear. She, Jake, Eric, and I were reclined against the gun cabinets in the back.

"She acts that way no matter what she's feeling inside," I said. "She got like that after Dad died." I always wondered how different she would've turned out if Dad was still here. Being the youngest, his passing had hit her the hardest—not to mention that she always got along better with him than with our mother.

Thoughts of Travis and Olivia surfaced in my mind, adding to my roosting guilt. I pushed them aside with a shake of my head.

Eric huffed. "She wasn't calm and collected that day at the high school."

I elbowed him. "What did you expect?"

He shrugged. "Just saying."

"What is the hole for?" Lucia asked, handing the box back.

"For the demon to enter. I will order it to go inside, then you'll use your powers to keep it inside. The box represents Jake," Damien said.

I glanced over at Jake, who shuddered at the words. He hadn't been here when the box blew up, and I still didn't know if I was glad about it. Maybe if he'd witnessed the explosion, he wouldn't be so bent on letting a demon enter his body.

"Isn't the box kind of small?" my sister asked.

"It isn't. You'll see. Besides, it's just a test. We're only trying to make sure that we can contain the demon and stop it from going for Jake's heart."

Lucia's expression tightened for a split second, but I noticed. And I wasn't the only one. Jake did too. He stepped away from the cabinet.

"Lucia," he said, "if at any point you don't want to do this, you'll tell us, right?"

My sister glanced up at him and answered carelessly, "Sure

thing."

"I'm serious. You don't have to feel obligated because of me."

"Or me," I piped in.

"It's cool, guys," she said. "Let me try first, and then we can talk."

Jake shook his head and threw a worried glance my way as if he was wondering whether or not we could trust her to be honest with us.

"It's fine," I mouthed. I knew my sister well. She would never do anything she didn't want to. But more importantly, she wouldn't do anything that would embarrass her. If at any moment, failure seemed like a possibility, she would make up an excuse to get out.

Damien cradled the boxes in his arms as if they were babies. "All right, is everyone satisfied with the pentagram?"

We all took some time to examine the lines, and after a quick inspection, gave it a go.

Setting the boxes on the floor, the mage stepped to the south end of the pentagram and stretched his neck. Lucia stood across from him while the rest of us took positions at the east and west ends.

Damien struck a match and tipped it toward Lucia. "Light the candles?"

She smiled crookedly and the match floated out of Damien's hand and lit each candle in no time while Lucia just stood there without moving a muscle.

"Impressive!" Damien said.

When she was little, she used to reach out with her hands to use her powers. It was how we discovered what she was. Even before she learned how to walk, she could procure her own pacifiers, blankets, teddy bears, or whatever it was she wanted. Things got particularly dicey when she became a toddler and tried to reach for absolutely everything she saw. Talk about baby proofing. Mom nearly went crazy. Good thing, by then, Daniella's healing abilities were well developed. She had to heal bruises, cuts, and even burns more than once.

Damien rubbed his hands together. "Now, my turn." He cleared his throat and spoke the conjuration. "From the depths of hell, I command you to come forth. The circle will bind you. The flames will charm you. Velthgrek, you are summoned."

When Velthgrek appeared, it still had six legs, fur, and one huge eye, but this time, he resembled a cat, a large one, black like a panther, but kind of cuddly-looking. It walked within the boundaries of the pentagram, waving its tail up in the air and purring loudly.

I watched my sister carefully, trying my best to read behind her chilled façade. To her credit, she kept most of her cool, though her eyes got wide when Velthgrek peered up at her with curiosity. Her mouth opened as if to say something, but she quickly bit her lower lip. She wasn't the kind to hold back when it came to piping in with witty comments, but I was glad she heeded Damien's advice to stay quiet.

"Velthgrek, show us your true form," Damien ordered.

Unlike the last time, Velthgrek obeyed right away, turning into a cloud of black smoke that hung in the air like car exhaust.

Carefully, the mage lowered the box into the pentagram using his magic while Lucia appraised him curiously, probably wondering how good he was with his telekinetic skill.

"Get in the box," Damien ordered as soon as it settled on the floor.

Again, the demon obeyed right away.

Next to me, Jake flinched as the tendril of smoke went in through the hole. Sometimes, he seemed to have ice in his veins, but unknown things unsettled him. I'd noticed this for the first time when we went to Elf-hame to hide the rhabo cure.

I reached for his hand and twined my fingers with his. He squeezed reassuringly but never took his eyes off the box.

Damien glanced at Lucia. "Ready?"

Lucia nodded.

"Don't let it get out."

She nodded again, her eyebrows scrunched up in concentration. Her fingers twitched at her sides, but she didn't lift her hands.

The mage turned to the box and commanded, "Velthgrek, get out of the box!"

I held my breath as the box vibrated. I expected it to explode again, but instead, it went completely still after only a short few seconds.

Damien blinked in surprise then nodded in approval, looking impressed. "Very good. Now, draw the demon out."

Lucia raised an eyebrow, the only indication that she was switching gears. Right away, the smoke snaked back out and hovered in midair.

"Beautiful, you make it look easy," Damien said.

I released a pent-up breath, also impressed by how smoothly and safely everything was going.

"Now, the real test." Damien walked to Jake, pulled a pocket knife out of his pants pocket, and handed it over. "I need some of your blood."

At the word blood, the demon's essence expanded and contracted, making me jump. It vibrated in place for an instant, then shot toward Jake. Rosalina gasped. Eric cursed, and I crouched, bracing myself. The demon's essence crashed against an invisible wall as it reached the pentagram's perimeter.

I puffed my cheeks and blew out in relief.

This time, Lucia's hands jerked toward the demon. Slowly, they moved as if pulling on a rope and led the demon back to the center of the pentagram. There, it floated, rapidly inflating and deflating like an anxious, beating heart.

"Good job, Lucia," Damien said. "But it's about to get harder, so brace yourself." He stared pointedly at the knife in Jake's hand, then gave a quick nod.

Jake unfolded the knife. Its edge glinted as he pressed it to the palm of his hand and cut himself without even flinching. Blood pooled quickly.

A small sound came from Lucia as she dug in her heels and bent her knees, no longer looking like this was a walk in the park. Her mouth pressed into a thin line, and her eyes narrowed in concentration. The demon was still floating around the middle of the pentagram, but it was putting up a fight and it was slowly inching closer to the outside of its invisible enclosure.

Damien produced a small porcelain bowl out of thin air and held it in front of Jake, who made a fist over it and squeezed. Blood trickled into the bowl. The mage nodded when he deemed it enough. Jake flexed his hand as the wound quickly closed.

The mage turned back toward the pentagram. His sharp copper eyes appraised the demon's position.

"Pull it back some," he instructed Lucia.

She inhaled sharply, took a step back, and pulled her hands toward her chest. Her fingers trembled with the effort, but the demon's essence drew back.

"Good." Nodding, Damien levitated the bowl into the pentagram.

As soon as it crossed inside its boundaries, Velthgrek went nuts, its essence practically doing calisthenics, its edges jutting out from every direction, forming all kinds of shapes that could put an inkblot test to shame.

Lucia started breathing heavily, air hissing through her clenched teeth.

Damien deposited the bowl on the floor, then focused on my sister as if by scrutinizing her he could help, but he'd explained his magic would only interfere with Lucia's abilities.

"Keep it steady," he said, inclining his head to better judge the distance between the demon and the bowl. They were about three feet apart.

"The demon will need some time to eat the curse out of Jake's blood," Damien explained as my sister took another step back and her fingers twisted inward, making a claw. "That means you'll need to hold it in place somewhere inside his body, a safe distance away from his heart. The more control you have over it, the better. Let's try this, give it some slack. Just a couple of inches."

Lucia inhaled audibly and let her fingers stretch forward. The demon advanced several inches toward the blood.

"Ah, ah, not so fast," Damien warned. "Hold it… hold it. Okay, a couple more inches. Good, good."

Sweat broke over Lucia's brow. Her face was twisted in near pain. I wanted to help somehow, but there was nothing I could do. Throughout all of this, I just felt useless.

Suddenly, the demon's essence coalesced into the smallest shape it had yet. It became as compact and smooth-edged as a bullet, and it began vibrating in place as if it contained the power of a nuclear weapon.

The shape jerked forward, cutting the distance to the blood by an entire foot. Lucia was jolted along with it, her feet skidding along the smooth concrete floor and taking her within inches off the pentagram. I lurched forward to grab her, but Damien put a hand up.

"Don't touch her! She's fine… she's fine," he said as Lucia's resolved expression hardened. "You got it?" the mage asked.

My sister gave a single nod, her eyes never leaving her target, her fingers curling back into claws.

"Steady, steady," Damien said.

The demon pitched forward a few more inches. I grabbed my head. My heart pounded like a drum, its quick beats loud in my ears. Lucia pulled back her hands. The demon retreated two inches.

A smile stretched on the mage's lips. "That's it. That's it."

Again the demon pressed forward, gaining some room, but my

sister—my stubborn, stubborn sister—pulled it back even further.

For a long minute, the battle of wills went on. My hope soared. Jake and I glanced toward each other, and I could see the same hope in his eyes.

"You're doing great," Damien praised. "Do you think you could hold another minute? It might be all it takes for the demon to eat the entire curse."

Lucia nodded, a small gratified smile appearing on her face. Her satisfaction hadn't finished materializing when the demon broke free and slammed into the bowl shattering to pieces and sending blood splattering everywhere.

She staggered forward, her converse hitting the edge of the pentagram. Her arms windmilled as she tried to stop herself from crossing into the inner circle. Acting on instinct, I fleeted over to her, snatched her hoodie, and pulled her back. She crashed into me, and I wrapped my arms around her and held her tightly.

"I got you. I got you," I said, letting out a huge exhale of relief.

She stayed in my arms for a long while, trembling slightly. We all stared, eyes wide, as Velthgrek sucked at the blood like a vacuum cleaner.

Damien snapped out of it and spoke in a quick breath. "Velthgrek, to the depths of hell, I command you to return!" With a snap, the demon disappeared.

Silent tension hung in the air.

"I'm okay," Lucia said after a minute, her voice steadier than I would've suspected. She disentangled herself from me and straightened her hoodie.

Jake moved into her field of vision. "You all right?"

"I'm fine. Perfect. Let's try that again. I wasn't expecting that. I'll be better prepared now."

I opened my mouth but Jake spoke first. "There won't be a next time."

"Bullshit!" Lucia protested. "Of course there will be. I can handle that fucker."

"Lucia!" I chided her, sounding just like Mom.

She rolled her eyes at me. "Seriously? You're worried about my language?"

"I'm worried about more than your language, young lady!"

"Young lady? You're only two years older than me."

"Yeah, but in that time, I've lived way more than you have in your entire life."

"Whatever. Tell yourself that. So do you still want me to help? Or not? Because I'm game. I promise you I can handle it. I know what to expect now. It won't take me by surprise again."

"I don't know." I rose to my feet. Everyone stared, waiting for an answer. "I don't fucking know."

Overwhelmed, I stomped out of there. Jake made as if to follow, but Rosalina shook her head. He frowned but stayed back.

In my bedroom, I crashed into bed and buried my face in the pillow. I wanted to scream but I managed to keep it to a groan.

If Lucia had fallen into the pentagram, she would've been possessed—or worse yet, dead. And I had done that. I had put her at risk. What was wrong with me?

Selfish. You're so selfish. You take and you take and you take.

I pressed harder into the bed. "Swallow me, please."

My bones and my consciousness felt heavy, leaden. Guilt was fucking heavy. My eyelids dropped, and the exhaustion from the past few days settled over me with a vengeance. There was no better escape than sleep.

Before I knew it, I was out.

CHAPTER 29

Rosalina's gentle voice called my name. "Toni, wake up." She tapped my shoulder.

I opened my eyes, blinking rapidly. When I caught sight of her, I sprang to a sitting position. "Shit, I fell asleep." I hadn't meant to. There was no time for sleep.

"Are you hungry?" she asked.

Not at all what I was worried about. I pushed my way out of bed. "How long did I sleep?"

"Only a couple of hours." She gave me a big smile. "C'mon, I made spaghetti and meatballs."

My stomach growled at that, surprising me.

Rosalina laughed. "I guess that's my answer." She headed out of the bedroom at a clipped pace. "There is a big bowl with your name on it, and a huge wedge of Parmesan to grate on top."

Parmesan! Yum!

Why didn't she lead with that? She knew how much I loved good cheese, and Parmesan was one of my favorites. There was also feta and asiago and gruyere and pecorino. The list went on and on.

When I walked out of the room, there was no sign of her in the hall. Whenever she took charge of something, she was all business.

In the kitchen, I found everyone milling about. They were chatting, pouring drinks, serving noodles, and ladling sauce on top of them. Jake had a grater in one hand and a wedge of Parmesan cheese in the other. Lucia walked up to him and presented her plate to him. He went to town grating until she had a thick layer of cheese on her food.

The mood in the room was upbeat, and it clashed with mine completely.

"What's going on?" I said, sensing something had changed.

Lucia perked up and turned to look at me. "Oh, nothing, just that I showed that demon who's boss. For over five minutes. And Damien said that should be more than enough to get the curse out of Jake." Her tone was smug, and not to mention her expression.

"What?! You tried again without my permission?!" I demanded. "Jake?!"

He put both hands up, holding the grater and cheese above his head. "Don't look at me. I'd come up here to help Rosalina with lunch."

Lucia glowered at me. "News flash, Toni, I don't need your permission. I'm eighteen, and neither you, Mom, Daniella, or Leo can tell me what to do. When are you going to get that into your thick heads?"

I seethed with anger, but there was nothing I could say because she was right. When *I* turned eighteen, I didn't listen to anyone.

I whirled to face Damien. "You should know better!"

"Should I?" he asked, cocking his head to one side.

My mouth opened and closed as I struggled with what to say. He was the same damn mage who had repeatedly put a restraining curse on my wolf for twenty years, so what else could I expect?

"You're wasting your anger, Sunder," Eric said. "This is what you and loverboy wanted."

"Exactly! Thank you!" Rosalina exclaimed, walking to the table to dig into her spaghetti.

Huh? This? From her?!

There were a few seconds of silence, then slowly everyone resumed what they'd been doing while I just stood there watching them cast furtive glances in my direction. Slowly, my outrage subsided. Eric was right. This was the reason I'd called Lucia here. Now I was upset because she'd accomplished it?

"Here." Rosalina pushed a large bowl of spaghetti into my hands. I took it to Jake who, knowing my love for cheese, promptly started grating a layer a lot thicker than the one he'd given Lucia. He held my gaze as he topped my plate with *yumminess* and smiled.

"I know it wasn't right, what they did," he said under his breath, "but…" His lower lip trembled with emotion.

"I'm glad they did it. All will be as it should be."

"Thank you," Lucia mumbled righteously, a lump of food squirreled away in her cheek.

I ignored her and pressed a hand to Jake's cheek. "I love you."

"I love you, too."

Eric groaned. "Don't make me regret helping you."

Everyone laughed, except for Eric, of course.

A moment later, we were all sitting at the table, enjoying the delicious food and amazing company. The mood was light and hopeful, and it felt incredible. Despite everything else that was going on, knowing that Jake would be free from the pact meant everything. I knew there were still risks, that something could go wrong. We were messing with demons, and it was not child's play. But, with Damien in charge, I felt confident everything would be all right. The man had resurrected, for Pete's sake.

We were laughing at Lucia slurping spaghetti like in *The Lady and the Tramp* when Jake reached for his vibrating phone. He stared at the screen with a frown and quickly answered.

"What's going on, Khal?" He listened intently while I did the same.

"Have you seen the news?" Khal asked on the other side.

"No."

"It's The Scourge. It's under attack. An army of hybrids and that witch are there. It's bad. K-Tech took a big hit. Huge loss. Some employees are dead."

"Fuck!" Jake jumped to his feet, and I followed suit. "I'll be right there."

Eric sighed and pushed his half-finished bowl of food aside. "No rest for the wicked. The Scourge, then?"

Jake started shaking his head, but I put a hand up. "Nope. You're not going by yourself, and you well know it."

His teeth clicked as he closed his mouth and swallowed his protest.

"What's going on now?" Damien asked.

"The witch and her hybrids are at it again," Eric said.

Lucia's fork clattered against her bowl. Panic etched her features and none of her usual cockiness showed anymore. It seemed the beasts had truly put the fear of God into her. At least she had *some* sense.

"At The Scourge?" Damien asked. "Really? What does she have against her own kind?"

The Scourge was a commercial district reserved for Skews. At night, it turned into the wild west, and Stales steered clear of it.

Jake ran stiff fingers into his hair. "Knight Industries owns several businesses there, and Khal said one of them got hit pretty badly."

"Avengers assemble!" Rosalina exclaimed, leaving the table and rushing out of the kitchen ahead of everyone. "Let's get that bitch!"

I put a hand on Lucia's shoulder and adamantly said, "You stay here, all right?"

She nodded several times without hesitation and, for once, I knew I didn't have to worry about her. We marched out of there, our steps quickly getting in sync as we went. I cracked my neck as Red bubbled to the surface, readying herself for a fight.

If we could, for once and for all, put an end to Mekare, and tomorrow, we broke Jake's pact, my life could go back to normal. More than that, my life would be near bliss.

I would have Jake, Rosalina, my family, and two unlikely friends in a flamboyant mage and a grouchy alpha.

Who could ask for more?

CHAPTER 30

When we got there, we found police barricades all around the perimeter of The Scourge. We tried several routes before we abandoned Eric's car and went on foot. We approached one of the barricades and watched from a distance.

Thunder rolled behind heavy clouds, obscuring the sun and enhancing the ominous feeling. *How appropriate!*

The sound of bullets reverberated in the distance. As we sat there trying to decide what to do, a couple of patrol cars with their sirens blaring came to a screeching stop in front of the barricade.

One of the drivers exchanged a few words with the men guarding the blockade, then the barriers were pulled aside, and the reinforcements sped through, their tires spinning for a bit and releasing acrid smoke into the air before taking off. As the policemen were distracted replacing the barriers, we slunk along the side of the building, crossed the street, and then pushed through the back door of a Chinese restaurant. Jake guided the way, looking like he knew exactly where he was going. He'd told me a bit about all the businesses Knight Industries owned, but if he'd mentioned K-Tech, I couldn't remember. The man had his hands full, for sure.

Crouching, we crossed through an empty kitchen with no signs of activity, except for the abandoned food items resting on the counters. There were vegetables on a cutting board, a large bowl filled with dark sauce, a wok with a half-cooked meal on the unlit stove, and several whole fish resting on brown paper, their round eyes staring emptily.

Pressing past a double door, we entered the customer area, which was also empty. I imagined the lunch rush-hour customers had gone out the back door as soon as all hell broke loose.

We exited the building through the restaurant's front door. The gunshots sounded louder, and now I could also hear battle cries as well desperate screams. Jake urged us forward. Rosalina was hot on my heels, wearing her leather trench coat, which she'd stuffed with guns and ammunition to the hilt. I glanced back to find that Eric was already in his wolf shape, bringing up the rear.

But where was Damien? He'd warned us he might go off on his own.

I was about to say something when I spotted him just exiting the restroom. He was lagging several yards behind, but he wasn't hurrying. The man didn't believe in walking in any way that wasn't dignified. He was too cool to skulk, sprint, or even crouch.

We followed the sounds of battle, weaving in and out through several alleys and going through two other private businesses. One of them was a tattoo parlor, where we found the workers and customers huddled in a corner, sitting on the floor. They startled when they saw us come in, but Jake set them at ease, making pacifying gestures with his hands to reassure them we meant them no harm.

I could smell their fear in the air and also a scent that let me know at least one of them was a werewolf. The other two gave out no scent, so I assumed they were vampires.

"Nice!" Rosalina whispered with a smile, pointing toward some very cool-looking tattoo designs displayed on posters on the wall.

"Thank you," a guy with a bushy beard mouthed.

Leave it to Rosalina to be nice even during dangerous circumstances. She would probably have compliments for people during the apocalypse.

"You guys can leave through the back alley." I pointed the way we'd come. "It's clear. Just head south and be careful."

They seemed hesitant at first, but when the guy with the beard stood, the others followed.

An electronic bell chimed when Jake pushed the front door open. He eased his tall frame halfway out to check if the coast was clear. The sounds of battle grew even louder. Glass breaking, something that sounded like a chainsaw, growls, and shouts.

Maybe *it was* the apocalypse.

"Where's Damien?" Rosalina asked.

I searched for him, but he'd already abandoned us.

Rosalina frowned, worry forming lines across her forehead.

"He'll be fine," I said.

After glancing left and right, Jake waved, and we tiptoed behind him. He pointed a finger down the street, directing our attention toward the battle.

We stood at the fringes of full-on war. The troops had been getting ready for this, and now they were here. For as far as the eye could see, chaos reigned. Hybrids, werewolves, vampires, witches, mages, and even a few Fae were engaged in a battle royale. It was all Skew, even the ones wearing badges and uniforms. This was no place for Stales. They wouldn't last a second in The Scourge—not even on regular days, much less during Armageddon.

A thick cloud of smoke hung above. Flames lapped out of buildings and cars. Heat radiated outward, making the air waver.

I scanned the chaos. "No sign of Mekare."

There were plenty of hybrids to go after, and as much as I would've liked to kill every single one of them, they weren't our target. If you cut the head of the snake, the body would follow. We had to get *her*. And a more urgent reason to find her? Damien had gone to her without us.

For an instant, I wondered what would happen to the hybrids without their master. Would they sit mindlessly waiting for orders? Then I remembered the story Ulfen had told us about their origin. The mage who'd created the first hybrids was killed by them, and afterward, the creatures had carried on with their violence. That was when ancestors of present-day packs hunted them down, killed them, and hid the Unholy Vessel.

My anger surged. Would all those werewolf lives be lost because of that insane witch?! Maybe someone could figure out a way to free them from the curse. Hopefully, they wouldn't be a lost cause like vampires on rhabo.

Eric stepped in front of us, scenting the air.

"Got something?" I asked.

He shook his tawny wolf head. *"Some help?"* his alpha voice asked.

Also catching the message, Jake nodded.

A second later our clothes lay in tatters on the sidewalk. Jake's immense wolf towered over Eric and me. I couldn't help but admire his massive shoulders and compare the size of his paws to mine. His were larger than softballs while mine didn't even get to tennis balls. He lifted his head up and sniffed the air.

"All I smell is smoke," he said. *"You try it, Toni. Your sense of smell has always been better."*

I did as he said and took a deep whiff. The acrid smoke hit me like a load of bricks. I held back a sneeze and tried to focus, to sense other things under the overpowering stench. Small hints of other scents were there too, though. I closed my eyes, and just like I did during my tracking trances, I started parsing the different smells. I gave a huge check mark to the sharp, overpowering smoke, acknowledging it, then pushed it aside and moved on to the next. With the tons of weapons being discharged, gunpowder was another strong one. Sweat was also there, and of course, the metallic tang of blood.

I pushed all of them aside and went deeper, riffling through my mental catalog. I discarded ten, twenty, thirty of them until finally, I caught the scent of strong magic. Though its sharpness was everywhere, I could detect different levels of concentration.

"I got it!" My eyes sprang open, and I moved forward, following my nose.

Rosalina walked behind me while Jake and Eric flanked her at either side. We moved cautiously as we approached the rim of the battle. If we were to get to Mekare, we had to do our best to avoid getting pulled into the melee. But that was easier said than done, considering the clusterfuck we had to wade through.

I shot a quick glance backward to check on my friends. Rosalina had two handguns at the ready, and her expression was as intent and confident as that of a professional killer. I doubted if we could find another brave Stale like her on the streets.

We crossed the street and prowled alongside the buildings. A few yards ahead a group of vampires surrounded a gigantic hybrid, bigger than any I had seen so far. One of the vampires had a sword in hand and kept going in and out, slicing, dicing, and chopping at the speed of light. Wounds appeared on the hybrid's body while it batted its huge arms around fast enough to avoid serious injury. The other vampires also went in and out attacking with their claws and fangs, trying to distract the beast, but even five of them didn't seem enough to put a dent in the monster. Good thing it was cloudy or the vamps would also be fighting mother nature and her beams of sunlight.

"They need weapons," Jake said.

They sure did. If they all had guns or at least swords, they would be doing much better. But many of these people were not warriors. They just worked here, one of them was wearing an apron, for Pete's sake. He'd probably been serving blood pints at some bar before all of this started. Good thing most of those fighting *were* prepared. The werewolves, at least, had been getting regular marching orders.

A few feet away, there was a similar situation. Though, instead of vampires, this hybrid was surrounded by a group of my kind—some in their wolf forms and others in their human form. I could tell they were all werewolves by their scent. They were doing better since those with opposable thumbs held guns and swords. They discharged a barrage of bullets on the beasts, then the ones with swords and sharp claws swarmed in to finish the job. As they were busy attacking, a second hybrid charged in. I was about to scream a warning when there was a loud *pop*, and a bullet hit it between the eyes.

"Sharpshooter!" Rosalina said, pointing toward the top of a nearby building.

The hybrid toppled to the ground like a heavy boulder. A man with a samurai sword was immediately on it, chopping at its head. It took several whacks before he separated the ugly mug from the massive body, but he managed. Then the group of them hurried to help the vampires.

More shots rang out. Hybrids growled in pain, a black wolf's body flew as if swatted like a fly and crashed against the façade of a building, leaving a blood trail on the wall as it slid down.

"It's a damn massacre," Eric said. *"I still don't understand how she can command so many hybrids at once. She's no alpha."*

I clenched my teeth as we pressed forward. *Our goal is more important. If we stop Mekare, we stop all of this.* It wasn't easy to convince my legs to keep moving, but I did it. A few yards ahead, the scene changed, and we encountered groups of vampires much better prepared for battle.

They fought with swords, guns, and axes. I even saw someone with a flail, its ball and chain twirling about her head. Surprisingly, werewolves and vampires fought together, helping each other. More surprisingly, they fought alongside uniformed Skews and Stales, which were never allowed in The *lawless* Scourge.

Unheard of!

We weaved around the battle as I followed the magical scent. It was getting stronger.

"We're getting closer," I said.

As we tried to pass through an area tight with bodies—some fallen and some still fighting—a hybrid with a chunk of patchy blond hair on top of its head noticed us and charged in our direction.

With practiced ease, Rosalina discharged her weapon.

Pop.

Her bullets grazed the beast's cheek as she tried to strike between the eyes. She squeezed the trigger again and again. A volley hit the hybrid's chest, bullet after bullet, fractions of a second part. The creature slowed. We prepared to jump it, but a leather-clad Fae female wielding a sword half her size came at the beast from behind and cut it down mercilessly.

I nodded in thanks and kept going. As we rounded the corner, the scene changed even more.

A rainbow of magical attacks crackled in the air, forming a giant sphere that made me think of Epcot Center. In the middle of it, Damien and Mekare battled it out as if trying to create the world's most dangerous Fourth of July fireworks display.

Except this was no celebration.

It was carnage.

Swimming in puddles of crimson, a multitude of bodies lay around the sphere's perimeter, wounds gaping, limbs torn, heads severed. Red rivulets ran down the street drains, and the stench of blood clogged my nose, making me gag. The tableau was so horrid, I was sure it would haunt my nightmares forever.

Tearing my eyes away, I focused on the mage and witch.

They were something to behold as their hands weaved at a prodigious speed and shot spell after spell at each other. Their protective shields blocked the attacks and projected them outward, however, causing the magical sphere around them to grow.

Eric took a step forward as if to cross into the sizzling bubble.

I blocked his path, afraid of what would happen if the magic hit him.

"We have to help them!" he protested.

"I know, but..." If he went in there, he might as well strap himself to an electric chair.

Rosalina planted her feet on the asphalt and aimed her guns at Mekare. Hell yeah, that seemed like a much better idea than stepping into that mess.

She aimed carefully at the witch, who stood with her back toward us. I held my breath. Just as Rosalina seemed ready to pull the trigger, the witch turned to smoke to avoid one of Damien's attacks.

Rosalina cursed under her breath.

The black haze suddenly disappeared.

My eyes flicked in every direction, looking for Mekare.

"Where did she go?!" Eric growled.

Rosalina brandished her weapon from side to side, seeking a target. Damien also appeared confused. He held out his hands, slowly retreating.

Between one blink and another, a mass of black smoke materialized behind Damien and instantly solidified. The witch towered over the mage, all six-foot-two of her. A smile slashed her face as she directed a hand at Damien's head.

"Watch out!" My warning came out as a bark.

Damien's eyes widened in surprise as he sensed her presence. Dark magic sparked in Mekare's fingers.

"NO!" Eric cried out.

A crack reverberated in my ears, then a bullet struck the witch's shoulder, sending her reeling backward. Damien whirled, already weaving a spell.

Mekare clutched her shoulder and bared her teeth in pain. Her attention shifted in our direction. She found me in an instant and a deep hatred disfigured her face.

"You will pay for this. All of you. AND SOON!" she said, her voice resounding as if from a megaphone. The last words were much louder, holding a promise.

My hackles rose from the threat, and I knew in my very bones that she would keep her promise, that we had to be ready.

Before her words finished echoing, she disappeared, vanished into smoke with no trace.

Damien backed away from the spot, his hands still up, his copper eyes roving all around. When it became evident she had fled, the mage twirled a hand up in the air and the electric cloud that hung over him dissipated.

"Damien!" Rosalina exclaimed and ran in his direction. She crashed into him, wrapping her arms around his neck, still holding her guns. An instant later, she pulled back and planted a kiss on his lips as he stood stiffly, eyes wide.

Taken aback by Damien's lack of response, Rosalina pulled away, looking embarrassed.

The mage searched her face.

"I'm… I'm sorry," Rosalina said, stepping back and starting to turn.

But before she got too far, he grabbed her wrist, pulled her back into himself, and pressed his mouth to hers in a passionate kiss that would curl any warm-blooded girl's toes.

Tearing my attention away from them, I occupied myself with scanning the area, making sure the Midnight Witch was truly gone. Jake and Eric did the same, fanning out and trolling in circles around the oblivious, kissing couple.

I shook my head. This was so *not* the place for this.

At last, they broke their heated kiss, then spent another instant peering into each other's eyes.

Taking Rosalina's hand, Damien started marching the way we'd come. "Let's go help!"

We jumped into the fray and fought alongside civilians and uniformed Skews alike. The battle lasted for hours, but gradually our sheer number overwhelmed even the most rabid hybrids.

In the end, The Scourge's streets ran red with blood. Werewolves, vampires, and Fae alike lay dead on the blacktop, next to the beasts that had blindly attacked them on a vengeful witch's command—a witch that had fled like a coward, leaving them behind.

There were many injured. Most healed on their own, if their wounds weren't too serious. But others needed help, and soon, the streets were teeming with paramedics and other emergency personnel.

In time, even Stales came. They helped find survivors among the bodies, administering first aid, and saving lives.

Exhausted, we made our way out of there, hobbling toward Eric's car after Damien healed our wounds as best as he could.

My paws were soaked with blood and my fur was starting to dry into clumps with the stuff. I was limping with phantom pains from a bite to my shoulder. A hybrid three times my size had mistaken me for a piece of kibble and chomped on me pretty good. I screamed and the beast shook me like a rag. If Damien hadn't zapped the monster in time, I might've met my maker tonight.

At the barricade, we found a bunch more police cars blocking the way.

"Hey, it's Tom," Rosalina said, noticing detective Freeman issuing orders to a few uniformed officers.

He also noticed Rosalina and the rest of us and approached us wearily, his dark eyes assessing us. "I should've figured you'd all be here." He glanced at Jake, Eric, and finally at me. "Toni?"

I flexed my ears and inclined my head.

He nodded and smiled. It was the first time he'd seen my wolf. "Did you get that bitch?" he asked.

"Not this time," Rosalina answered. "But maybe next."

Yes, next time. At least, all her hybrids were dead. They had to be because it looked like she'd brought all of them here. It would take her time to make more.

He sighed in frustration and rubbed the back of his neck. "When is this mess going to end?"

That was what *I* wanted to know.

"Y'all get out of here." The detective tiredly waved a hand, urging us away. "Somebody might start asking questions I don't want to answer. It's not like you're inconspicuous." He scanned Damien with his flashy, blood-dripping cloak. "I already had to deal with that the last time y'all got involved. *Shoo, shoo!*"

Rosalina gave him a military salute. "You don't have to tell us twice."

She was right about that. I was tired and so was everybody else. We needed to rest, badly, especially Jake and Damien. And I really hoped Lucia was already in bed, though knowing her…

Saying that tomorrow would be hard for them was an understatement. If only I could lend them some of my strength.

CHAPTER 31

Eric drove us back, and I was, yet again, jealous of his shifter ring. Jake and I stayed in our wolf forms while Eric cringed at the blood we smeared on the leather seats. When we got to his house, he brought our clothes along with towels out to the garage so we could clean before going in.

Upstairs, I checked on Lucia and was surprised to find her asleep on my bed. I left quietly and chose a different room out of the many vacant ones in the house, making sure it had its own bathroom—there was no shortage of them either.

I went back out into the living room and found Jake on the phone. No one else was in sight.

"I already told you, we're doing it tomorrow," Jake was saying with a slightly aggravated tone. "My guess is as good as yours."

I chose to listen to the other side of the conversation and carefully focused my werewolf hearing.

"...managed to control the demon today?" Allison asked.

"She did, and Damien thinks it'll work."

"You have to let me come. I want to be there."

"We already went over this, Allison. There's nothing you can do to help."

"I just want to—"

"I'll call as soon as we're done. If I don't, it won't matter. Either way, you'll be free."

I cringed at the last bit and found myself hating Allison all over again. She seemed desperate to make sure Jake went through with the cleansing so she could be free of the pact, but she wasn't risking *her* neck or doing anything to be with the man she loved. *Bitch!* She was back on my shit list for sure.

Allison started to say something, but Jake disconnected the call.

"She sucks!" I exclaimed, walking to him and wrapping my arms around his waist.

He leaned into me and placed a kiss on the top of my head. He smelled of smoke and blood, just the way I did.

I glanced about. "Where are the others?"

"They all disappeared." We pulled apart. "Rosalina went with Damien," he said, wiggling his eyebrows.

"Good for them."

"About time, don't you think?"

I nodded. "Now, how about you come with me?" I interlaced my fingers with his and guided him to the bedroom I'd scoped out.

"Oh?"

I looked him up and down. "You're filthy. You need a good scrubbing."

"Hmm, I think you're right."

Once in the bedroom, I locked the door behind us and guided him to the bathroom. I got the water running in the shower and set it to the right temperature.

Returning my attention to Jake, I grabbed the hem of his shirt. He lifted his arm as I pulled it off. His muscles rippled and flexed exquisitely. There was dry blood on his torso and strong arms. I would make sure to wash every last bit with much care.

Next, I unbutton his pants. They dropped from his narrow hips and puddled at his feet. I gasped when I saw he was wearing no underwear and was more than ready for me. I bit my lower lip as I admired him. He was so beautiful. I ached in my core.

"Your turn." He made quick work of my T-shirt and basketball shorts. I *had* opted to wear panties and a bra, but he got rid of those as his silver gaze tracked me one inch at a time.

Hands roving over each other, we stepped into the shower together and slid the glass door shut. The water was perfectly delicious. There was a handheld shower head, which I removed from its base and aimed at Jake's chest. With the tips of my fingers, I rubbed his pecs and abs, removing all traces of the battle from his skin. When I was done, he did the same with me. He started with my hair, massaging my scalp with the tips of his fingers.

"It looks like the pink is washing off," he said as he rubbed a strand of hair against his palm and sprayed it thoroughly.

"I know. I haven't had time to go to the hair salon. I need a haircut badly, too."

"I like your hair brown better."

I tipped an eyebrow at him. "And I like it pink."

"Fine, fine," he chuckled. "I'm not gonna try to tell you what to do Ms. Alpha."

"That's right." I poked his pec with one finger. He flexed it, and it felt like poking a wall. "Ouch." I shook my hand.

He grabbed it and kissed it better.

Once we washed all the blood away, we went through the same steps again, but this time with soap and shampoo. At some point, the cleaning *and* the foreplay ended, and Jake picked me up and pressed my back against the wall. I wrapped my legs around him as he kissed me and made love to me with patience and tenderness as if we had nothing to fear in the hours ahead.

I traced every inch of his body, doing my best to believe we would be like this forever. I managed to fool myself until we were lying in bed, our naked bodies pressed together. That was when silent tears spilled out, and he discovered them when they splashed onto his smooth chest.

"Hey!" He hooked a finger under my chin and guided me to meet his gaze. "It'll be all right. You have to believe that."

"I know."

He kissed my forehead and smoothed my still-damp hair.

"You fight that fucking demon, okay?"

"I will. I won't let it keep me from you. Lucia will do great. She's strong, like you. You all get it from your mom."

"Yeah, I guess. Luckily we didn't get the lying gene, too." Part of me was still angry at her. Would the resentment ever go away?

"With time, you'll forgive her," Jake said as if he'd read my thoughts.

"I think Travis hates me. Not that I care."

"Don't blame him. He'll need time, too. He must be in awful pain after losing his daughter. He must also be conflicted about his emotions."

"That damn witch!"

"We'll get her. After tomorrow, we'll focus on ridding the city of her and her pests."

I nodded and rested my cheek on his chest. I listened to his heart and prayed, begging Velthgrek didn't get a chance to come near it. After several quiet minutes, I let out a heavy sigh and allowed his heart's steady rhythm to lull me to sleep.

CHAPTER 32

In the morning, we all met in the kitchen for a strong cup of coffee and a breakfast of eggs and toast. I was up before everyone since I wanted time to cook the customary mountain of food needed for three werewolves, one mage, and a hungry telekinetic teen. Rosalina was a dainty eater, so she wasn't much of a concern, come to think of it, neither was Damien.

Rosalina was the first one to walk into the kitchen, which was a surprise since she normally liked sleeping late. Shuffling her feet, she went straight for the coffee and poured herself a tall cup.

"Good morning," she mumbled.

I assessed her through narrowed eyes. "Busy night?" I asked, suggestively.

A twinkle appeared in her eyes and a smile on her lips.

I clasped my hands together. "Oh, my gosh, you two… did the ugly?"

Her smile deepened as she nodded.

As excited as a schoolgirl, I grabbed her hand and dragged her to the table, where we sat facing each other. "How was it?"

Her answer was a sigh and a dreamy look in her green eyes.

"That good, huh?"

She nodded.

"Did he… use magic?" I'd always been curious about this. Mages and witches could really make sex interesting with their powers.

"Mmm, maybe. I'm really not sure." She blushed.

"Shit!" I blinked repeatedly, considering her answer. From the sounds of it, it *had* felt magical, but she couldn't tell one way or the other if he'd used it. "Oh, he's good!" I said. "You lucky girl." I mock-punched her arm.

I was about to ask for more details when Lucia bounced in, looking freshly showered and perky.

"Yay, finally, someone's up. Umm, coffee." She lifted both arms and walked mummy-like toward the coffee machine.

When Leo, Dani, and I were Lucia's age, Mom didn't allow us to drink coffee at all, assuring us that it would stunt our growth. With her youngest, however, Mom seemed to forget all her convenient lies. She'd let Lucia start drinking caffeinated stuff at thirteen. No wonder Lucia was thoroughly addicted to it now, and not to mention an inch taller than me.

"Been up for a while?" Rosalina asked.

"'Bout an hour. Um, eggs. Lots of them." She spooned eggs on one of the plates I'd set out then added two pieces of toast on top.

"You could have made breakfast, you know?" I said.

She scrunched up her face as if I'd suggested she could have drilled holes in her head. She sat and attacked her food right away. Rosalina cut a sharp glance in her direction then back at me.

"This is what happens when you're the baby of the family," I said. "You expect everyone else to do everything for you."

Lucia kept eating as if I hadn't said anything.

I huffed. "And you don't give a shit."

Instead of acknowledging me, she asked, "When do we start?"

Man, was she eager to let a demon start munching on my

boyfriend or what? I continued my former train of thought about the callousness of younger siblings. "Oh, and what's more, you grew up to be reckless."

Lucia finally acknowledged me by rolling her eyes and saying, "Give it a rest, will ya? I'm here to help you, so show some gratitude."

I opened my mouth to argue but quickly clamped it shut. Lucia had a temper, and at the moment, it wasn't in my best interest to get it going. Instead, I swallowed the biting words that perched on my tongue and replaced them with something nice.

"That's right. You're helping Jake and me, and I'm grateful for that."

My sister raised an eyebrow and, looking satisfied, went back to her food.

Thirty minutes later, Jake was the next one up. I was glad he got to sleep a little longer since he was in for a rough day. I greeted him with a kiss, ordered him to sit, and served him breakfast.

"Thank you," he said, looking surprised. "I feel like a king."

"Today, you are one," I said, planting a quick kiss on his lips. "But don't let it get to your head."

Eric walked in at that moment, made a disgusted sound, turned on his heel, and left. Thinking he might be joking, I waited for him to come right back around, but he didn't.

"Seriously? That man is a grump!" I exclaimed. "Isn't there a spell or something that could help him lighten up?"

"There isn't," this from Damien, who was strolling in, a huge smile stretching his mouth from ear to ear. "Trust me, I've tried." He made a beeline toward Rosalina. "Good morning, beautiful." He kissed her full on the lips, showing no hint of his previous reticence.

"Gah! I'm with Mr. Eric Grump," Lucia put in. "The *ambiance* in this kitchen is getting more unbearable by the second."

"One day, you'll understand," I said.

"I seriously doubt that. Unless *syrupiness* comes with age."

It was a truth universally acknowledged, that a teen girl with a bad attitude, must be in want of an ass whooping.

"Oh, I forgot we had a teen in the house," Damien said. "When I was her age, I remember thinking that everyone who wasn't a teen was positively geriatric."

"You remember that far back?" Lucia asked.

"Dear, I remember everything. Even you in diapers and reaching in the back of them, proclaiming you'd gone number two. It wasn't pretty when you took your hand out."

I busted out laughing and so did Jake and Rosalina.

Lucia grew red but managed to keep her temper in check.

Damien gave me a quick wink. I couldn't believe how much lighter his mood was. But I shouldn't have been surprised. Love kind of has that effect on people. It makes everything so much better.

After we ate breakfast, we set out to make all the necessary preparations for the cleansing. Damien brushed away the old chalk pentagram and redrew it, while Eric and I moved a long table from an upstairs room into the garage. It was for Jake to lie on during the process. We attached a long stick to the head of the table from which we hung a blood bag. We had more in the small fridge and had bought them at a vampire bar, making sure the type was correct. We also had ropes to tie him down and make sure he stayed in place and didn't hurt himself. It was all improvised since we didn't have much time to prepare.

I wanted the preparations to last and last and last, but the moment came when we couldn't put it off anymore. Jake had spent some time in solitude to center himself, and now, he glanced around at everyone, at the table, and the pentagram. His stance was firm and so was his expression. Nothing about him revealed uncertainty or fear. Slowly, he unbuttoned his shirt and set it aside. He hopped on the table and quickly lay down.

I picked up one of the ropes and began at his feet, coiling it around his ankles and tying the ends to the table legs. When I was done, I took his right hand and wrapped the rope around his wrist, then pulled his arm over his head.

"I think I like this," he said under his breath.

"*Shh!* Hush, or you'll send Eric into a tizzy."

He chuckled.

I secured his other wrist in place and tied that end to the table as well. "Is it too tight?"

"No, it's fine."

As I placed a gentle kiss on his forehead, my heart squeezed tightly. The back of my eyes stung, and I had to clench my teeth not to cry.

"It will be all right, Toni," he reassured me for the *nth* time.

He was the one tied to a table, moments away from being invaded by a demon, and yet, he remained courageous and able to offer me the support I needed. I inhaled deeply and pushed my turbulent emotions out of the way. I had to keep my cool. I couldn't let fear get the best of me.

"It will," I said, conjuring every bit of self-assurance I could muster.

Jake nodded and smiled, and I could tell by the small measure of relief that entered in his expression that he'd also found comfort in my words.

Slowly, everyone took their places around the pentagram. My pack, the people I loved. Damien cracked his fingers, then flexed them. He craned and loosened his neck, moving his head in small circles several times. Bones popped as he made circles with his arms and bent his knees to perform several squats.

"I'm a little stiff," he said when he noticed everyone watching him with interest.

I smirked suggestively in Rosalina's direction.

"He's actually *a lot* stiff," she whispered, then snickered.

When he was done with his calisthenics, which was exactly what they looked like—just the thing that had been in vogue during his prime, no doubt—Damien turned to Lucia.

"Are you ready?"

"I am," she answered, quickly lighting the candles like before.

I was glad for her simple response and absence of bravado, which were so common in her. It meant she was taking this moment seriously as she should.

Damien inhaled deeply and conjured the demon. "From the depths of hell, I command you to come forth. The circle will bind you. The flames will charm you. Velthgrek, you are summoned."

The demon appeared in its dog guise again. It blinked its big eye and wagged its stubby tail.

Keeping the fiend under control, Damien turned to Eric and nodded firmly. Eric started toward Jake, a dagger in hand. Reluctant to cause Jake pain, I had asked Eric to make the cut where the demon would enter, but now that I saw Eric approach with the blade, I realized I was being a coward. As upsetting as it would be to inflict pain on my mate, I had to be the one to do it. He was about to put himself through hell for me, for *us*. I needed to walk the path with him for as long as I could.

I hurried forward and touched Eric's shoulder to get his attention.

"I'll do it," I mouthed.

He frowned as if asking *are you sure?*

I nodded, took the blade from his hand, and walked to Jake's side. My eyes met his, and I tried to tell him how much I loved him. I didn't want to hurt him, but I needed to be brave. Jake was the one facing the true challenge, and he hadn't once shied away from it. It was only right for me to face this small task with courage.

I lifted the blade, making sure my hand didn't shake as I pressed its sharp tip to the inside of Jake's right biceps. Pausing, I held steady until he gave me the go-ahead with a single nod.

Exerting a moderate amount of pressure, I slid the blade downward. Its sharp edge made a clean, straight cut. Blood immediately seeped from the wound, sliding around his thick muscles.

Behind me Velthgrek went crazy, making snarling sounds and pawing at the concrete floor.

Quickly, before the wound healed, I stepped aside. Damien's gaze went around the circle, letting us know he was about to release the demon. His copper eyes remained locked with Lucia's, who bent her knees and stretched her arms toward Velthgrek, her expression pinched in concentration.

"On the count of three," Damien said. "One… two… three!" He flicked a hand down toward the edge of the pentagram and, using magic, swept a section of the chalk away, breaking the circle's integrity.

A split second later, Velthgrek turned to smoke and shot toward Jake. I gasped and hugged my arms around my torso to stop myself from running to his side.

As the demon zipped past, I panicked, afraid Lucia would not be able to get hold of Velthgrek again, but the jetting smoke drew to a near halt a beat later. My sister grunted with the effort but held fast.

"Good," Damien said. "Now, let it in slowly."

Jake's wound had healed halfway, but as Lucia allowed the demon to reach his arm, Velthgrek had no trouble seeping under his skin.

At the sight of the evil essence slithering with such relish into the man I loved, I almost screamed. My heart rattled my ribcage, and cold sweat traced a line down my back. Just like the day Damien had lain dying on the floor of the agency, I felt useless. That day, I'd wished for Dani's healing abilities, and today, I wanted nothing more than to be a telekinetic like Lucia. But I was none of those things, and all I could do was stand here and watch while the demon wormed itself inside of Jake like a parasite.

"A little more," Damien instructed. "All of it needs to go in. Good, good. Now, keep it there. Keep it there. Don't let it go any further."

Lucia gave one nod and continued exerting her power on the hellish creature.

The skin in Jake's biceps stretched and contracted. The area changed shapes as the demon writhed inside. The bastard was struggling against Lucia's staying force, doing its best to break free and go straight for Jake's heart.

My eyes were glued to his arm. My heart slowly turned to ice as Jake's legs began twitching and his face contorted in pain.

Images of a dim future flashed before my eyes.

Without him, there would be no real joy. Whatever life I made for myself would be filled with the phantom of happiness, a see-through façade that would not hide my awful reality. I knew deep in my heart that time would not heal his loss, that nothing and no one would ever replace him. My friends and family would be there, and their presence would help ease the pain, but not even their love and support would give my life the meaning it now had. Perhaps if Jake had never come back, I might've been able to fool myself into believing I had all I needed. But now, with the knowledge that he loved me unconditionally and I was his true mate, there was no amount of lies I could tell myself to believe the trudge of life was worth anything without him.

Please, Jake, be strong!

Lucia, hold on. Fight. Win.

An eternity ticked by, or maybe it was only a minute.

Lucia started panting, her chest visibly rising and falling. Her fingers slowly curled inward as her arms trembled with the effort of keeping the demon in place.

Just a little longer.

Suddenly, a heart-stopping screech echoed all around us.

For a second, I thought the world was ending, that we had messed with the other realm one-too-many times, and Lucifer himself had decided to pay us a visit.

My frozen heart came back to life, pounding out of control as I glanced behind us toward the garage doors. A huge hybrid was tearing through one of the doors, its large head half in as it roared. My heart froze again.

No, not here! Not now!

How were they able to get through all the protection spells and the Stale security system? But I figured that was a stupid question. Mekare was here. She'd deactivated them.

Frantically, my attention returned to Jake and Lucia. The right side of Jake's torso was now writhing with the demon's essence.

God, No!

No. No. No.

Shifting in a heartbeat, Eric jumped in front of the hybrid. He attacked, swatting at its face with razor-sharp claws. Rosalina ran toward the gun cabinet and pulled out a couple of handguns. I rushed to Jake's side, determined to protect him while he lay helpless on the table.

Up close, the sight was even more gruesome. Jake's skin was squirming as if he had a den of snakes under it. His eyes circled and circled behind reddened lids, as tears slid down his face.

Oh, Jake!

"Steady, Lucia!" Damien said in a commanding tone.

My sister clenched her teeth and let out a hiss as she pulled back. Velthgrek retreated back into Jake's arm.

"Now, take it out," Damien ordered.

It was too soon. The blood curse wasn't out of his system, but what else could we do? We were under attack.

Despite Eric's effort to keep the beast back, the hybrid broke through the hole while daylight and a second beast followed on its heels.

"Take it out!" Damien ordered again, his hands weaving a spell that he quickly shot at the second hybrid. The magic hit the creature square in the chest and sent it skidding backward.

"I can't," Lucia cried out, breaking the rule not to talk. "I'm trying, but I can't."

Jake's skin grew sallow, and beads of sweat covered his entire torso and face. His head turned from side to side as if a terrible nightmare were ravaging his dreams.

A tug-of-war began between the demon and my sister. By degrees, Velthgrek pushed into his chest again, inching closer to the sternum. I clenched my hands to stop them from attempting to push the damn thing out of him, but if I touched him, it would only make things worse. Damien had warned us against it.

Lucia hissed through gritted teeth, renewing her efforts. The demon retreated back into Jake's arm.

A keening sound escaped through Jake's half-opened mouth as his eyes rolled into the back of his head.

I stood there, my fingers flexing, useless, unable to do a thing.

A third hybrid broke in, tearing a second hole in the door. The beast trampled in, growling and thrashing. Rosalina discharged her gun, but the bullets could've been gnats for all the harm they were doing.

We're fucked. Fucked!

I locked eyes with my sister, begging her to take the demon out of Jake. She shook her head even as she renewed her efforts and the tug-of-war went on and on.

Rosalina continued shooting, careful to avoid Eric as he weaved between the three hybrids, biting and clawing wherever he could, buying us time. She hit one, then another, discharging an entire cartridge. Their bodies twitched, and they slowed but didn't go down. She switched guns and focused on the third one, but Damien's magic hit it first, dropping one at last. The beast twitched for a moment, then went still. It seemed the mage had found the right magic spell to put them out of commission.

Movement caught my eye at the hole at the garage door. *God, no!* How many more were coming? And where was Mekare? Surely, she wasn't far behind.

As if I'd conjured her, instead of another hybrid, the witch walked in, a sphere of magic surrounding her, protecting her from Damien's spells.

A satisfied grin slashed across her face as she said, "You started the cleansing without me? How rude! Let me give you a hand." Wasting no time, she weaved a magic spell and shot it straight at Jake.

CHAPTER 33

A scream vaulted from my throat as Mekare's black magic flew in our direction. Instinctively, I shifted, though it was useless. Neither Red nor I could do anything against the blast of magic headed our way.

But that didn't matter. I only wanted to protect Jake.

In the split second that my torn clothes fell to the floor, I leaped forward on my way to a head-on collision with a crackling ball of energy.

I closed my eyes as I sailed through the air. I waited for the blast to rip me to pieces but it never came. Instead, there was a hiss and a pop, and when I looked again, the magical attack was dissolving, falling down like spent fireworks. Purple remnants of magic mixed with black.

Damien had blocked her.

My front paws hit the floor, and I leaped again, this time aiming my sharp fangs at the witch's neck. She blinked in surprise, then turned to smoke with a flick of her wrist. My jaws closed around nothing but air as I flew past and landed on the other side.

Digging my claws into the concrete I whirled around, frantically searching for her. My eyes roved around, taking in the scene for a split second.

Eric was circling around a fallen hybrid, trying to go for the beast's neck as the creature's bulging arms flailed about defensively, grotesque claws intent on shredding the tawny wolf. Rosalina was repeatedly pulling the trigger, discharging as many bullets as she could on the second and third hybrids. Damien was scanning the garage, a ball of magic sitting in his hand ready to be launched at the first sign of the witch. He was slowly walking closer to Jake and Lucia, who was still fighting to pull the demon out of Jake.

Trusting Damien to take care of Mekare the moment she reappeared, I lunged toward one of the hybrids stalking Rosalina and clamped my jaw around the back of its thick calf. The beast roared as my teeth sank in. I shook my head and pulled back, ripping sinew off of bone and spitting it out. The creature whirled as blood spilled onto the floor. I peered past its massive body to check on Rosalina. She had felled the second hybrid and was now dashing to help Eric, holding a sword above her head.

Holy shit!

She was like Xenia, Warrior Princess. She even let out a war cry to match. Seeing her out of the corner of his eye, Eric stepped back from the hybrid he'd knocked to the floor as she swung down and hacked at its neck. One, two, three times until she decapitated it.

I tore my eyes away from the scene as the hybrid I'd attacked limped in my direction, teeth bared, black veins bulging in its neck and face. I'd pissed it off. Big time. Well, I was pissed off too. With my mouth opened wide, I let out a blood-curdling roar and fleeted around the hybrid. The beast's head swiveled around, searching for me. But it didn't pinpoint my location until I took a bite out of his other calf.

The creature roared in pain, throwing its head back. I spit out the foul-tasting chunk of meat as it fell to its knees and Rosalina sprang in front of it, swinging her sword with such force that she cut the massive head clean off. The hideous thing thudded to the floor and rolled off to the side, leaving a trail of blood in its path. The body followed an instant later.

With the three hybrids dead and Mekare nowhere to be seen, we all gathered around Jake. At least there'd been only three of the monsters. Hopefully that was all she'd been able to make since last night.

Lucia was still fighting against Velthgrek, and it seemed she was winning. Half of the demon's essence was out of Jake's body. The skin around his biceps was still writhing, but not bulging as much.

"You almost got it," Damien said. "You can do it."

How long had passed since the demon first went into Jake? Maybe enough that it'd had a chance to get rid of the curse? No, I didn't think so. But that didn't matter anymore, not when that fucking Midnight Witch was—

Without warning, Lucia yelled as something hit the back of her legs and she fell to her knees, losing control of the demon. In the blink of an eye, Velthgrek slithered back into Jake. With a grunt, he started thrashing violently at the shock of the reentrance.

A surge of panic hit my chest, paralyzing me. My mouth opened, but no sound came out.

Dead. He's dead.

Crippling despair reared its ugly head, and once more, I had a glimpse of a future without joy, without meaning.

But then, with a punch of her power toward the floor, Lucia was back on her feet. She seemed to levitate for an instant, then as her feet settled back down, she extended her hands forward and quickly pulled back, taking hold of the demon once more. Velthgrek had made it into Jake's chest, but she stopped its progress and pulled it into Jake's arm once more.

Another magical attack came at Lucia, but this time, Damien was ready and blocked it.

"Show your face, you ugly bitch," the mage spat.

"Very well," Mekare's voice echoed through the garage, then she appeared in front of us, framed by the garage doors.

Her two-tone bangs swayed as she settled. She wore leather pants with buckles around her thighs, a laced bra, and an unzipped jacket on top.

I growled and took a step in front of my friends. If hatred could kill, she would've dropped right then and there. I'd never hated anyone this much in my life.

"That little girl is wasting her time," the witch said, gesturing toward Lucia. "Your beloved is dying, Toni. Isn't that right, Damien?"

I shook my head so violently, my ears flapped.

Not true. Not true, I repeated inside my head.

There was no answer from Damien. Fear crept into my bones like venomous spiders even as my sister grunted with the effort of controlling Velthgrek.

"You're nothing without your hybrids, bitch!" Rosalina exclaimed, switching the sword for a gun and aiming it at Mekare's head.

With a flick of the witch's wrist, the gun flew from Rosalina's hand and clattered to the floor.

"Pathetic Stale," the witch spat. "You and your kind are a waste of space. Don't you know weapons are worthless against Skews like me?" She paused, then answered her own question. "Of course you don't. You're stupid." Grinning like a maniac, she raised her arms to the heavens. "And I'm *not* nothing. I am *everything.* With or without hybrids. Right babies?" she asked over her shoulder.

Behind her, the garage doors shook and clattered, sounding as if thousands of fists were beating on them. With the twist of metal and wood, new holes were punched through by massive claws. In an instant, the doors were reduced to splinters and a throng of hybrids pushed in, so many that they stretched as far as I could see, flooding the street outside, standing on Eric's fancy cars and pounding on them like incensed gorillas.

Oh, God. I'd been wrong, so wrong. She had another army of them.

At her command, they all roared, looking ready to turn us into confetti.

This was it. The end of everything, but it didn't matter.

Jake was dying, and I was going down with him.

CHAPTER 34

I sprang toward the witch, heedlessly. Jake and I had lost the war, and I was going to make sure she lost it with us.

"Sunder!" Eric screamed in my head. He charged from the side and knocked me sideways just a ball of fire from Mekare's fingers singed my tail. *"Are you trying to die?!"*

I lurched to my feet, snapped at Eric, then whirled on the witch again. She smirked and made a second ball of fire. She flicked it at us, but it hit an invisible barrier as soon as it left her hand. Her dark gaze shot toward Damien.

"You'll go down with us," the mage said, his words a promise.

Shots spat from Rosalina's guns. Magic trailed from Damien's fingers.

Eric stalked in her direction. *"We do this together,"* he said in my mind.

The Midnight Witch let out a derisive cackle. "You are *so* deluded. You can't beat me." She lifted a hand, snapped her fingers, and gave the orders. "Attack!"

Outside, the hybrids howled at the sky, then charged.

Teeth and claws were nothing against her magic. Magic and

weapons paled in the face of so many hybrids. Two or three we could take down, but the hundreds that stood outside would leave no trace of life after they were done with us.

Only a command from Mekare would save us now.

My eyes shut wide as a thought suddenly ripped through my brain.

"She's not an alpha, so how can she command them?" Eric's question from days ago resonated with the same intensity as it had the first time.

The hybrids stampeded into the garage, growling and striking at each other as their huge number tried to push through the too-narrow doors.

I had a second, maybe two.

Mekare flinched and took a step back as she blocked Rosalina's bullets and a magical attack from Damien. Taking advantage of her distraction, I fleeted toward her and clamped my jaws around her ankle before she could turn to smoke.

My teeth sank into flesh. Mekare cried out and aimed a spell at my head.

Anticipating the agony that would follow my memories, I opened the floodgates.

I huddle under a bridge, hugging my shoulders, shivering violently. My toes ache. My fingers and my head, too. I might die tonight.

Damn you! Damn you!

The water running under the bridge stinks of death, the awful smell has become part of me. Rats squeak nearby. They try to get near but I kick at them, and now they wait. Maybe they know my fate, they know I will *die tonight.*

The sound of tires repeatedly hitting the bridge's uneven pavement fills my ears. The traffic never stops. The city can never sleep. Neither can I. Closing my eyes, I try to drift away, but my stomach twists with hunger. I hear the shouts and screams of men nearby. None of them my friends. I stare at the dark, flowing water, at the light being absorbed to its depths. It is moonlight and lampglow being consumed by darkness.

It is the glow of Jake's callous, silver eyes.

My heart twists more violently than my stomach.

There's only self-loathing and resentment inside it, like foul worms eating at it.

I will die tonight, and I don't care.

The certainty of death resonated through time, through memory, through resignation.

It's okay. You'll be with Jake. It's okay.

Even as the witch's magic left her finger, I didn't let go. Instead, I allowed my alpha tracker skills to combine and push everything I was feeling into the witch.

The cold and the pain it gave. The high-pitched squeak of rats and the fear of their teeth on flesh. The insistent and repugnant thudding of tires. The cloying stench of car exhaust and putrid water. The feel of tears frozen on stiff cheeks. The wavering sights perceived through tired, bloodshot eyes. The reek of human refuse, of dirty clothes, dirty hair, dirty hands that tried to squeeze out the anguish.

I felt it all transfer into the witch like a transfusion of misery. A split second later, I sensed the hybrids inches away from running all of us over like a stampede of wild dogs. I issued an unequivocal alpha command.

"Stop!"

The swarming hybrids froze in place. I saw them out of the corner of my eye and couldn't believe my hunch had been right. The witch was the hybrids' leader, their alpha. Except, she wasn't one, not really, not like me. She had no business leading werewolves, even if they were half vampires. I, on the other hand, was meant to be a pack leader. I could make them do whatever I wanted.

Couldn't I?

Mekare convulsed as my sensory assault ripped through her.

I clamped my teeth harder around her ankle, grinding at the bone, and—with all my strength and will and desire to save my friends—I unleashed a second sensory attack at the same time that I pushed one overpowering command into the witch.

"Die!"

Energy coursed through me like a mighty river, flowing with single-minded determination and making my skin glow. All the sights, sounds, scents, flavors, textures that I'd seen, heard, smelled, tasted, and touched in my life came to me with clarity.

There was the smell of grease while Dad and I worked on the Camaro. The taste of Mom's creamy tortellini. The intense reds of a St. Louis summer sunset. The ring of Rosalina's voice. And the feel of Jake's silky hair between my fingers.

In an instant, I knew every single one of those sensations as they passed through me. But I held those good memories back, and for the witch, I focused only on the bad. All the awful things I'd been through in my life poured out. I experienced a total awareness of every sense, every recollection, individually and at once. It was a new awakening of my powers, something I had never imagined possible.

In the end, so many terrible things passed through me, so much pain and dreadful anguish that when it was all gone it felt like the dawn of something different.

The onslaught lanced into the witch like sharp knives. And from her, I willed it with my alpha powers to flow directly into the hybrids' sheep-like minds.

A host of deafening roars went up into the air as the hybrids clenched their heads in an orchestrated dance.

Doubling down, I pushed harder, giving it my all.

Mekare screamed with an inhuman quality. Bodies thudded to the floor inside and outside of the garage. I had once killed a single hybrid like this, and now I was killing hundreds. All at once. I felt their lives slip away through my link with the witch.

I relished their pain as they howled and twisted, their minds bombarded with more than they could handle.

A moment later, I felt empty. An uneasy quiet fell over me, a different kind of dawn. Through Mekare and the hybrids' minds, I saw my life play out like a movie, memories of sound and sight, ecstasy of taste and touch. It had been a good life. I had experienced many things.

But most important of all, I had loved, and I would die loving. Fiercely and entirely.

My jaw went slack and released its hold on the witch. Staggering backward, my hind legs barely holding me up, I blinked through tear-filled eyes. For an instant, I saw nothing and imagined myself in limbo. Maybe heaven or more likely hell.

I continued to blink at the tears. My eyes finally cleared and took in the tableau of the witch and the immobile bodies of her hybrids strewn all around her statue-like shape.

My legs trembled and I collapsed, head swimming.

I'd done it. I'd stopped the hybrids, killed them.

And Mekare? I had… what? Turned her to stone?

To prove me wrong, the witch stirred and groaned as if waking from a long slumber.

No!

She wasn't dead. I tried to stand, tried to attack once more, but I couldn't move.

She glanced all around, her jaw going slack with incredulity at the sight of all her dead monsters. Judging by her reaction, she hadn't been aware of what I was doing while I shot my entire being into her.

And yet, it hadn't been enough.

She blinked and her dark eyes landed on me, shooting back all the hatred I'd given her. Shakily, I pushed to all fours. My joints shook and ached with the effort. I would fight her with my last breath.

"What have you done?!" she demanded, her voice wavering with fury.

I bared my teeth in a wolfish grin to rub in my satisfaction.

She shook her arms and grunted in anger, a weird action that she seemed to use to shake off her frustration. "It doesn't matter. I will make more, and I will kill you and your mate…"

With dramatic flair, she cocked her head to one side and made a show of listening intently.

"Never mind," she said with a grin. "He's already dead. His heart stopped beating."

No!

I whirled to face the table where Jake lay. He wasn't moving, the twitching that had ravaged his body was gone and replaced by utter stillness. Forgetting all about Makare, I staggered to him. Lucia was still wrestling with the demon, pulling the last bit of its essence from the hole in Jake's arm.

With stuttering slowness, I shifted, stretched to my full height to reach him, to lay my hands on his neck and search for a pulse. My fingers trembled as I extended my hand.

"Jake, Jake!"

"Don't touch him!" Damien warned as my sister, at last, finished pulling Velthgrek out. The demon's dark essence hovered in midair, pulsing as if in anger. The pentagram was totally gone, smeared by the scuffle.

But I didn't care. I only cared about Jake.

I pressed two fingers to his neck. His skin was cold and clammy. There was no pulse. I grabbed his shoulders and shook him.

"Did the demon reach his heart?!" I asked, desperation sinking its teeth into my own heart.

"No," Lucia said with certainty.

Relief flashed through me for a second, then I snatched the needle attached to the tubing and blood bag, quickly searched for a vein in his arm, and stabbed him. Next, I cupped my hands and pressed them to his chest to perform CPR, except I needed leverage. Clumsily, I climbed on the table and knelt by the edge.

Mekare laughed. "Look at you, so pathetic. Gods, you've made it so easy with your gullible ways. I've known what you've been up to every step of the way."

What?! Her words registered at some base level, even as I continued pumping, trying to jump-start Jake's heart.

How had she known? I glanced up and got my answer. Slowly, Mekare shrank an entire foot, her hair shortened and turned entirely green. A moment later, Em stood in front of us.

"You!" Rosalina exclaimed.

The witch smiled innocently. "*Em* is for Mekare," she said in a sweet tone. "Lovely home you have here Eric Lone." Her hand gestured around vaguely.

Oh, God! She'd been here twice, by our own invitation. The first time after Damien's daughter was killed, and the second after we got Rosalina and Gonira back. That last time, she must have pretended to sleep while we drank oakfire and talked all night.

"You left spells to spy on us," Damien said, anger making his voice quake.

"Of course, I did. And how about that trigger I put in your lovely little head?" She directed the question at Rosalina and mockingly added, "*Bach playing faintly beyond the walls.*" She laughed.

So that was how she'd laid the trap, how she'd fooled us into going to that warehouse. My blood boiled.

"You twisted bitch!" Rosalina raised her gun and pulled the trigger. The bullet disappeared in midair.

The witch rolled her eyes and regained her true shape. "You are like a troop of clowns."

"Maybe," Damien said, his voice resonating with hatred. "But you, standing there full of glee while bleeding on the floor, take the top prize. Velthgrek, take *her* blood!"

For a second, as Lucia still held the demon in place, its essence vibrated. Then, realizing what was required of her, she dropped her hands and released it. Like a bullet, the hungry tendril of smoke shot toward Mekare and, finding the wound in her ankle, slithered into her.

Without Lucia's powers to hold it back, the demon had free range to go wherever it pleased. An instant later, the witch's eyes went wide, and her hands flew to her chest. Her back arched as she cried out in pain. For several interminable seconds, she quaked on the spot, a wet, squelching sound coming from within her. At last, she went still, then fell face-first to the floor and didn't move again.

Allowing myself only a second of relief and satisfaction, I pressed my hands to Jake's chest and began applying one compression after another. I counted desperately, the way I'd been taught in high school, then lowered my mouth to his and blew, determined to breathe life back into him.

I pumped and pumped, but I was weakening quickly. I glanced around, a silent cry for help.

"I'll do it," Eric said as he shifted to his human form.

I started to move out of the way when I realized I had more to give, one last bit of my energy, of life, to transfer to Jake. I only cared if *he* lived. Nothing else mattered.

Taking a deep breath, I reached for the things I'd held from Mekare, all the good, the love. Then, exhaling, I released everything into him, pushing the energy through my hands and pumping one last time.

As my strength vanished, my eyes rolled into the back of my head, and the world went dark.

ഇൽ

"Hey, you," Jake said as I opened my eyes.

He was lying down next to me, his head resting on a pillow.

I stared into his silver eyes, marveling at their clear beauty.

"Hey, you," I responded in a hoarse voice. "Is it time for the cleansing?"

A vertical line appeared between his eyebrows. "You don't remember?"

"Remember what?"

As soon as the question crossed my lips, everything rushed back with such violence that I gasped. I sat up as if spring-loaded.

"Jake!" I took his face in my hands and turned it this way and that. He looked all right. I patted his neck, his torso, his arms. He was whole, unharmed.

"You're alive. You're alive!" I exclaimed, wondering if I was in some sort of dream.

Jake sat up, smiling. "I am. All thanks to you. It's over. It's all over, Toni. We did it. You saved us all. Even the city."

I shook my head, unable to believe what he was saying. This *had* to be a dream. Tears slid down my face. Jake wiped them away, pulled me into his lap, and held me tight.

"*Shh*, it's over. It's truly over."

He soothed me, gently caressing my back and rocking back and forth.

"I love you," he said. "I love you, and for the rest of my life I will do my best to repay everything you've ever done for me."

I cried, not caring about any of that. He was all I wanted, and I had him. I had him.

EPILOGUE

Images of Mekare's defeat and the cleansing floated in my mind as Jake helped me walk into Eric's study where everyone waited.

Rosalina and Lucia rushed toward me as I limped in and fussed over me.

"Are you all right?"

"How do you feel?"

"Can I get you anything?"

I shook my head, smiling. "I'm all right, I promise you."

Jake helped me sit on the sofa, across from Eric and Damien. They both scanned me from head to toe and seemed relieved as they confirmed I was in one piece. Eric leaned back in the armchair and exhaled while Damien peered into the depths of the unlit fireplace.

For a long minute, we sat embedded in thick silence, steeped in a heavy dose of incredulity and relief. It had been a couple of hours since Damien unleashed Velthgrek on Mekare, and the demon devoured her blood *and* heart. It had happened so quickly that the witch had no chance to do anything to save herself.

Every few minutes, I had to glance over at Jake to make sure he was really there, safe and sound. He was pacing behind the sofa, mental wheels turning behind his clear eyes.

Suddenly, something occurred to me. "Damien, how did you send Velthgrek back without a pentagram?"

He blinked, startled out of his reverie, and said, "I didn't."

"What?!"

"I'm afraid that demon is… at large."

My eyes flicked toward Eric. "Is he for real?"

"I'm afraid so."

"After feasting on the witch," Lucia said, "it munched on a couple of hybrids and took off."

I pressed a hand to my mouth and mumbled. "You have to find it and send it back."

Damien rolled his eyes. "Of course, you don't think I'll let it roam free indefinitely. Let me rest some, then I promise I'll go after it. It can't do much damage for now—not after it gorged itself."

"Are you sure?"

The mage nodded and went back to looking pensive.

"What's bothering you?" Eric asked.

Damien glanced back. "Who? Me?"

"Yeah, you."

"Just thinking about Mekare's powers and wondering if she was using demon magic."

"What?!" We all exchanged confused glances.

"There are many ways to accomplish advanced magic, some harder than others. Demon magic doesn't come without risks, but for those willing to take the risk, it can make things easier. I'm sure you noticed how similar her 'turning to smoke' trick was to Velthgrek's essence."

I certainly *had* noticed it.

"And at the warehouse," he continued, "that mental attack was very much like what we experienced with the fearmonger."

"Yeah," Jake said. "It sure was."

Damien made a flourish. "But never mind all of that. It doesn't matter now. She's gone."

"And what about the Unholy Vessel?" Rosalina asked.

"It's what I've been wondering about," Jake said. "Among other things."

"We *must* find it," Eric said, adamant.

Jake nodded. "We will. If we have to move heaven and earth."

With his detective skills, Jake would figure it out. I was sure.

Eric glanced into his phone for the third time since I'd come in. "They're still dead." He turned the screen and showed us a camera view of the garage where the hybrids and their leader lay dead. "How about you call your detective friend. We can explain what happened, then they can clean this mess. We already did the hard part for them."

Feeling less shaky, I rose from the sofa. "I'll call Tom." I took the hand that Jake extended my way. "Walk with me to get my phone."

On our way to the bedroom, I squeezed Jake's hand and said, "You're worried about Craig," a statement, not a question.

"He's going to be pissed, very pissed. I might've just made my first enemy among the St. Louis alphas. Not a good thing since my pack is not as strong as it used to be."

"Maybe he'll let you explain..." I trailed off. That sounded ridiculous even to my own ears.

With a sideways hug, he drew me closer as we kept walking. "It's nothing for you to worry about. In fact, as soon as you feel better, we'll celebrate."

Once in the room, Jake closed the door behind us and pulled me into his arms. "God, Toni. I would be nothing without you. You saved me. You..." His voice broke, and he swallowed hard. "I love you so much."

I melted in the heat of his love, my weakened body draping

against his. Despite my shakiness and everything we'd had to go through to get here, it was the best feeling in the world.

"I love you, too."

ꕥ

I called Tom, and he came with a battalion of cops and forensic personnel. His jaw fell open when he saw the massacre, but to his credit, he recovered quickly and set to work issuing orders and making decisions.

Once the team was full at work, he left his partner in charge and came to me.

"What's with you and leaving blankets of bodies behind? Please tell me this is the last one."

I chuckled sadly. "I'm pretty sure it is." I inclined my head toward the door that led into the house from the garage. "Want a cup of coffee while we talk?"

"Got anything stronger?"

"Sure do."

"This Eric's place?" Tom asked as we made our way upstairs.

"Yes." Everyone had made themselves scarce. We figured it would be better if I explained everything first, then if Tom wanted to talk to the others, he could do it later at the station.

Back in Eric's study, I poured a glass of the Scotch Damien seemed to prefer and offered it to the detective.

He took a sip, worked it in his mouth, and stared back at the glass appreciatively. "Damn, so this is how the stuff I can't afford tastes?"

We sat in front of the fireplace.

Tom appraised me with his dark gaze. "So what's it gonna be this time, kiddo? Lies? Or omission?"

I shook my head. "None of that. I'll tell you everything."

He blinked in surprise. "Everything?"

"Yes. You deserve to know, and I trust you'll know how much to divulge."

Setting the glass down on the coffee table, he removed his jacket, rolled up his sleeves, and pushed to the edge of his seat. "Let me have it, then."

For the next hour, I gave Tom enough information to keep his head spinning for an entire month. When I was done, I felt lighter *and* stupid for not trusting him earlier. He was a dear friend whom I loved and cherished. After Dad died, he became an important father figure, someone I could confide in. I made a mental note never to let anything spoil that again.

Poor Tom, he looked like I'd given him a headache. "Holy mother of God," he said, squeezing his temples. "That was…" He scrubbed his goatee next. "That was messed up. So Em was that Midnight Witch all along. You'll have to go over all of that one more time."

"Not now? I'm exhausted."

"Okay, fine, but we can do it at the station tomorrow." He stood to leave.

"Sounds good." I wrapped him in a tight hug.

He chuckled, patted my back, then held me at arm's length. "Thank you for trusting me." His smile was gentle and his gaze fatherly, like I hadn't seen in some time.

Yep, I was never doing that again!

ജ്ഞ

The next day, I sat in the passenger seat of Rosalina's car in front of a tall office building in the middle of downtown. My finger tapped nervously on my thigh as I bounced my knee.

"Take deep breaths, Toni," she reminded me.

I was startled back into the moment and tried to do as she said. My stomach clenched with nerves.

"You don't have to do this," she said.

"I know."

"You did the right thing."

"I know."

She reached over and gave my hand a squeeze. "And either way it goes today, you're doing the right thing again."

That was exactly why I was here. After almost dying, my perspective about a lot of things had changed. I didn't want any regrets. It was the reason I had told Tom the truth, and the reason I was here.

Our phones dinged at the same time. We picked them up in unison and checked our messages.

"It's Jake," I said.

"It's Damien," she said.

We smiled and then said at the same time, "They got it!"

I raised my hand for a high five, she hit it with gusto. It was damn good news. Jake, Eric, and Damien had gone to what they believed had been Mekare's true hideout, and, thanks to the witchlights, they'd found the Unholy Vessel.

Using a strand of the witch's hair Damien had a friend track the place. The friend was a different kind of tracker—one who, given an object from a mark, could trace the last few places that person had visited. It seemed one of the locations turned out to be the right one. He'd also tracked that pesky demon earlier today, so this was the cherry on top.

"I'm glad your boyfriend thinks of everything," I told Rosalina. He'd cut a section of Mekare's hair before the police arrived, planning ahead.

We sat in silence for a moment. A string of words crowded my mouth and before I talked myself out of it, I asked the question that had been on my mind since Mekare blew up our agency.

"Do you think… rebuilding the agency is a good idea?"

Rosalina did a double-take of surprise. "What kind of question is that? Of course, it's worth it! Don't tell me you're having second thoughts."

"No, I'm not, but I was worried you might. It wasn't going too well."

"Toni, it can take from two to three years for a business to become profitable. We were in diapers. Of course, we'll rebuild."

We'll rebuild! My heart jumped for joy. I laughed like an idiot, relieved that she hadn't given up on our dream. I hadn't either, but it meant the world that she was still vested.

"I was afraid you might decide to join a mercenary squad instead," I joked.

She laughed, shaking her head.

"But you're okay, right?" While I was at it, I could vent all my concerns. "Mekare didn't turn your soul into a shriveled mushroom? And you're not going to need to go all *Kill Bill* every blue moon?"

"What are you talking about?" She looked truly puzzled.

"Um, nothing! Forget I ever said anything." It seemed I'd been worrying for no reason. I hadn't seen that darkness in her eyes in the last couple of days, so it seemed she was back to normal.

"Hey, that's them!" she said, suddenly pointing out of the window.

I followed her finger and saw Travis and Marcus walking side by side. They were both dressed in suits, ready to take over board meetings everywhere.

Steeling myself, I hopped out of the car and took a few tentative steps in their direction. I almost turned back to the car, but Red reminded me that alphas didn't do that. So I squared my shoulders and marched forward firmly.

As soon as I caught their scent in the air, they caught mine and glanced sharply at me. A part of me expected them to bare their teeth, grimace, or at least slightly cringe. They did none of those things.

"Hi," I said, stopping a few paces away in front of them.

Marcus replied with a friendly enough *hello* while Travis only inclined his head.

"I… I don't mean to take more than a few seconds of your time," I said. "I just wanted to say I'm sorry that—"

Travis put a hand up to stop me.

The words I'd planned to say turned stale in my mouth. I swallowed hard.

"I appreciate you coming here," Travis said, "but it wasn't necessary."

Tears pricked in the back of my eyes. I hated myself for caring, for remembering the night of the Pack Rule meeting and the way he'd seemed willing to create a connection. Peter Sunder would always be my father, but it would be a lie if I didn't admit that I felt a part of me had been cheated out of an important facet of who I was meant to be.

I took a step back, inclining my head.

"You have nothing to be sorry about," Travis said.

My gaze snapped to him.

Smiling, Marcus gave his father an approving nod as if these weren't the words he'd been expecting to hear, but he was very glad for them.

"I'm the one who should apologize." He offered me a smile that resembled his son's. It was a little stiff but genuine enough. Travis cleared his throat. "Marcus and I were headed to lunch. Would you like to join us?"

My chest swelled in a weird way I hadn't anticipated. "Yes, I would."

As we left, I lingered a step behind and gave Rosalina the thumbs up. She grinned, looking happy for me. I sent her a quick text to tell her she didn't need to wait for me and hurried forward.

"I heard you defeated that fucking witch," Travis said, a note of satisfaction in his voice.

"We did. She's gone for good."

"You'll have to tell me all about it over the best damn tuna steak in the city."

We walked down the sidewalk, moving in sync. Red seemed to brim with a certain pride, and I imagined it wouldn't be long until I felt exactly as she did.

ꕤ

Mom was crying, and Lucia was callously rolling her eyes. Maybe, a couple of years back, I would have done the same, but I understood Mom all too well now.

The baby of the family was graduating and would soon be leaving us for New York City to attend the League of Demon Hunters.

Her Converse peeked from under her black graduation gown. Her cap was decorated with the words: *"Sorry, not sorry, for all those times* I *raised* your *hand in class."*

I shook my head. Classic Lucia!

She kept glancing over her shoulder, eager to run to her friends. We were in the same gym where Leo, Dani, and I had received our diplomas. The same place the hybrids had invaded a week ago.

Lucia's hell of an ordeal with us had definitely swayed her to take the scholarship at the LDH. They'd even provided a plane ticket for her to fly at the end of July. She would have room and board, and a cafeteria plan with all her textbooks included. A full ride. It was really something to be proud of, if only because of her innate skills since her grades hadn't been all that stellar. It paid to be a Skew with rare powers.

Dani hugged our little sister and slipped an envelope in her hand. "Don't spend it all at once."

Knowing Lucia, she would have nothing left by tonight. But heck, we'd all been there. We could warn her until we went blue in the face, but she had to learn the hard lessons on her own.

Rosalina also hugged Lucia and offered her another envelope.

Lucia beamed, likely imaging all the things she would buy.

Jake draped an arm across my shoulders and smiled. He looked very handsome in his dark suit, with his brown hair perfectly combed back and shining under the fluorescent lights. I drank in his features, unable to believe he was mine. Maybe there would be trials to come. I had to adjust to pack life, and we had to watch out for Craig Blackridge, but after what we'd been through, I knew we could face anything together.

"Sorry I'm late," a deep voice said behind us.

My heart skipped a beat. I froze. My mom and sisters seemed to freeze too. I turned around slowly, holding my breath, willing it to be true.

Tall and handsome, my big brother stood there smiling from ear to ear.

"Leo!" I exclaimed and, in two strides, I was on him, hanging from his neck as I hugged him tightly.

In an instant, Mom, Dani, and Lucia were there, also wrapping their arms around Leo, trapping me there, and it was the best feeling ever.

The first thing that got through to me, after my surprise, was that he smelled wonderful, like home.

We pulled away from him, and the questions poured out.

"Why didn't you tell us you were coming?" from Mom.

"Where have you been?" from Dani.

"When did you get in?" from Lucia.

"Woah, woah!" Leo put both hands up. "One at a time."

"You're eyes!" I exclaimed, forsaking all questions.

When he'd left, they'd been brown like mine, but now they glowed with an inner green light, which meant… he was an Emerald Mage!

He smirked and ran a hand through his dark brown hair a bit

subconsciously. It was shorter than when he left. He'd also grown broader at the shoulders, and his skin was a shade darker, bringing it to a honey tone. *Dang!* If I was being objective, he was handsome as hell.

"Leonardo Sunder." Jake stepped forward, clasped Leo's hand, then went in for a man hug.

"Jacob Knight. I see you didn't listen to me." Leo's gaze flicked in my direction. "I told you to stay away from my sisters." There was menace in his voice.

Jake's jaw clenched and twitched as he seemed to hold his breath.

Leo threw his head back and laughed. "I did have a feeling it would be inevitable. You always had it bad for Toni." Smiling, he turned to Lucia. "So where's the celebration, baby girl?"

Lucia's face lit up. She didn't mind Leo calling her that. "I want a big old steak," she declared. "You all figure out where to get it for me."

She wasn't worried about her friends anymore. She was in the here and now, ready to let us be a family. *If only Dad was here the moment would be complete.*

I pushed the sadness away. I still had *so* much to be grateful for, despite his absence.

In truth, I had everything I needed to be happy.

WWW.INGRIDSEYMOUR.COM

www.ingramcontent.com/pod-product-compliance
Lightning Source LLC
Chambersburg PA
CBHW020336310726
48979CB00015B/2386/J

* 9 7 8 1 7 3 6 0 6 1 2 4 4 *